"Do you have a name?"

"Yeah, I've got a name. Cooper Landry. But this isn't a garden party so forgive me if I don't tip my hat and say, 'Pleased to meet you.'"

For two lone survivors of a disastrous plane crash, they were off to a bad beginning.

"What's with you?" she demanded angrily. "You act as though the crash was my fault."

"Maybe it was."

Rusty gasped with incredulity. "What? I was hardly responsible for the storm."

"No, but if you hadn't dragged out that emotional, tearful goodbye to your sugar daddy, we might have beat it. What made you decide to leave ahead of him— the two of you have a lovers' spat?"

"None of your damned business."

His expression didn't alter. "And you had no business being in a place like that—" his eyes roved over her "—being the kind of woman you are."

"What kind of woman is that?"

"Drop it. Let's just say that I'd be better off without you."

Also available from Mira Books and
SANDRA BROWN

Previously published under the
pseudonym Erin St. Claire

THE DEVIL'S OWN
THE THRILL OF VICTORY

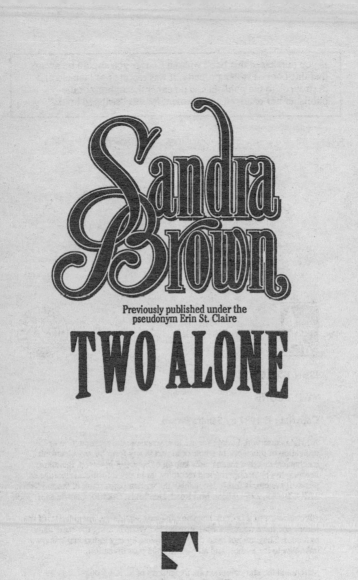

Sandra Brown

Previously published under the
pseudonym Erin St. Claire

TWO ALONE

MIRA BOOKS

MIRA

ISBN 1-55166-049-0

TWO ALONE

Copyright © 1987 by Sandra Brown.

MIRA and the star colophon are trademarks of MIRA Books.

Printed in U.S.A.

TWO ALONE

One

༺⚬⚬⚬༻

They were all dead.

All except her.

She was sure of that.

She didn't know how long it had been since the impact or how long she'd remained bent over with her head in her lap. It could have been seconds, minutes, light-years. Time *could* stand still.

Endlessly, it seemed, torn metal had shifted before settling with a groan. The dismembered trees—innocent victims of the crash—had ceased to quiver. Hardly a leaf was stirring now. Everything was frightfully still. There was no sound.

Absurdly she thought of the question about a tree falling in the woods. Would it make a sound? It did. She'd heard it. So she must be alive.

She raised her head. Her hair and shoulders and back were littered with chips of shattered plastic—what had previously been the window next to her seat. She shook her head slightly and the chips rained off her, making tinkling, pinging little noises in the quiet. Slowly she forced herself to open her eyes.

A scream rose in her throat, but she couldn't utter it. Her vocal cords froze. She was too terrified to scream. The carnage was worse than an air-traffic controller's nightmare.

The two men sitting in the seats directly in front of hers—good friends, judging by their loud and rambunctious bantering with each other—were now dead, their joking and laughter forever silenced. One's head had gone through the window. That fact registered with her, but she didn't look too closely. There was a sea of blood. She slammed her eyes shut and didn't open them until after she'd averted her head.

Across the aisle, another man lay dead, his head thrown back against the cushion as though he'd been sleeping when the plane went down. The Loner. She had mentally tagged him with that name before takeoff. Because the plane was small, there were strict regulations about weight. While the passengers and their luggage were being weighed before boarding, the Loner had stood apart from the group, his attitude superior and hostile. His unfriendliness hadn't invited conversation with any of the other passengers, who were all boisterously bragging about their kills. His aloofness had segregated him—just as her sex had isolated her. She was the only woman on board.

Now, the only survivor.

Looking toward the front of the cabin, she could see that the cockpit had been severed from the fuselage like a bottle cap that had been twisted off. It had come to rest several feet away. The pilot and copilot, both jovial and joking young men, were obviously, bloodily, dead.

She swallowed the bile that filled the back of her throat. The robust, bearded copilot had helped her on board, flirting, saying he rarely had women passengers on his airplane and when he did, they didn't look like fashion models.

The other two passengers, middle-aged brothers, were still strapped into their seats in the front row. They'd been killed by the jagged tree trunk that had cut into the cabin like a can opener. Their families would feel the tragedy with double intensity.

She began to cry. Hopelessness and fear overwhelmed her. She was afraid she would faint. She was afraid she would die. And she was afraid she wouldn't.

The deaths of her fellow passengers had been swift and painless. They had probably been killed on impact. They were better off. Her death would be long in coming because as far as she could tell, she was miraculously uninjured. She would die slowly of thirst, starvation, exposure.

She wondered why she was still alive. The only explanation was that she was sitting in the last row. Unlike the rest of the passengers, she had left someone behind at the lodge on Great Bear Lake. Her goodbye had been drawn out, so she was the last one to board the aircraft. All the seats had been taken except that one in the last row.

When the copilot assisted her aboard, the rowdy dialogues had ceased abruptly. Bent at an angle because of the low ceiling, she had moved to the only available seat. She had felt distinctly uncomfortable, being the only woman on board. It was like walking into a smoke-filled room where a heated poker game was in progress. Some things were innately, exclusively male, and no amount of sexual equality was ever going to change that. Just as some things were innately, exclusively female.

An airplane leaving a hunting and fishing lodge in the Northwest Territories was one of those masculine things. She had tried to make herself as inconspicuous as possible, saying nothing, settling in her seat and staring out the window. Once, just after takeoff, she had turned her head and inadvertently made eye contact with the man sitting across the aisle. He had looked at her with such apparent disfavor that she had returned her gaze to the window and kept it there.

Besides the pilots, she was probably the first one to notice the storm. Accompanied by dense fog, the torrential rain had made her nervous. Soon the others began to notice the jouncy flight. Their braggadocio was replaced with uneasy quips about riding this one out and being glad the pilot was "driving" instead of one of them.

But the pilots were having a difficult time. That soon became apparent to all of them. Eventually they fell silent and kept their eyes trained on the men in the cockpit. Tension inside the aircraft increased when the two-man crew lost radio contact with the ground. The plane's instruments could no longer be depended upon because the readings they were giving out were apparently inaccurate. Because of the impenetrable cloud cover, they hadn't seen the ground since takeoff.

When the plane went into a spiraling nosedive and the pilot shouted back to his passengers, "We're going in. God be with us," they all took the news resignedly and with an amazing calm.

She had bent double and pressed her head between her knees, covering it with her arms, praying all the way down. It seemed to take an eternity.

She would never forget the shock of that first jarring impact. Even braced for it, she hadn't been adequately prepared. She didn't know why she had been spared instantaneous death, unless her smaller size had allowed her to wedge herself between the two seats more securely and better cushion the impact.

However, under the circumstances, she wasn't sure that being spared was a favorable alternative. One could only reach the lodge on the northwestern tip of Great Bear Lake by airplane. Miles of virgin wilderness lay between it and Yellowknife, their destination. God only knew how far off the flight plan the plane had been when it went down. The authorities could search for months without finding her. Until they did—if ever—she was utterly alone and dependent solely on herself for survival.

That thought galvanized her into action. With near-hysterical frenzy she struggled to release her seat belt. It snapped apart and she fell forward, bumping her head on the seat in front of her. She eased herself into the narrow aisle and, on hands and knees, crawled toward the gaping tear in the airplane.

Avoiding any direct contact with the bodies, she looked up through the ripped metal seam. The rain had stopped, but the low, heavy, dark gray clouds looked so laden with menace they seemed ready to burst. Frequently they belched deep rolls of thunder. The sky looked cold and wet and threatening. She clutched the collar of her red fox coat high about her neck. There was virtually no wind. She supposed she should be grateful for that. The wind could get very cold— But wait! If there was no wind, where was that keening sound coming from?

Holding her breath, she waited.

There it was again!

She whipped her head around, listening. It wasn't easy to hear anything over the pounding of her own heart.

A stir.

She looked toward the man who was sitting in the seat across the aisle from hers. Was it just her wishful imagination or did the Loner's eyelids flicker? She scrambled back up the aisle, brushing past the dangling, bleeding arm of one of the crash victims. She had studiously avoided touching it only moments ago.

"Oh, please, God, let him be alive," she prayed fervently. Reaching his seat, she stared down into his face. He still seemed to be in peaceful repose. His eyelids were still. No flicker. No moaning sound coming from his lips, which were all but obscured by a thick, wide mustache. She looked at his chest, but he was wearing a quilted coat, so it was impossible to tell if he were breathing or not.

She laid her index finger along the top curve of his mustache, just beneath his nostrils. She uttered a wordless exclamation when she felt the humid passage of air. Faint, but definitely there.

"Thank God, thank God." She began laughing and crying at the same time. Lifting her hands to his cheeks, she slapped them lightly. "Wake up, mister. Please wake up."

He moaned, but he didn't open his eyes. Intuition told her that the sooner he regained consciousness the better. Besides, she needed the reassurance that he wasn't dead or going to die—at least not immediately. She desperately needed to know that she wasn't alone.

Reasoning that the cold air might help revive him, she resolved to get him outside the plane. It wasn't going to be easy; he probably outweighed her by a hundred pounds or more.

She felt every ounce of it as she opened his seat belt and his dead weight slumped against her like a sack of conerete mix. She caught most of it with her right shoulder and supported him there while she backed down the aisle toward the opening, half lifting him, half dragging him with her.

That seven-foot journey took her over half an hour. The bloody arm hanging over the armrest snagged them. She had to overcome her repulsion and touch it, moving it aside. She got blood on her hands. It was sticky. She whimpered with horror, but clamped her trembling lower lip between her teeth and continued tugging the man down the aisle— one struggling, agonizing inch at a time.

It struck her suddenly that whatever his injury, she might be doing it more harm than good by moving him. But she'd come this far; she wouldn't stop now. Setting a goal and achieving it seemed very important, if for no other reason than to prove she wasn't helpless. She had decided to get him outside, and that's what she was going to do if it killed her.

Which it very well might, she thought several minutes later. She had moved him as far forward as possible. Occasionally he groaned, but otherwise he showed no signs of coming around. Leaving him momentarily, she climbed through the branches of the pine tree. The entire left side of the fuselage had been virtually ripped off, so it would be a matter of dragging him through the branches of the tree. Using her bare hands, she broke off as many of the smaller branches as she could before returning to the man.

It took her five minutes just to turn him around so she could clasp him beneath the arms. Then, backing through the narrow, spiky tunnel she had cleared, she pulled him along with her. Pine needles pricked her face. The rough bark scraped her hands. But thankfully her heavy clothing protected most of her skin.

Her breathing became labored as she struggled. She considered pausing to rest, but was afraid that she would never build up enough momentum to start again. Her burden was moaning almost constantly, now. She knew he must be in agony, but she couldn't stop or he might lapse into deeper unconsciousness.

At last she felt cold air on her cheeks. She pulled her head free of the last branch and stepped out into the open. Taking a few stumbling steps backward, she pulled the man the remainder of the way, until he, too, was clear. Exhausted beyond belief, the muscles of her arms and back and legs burning from exertion, she plopped down hard on her bottom. The man's head fell into her lap.

Bracing herself on her hands and tilting her head toward the sky, she stayed that way until she had regained her breath. For the first time, while drawing the bitingly cold air into her lungs, she thought that it might be good to still be alive. She thanked God that she was. And thanked Him, too, for the other life He'd spared.

She looked down at the man and saw the bump for the first time. He was sporting a classic goose egg on the side of his temple. No doubt it had caused his unconsciousness. Heaving his shoulders up high enough to get her legs out from under him, she crawled around to his side and began unbuttoning his bulky coat. She prayed that she wouldn't uncover a mortal wound. She didn't. Only the plaid flannel shirt that no game hunter would be without. There were no traces of blood on it. From the turtleneck collar of his undershirt to the tops of his laced boots, she could find no sign of serious bleeding.

Expelling a gusty breath of relief, she bent over him and lightly slapped his cheeks again. She guessed him to be around forty, but the years hadn't been easy ones. His longish, wavy hair was saddle brown. So was his mustache. But it and his heavy eyebrows had strands of blond. His skin was sunburned, but not recently; it was a baked on, year-round sunburn. There was a tracery of fine lines at the corners of his eyes. His mouth was wide and thin, the lower lip only slightly fuller than the upper.

This rugged face didn't belong in an office; he spent a good deal of time outdoors. It was an agreeable face, if not a classically handsome one. There was a hardness to it, an uncompromising unapproachability that she had also sensed in his personality.

She wondered uneasily what he would think when he regained consciousness and found himself alone in the wilderness with her. She didn't have long to wait to find out. Moments later, his eyelids flickered, then opened.

Eyes as flinty gray as the sky overhead focused on her. They closed, then opened again. She wanted to speak, but trepidation held her back. The first word to cross his lips was unspeakably vulgar. She flinched, but attributed the foul language to his pain. Again he closed his eyes and waited several seconds before opening them.

Then he said, "We crashed." She nodded. "How long ago?"

"I'm not sure." Her teeth were chattering. It wasn't that cold, so it must have been from fear. Of him? Why? "An hour, maybe."

Grunting with pain, he covered the lump on the side of his head with one hand and levered himself up, using the other hand as a prop. She moved aside so he could sit up straight. "What about everybody else?"

"They're all dead."

He tried to come up on one knee and swayed dizzily. She reflexively extended a helping hand, but he shrugged it off. "Are you sure?"

"Sure they're dead? Yes. I mean, I think so."

He turned his head and stared at her balefully. "Did you check their pulses?"

She changed her mind about his eyes. They weren't like the sky at all. They were colder and much more foreboding. "No, I didn't check," she admitted contritely.

He nailed her with that judgmental stare for several seconds, then, with a great deal of difficulty, pulled himself to his feet. Using the tree behind him for support, he struggled to stand up and regain his equilibrium.

"How . . . how do you feel?"

"Like I'm going to puke."

One thing about him, he didn't mince words. "Maybe you should lie back down."

"No doubt I should."

"Well?"

Still holding his head in one hand, he raised it and looked at her. "Are you volunteering to go in there and check their pulses?" He watched the faint color in her cheeks fade and gave her a twisted smile of ridicule. "That's what I thought."

"I got *you* out, didn't I?"

"Yeah," he said dryly, "you got me out."

She didn't expect him to kiss her hands for saving his life, but a simple thank-you would have been nice. "You're an ungrateful—"

"Save it," he said.

She watched him lever himself away from the tree and stagger toward the demolished aircraft, pushing aside the branches of the tree with much more strength than she could have garnered in a month.

Sinking down onto the marshy ground, she rested her head on her raised knees, tempted to cry. She could hear him moving about in the cabin. When she raised her head and looked, she saw him through the missing windshield of the detached cockpit. He was emotionlessly moving his hands over the bodies of the pilots.

Minutes later, he thrashed his way through the fallen tree. "You were right. They're all dead."

How did he expect her to respond? Nah-nah-nah? He dropped a white first-aid box onto the ground and knelt beside it. He took out a bottle of aspirin and tossed three of them down his throat, swallowing them dry. "Come here," he ordered her rudely. She scooted forward and he handed her a flashlight. "Shine that directly into my eyes, one at a time, and tell me what happens."

She switched on the flashlight. The glass over the bulb was cracked, but it still worked. She shone the light directly into his right eye, then the left. "The pupils contract."

He took the flashlight away from her and clicked it off. "Good. No concussion. Just a rotten headache. You okay?"

"I think so."

He looked at her skeptically, but nodded.

"My name's Rusty Carlson," she said politely.

He barked a short laugh. His eyes moved up to take in her hair. "Rusty, huh?"

"Yes, Rusty," she replied testily.

"Figures."

The man had the manners of a pig. "Do you have a name?"

"Yeah, I've got a name. Cooper Landry. But this isn't a garden party so forgive me if I don't tip my hat and say, 'Pleased to meet you.'"

For two lone survivors of a disastrous plane crash, they were off to a bad beginning. Right now Rusty wanted to be comforted, reassured that she was alive and would go on living. All she'd gotten from him was scorn, which was unwarranted.

"What's with you?" she demanded angrily. "You act as though the crash was my fault."

"Maybe it was."

She gasped with incredulity. "What? I was hardly responsible for the storm."

"No, but if you hadn't dragged out that emotional, tearful goodbye to your sugar daddy, we might have beat it. What made you decide to leave ahead of him—the two of you have a lovers' spat?"

"None of your damned business," she said through teeth that had been straightened to perfection by an expensive orthodontist.

His expression didn't alter. "And you had no business being in a place like that—" his eyes roved over her. "—being the kind of woman you are."

"What kind of woman is that?"

"Drop it. Let's just say that I'd be better off without you."

Having said that, he slid a lethal-looking hunting knife from the leather scabbard attached to his belt. Rusty wondered if he was going to cut her throat with it and rid himself of the inconvenience she posed. Instead, he turned and began hacking at the smaller branches of the tree, cutting a cleaner path to make the fuselage more accessible.

"What are you going to do?"

"I have to get them out."

"The . . . the others? Why?"

"Unless you want to be roommates with them."

"You're going to bury them?"

"That's the idea. Got a better one?"

No, of course she didn't, so she said nothing.

Cooper Landry hacked his way through the tree until only the major branches were left. They were easier to step around and over.

Rusty, making herself useful by dragging aside the branches as he cut them, asked, "We're staying here then?"

"For the time being, yeah." Having cleared a path of sorts, he stepped into the fuselage and signaled her forward. "Grab his boots, will ya?"

She stared down at the dead man's boots. She couldn't do this. Nothing in her life had prepared her for this. He couldn't expect her to do something so grotesque.

But glancing up at him and meeting those implacable gray eyes, she knew that he did expect it of her and expected it of her without an argument.

One by one they removed the bodies from the aircraft. He did most of the work; Rusty lent him a hand when he asked for it. The only way she could do it was to detach her mind from the grisly task. She'd lost her mother when she was a teenager. Two years ago her brother had died. But in both instances, she'd seen them when they were laid out in a satin-lined casket surrounded by soft lighting, organ music, and flowers. Death had seemed unreal. Even the bodies of her mother and brother weren't real to her, but identical replicas of the people she had loved, mannequins created in their images by the mortician.

These bodies were real.

She mechanically obeyed the terse commands this Cooper Landry issued in a voice without feeling or inflection. He must be a robot, she decided. He revealed no emotion whatsoever as he dragged the bodies to the common grave that he'd been able to dig using his knife and the small hatchet he found in a toolbox beneath the pilot's seat. He piled stones over the shallow grave when he was finished.

"Shouldn't we say something?" Rusty stared down at the barbaric pile of colorless stones, put there to protect the bodies of the five men from scavenging animals.

"Say something? Like what?"

"Like a scripture. A prayer."

He shrugged negligently as he cleaned the blade of his knife. "I don't know any scriptures. And my prayers ran out a long time ago." Turning his back on the grave, he stamped back toward the airplane.

Rusty mouthed a hasty prayer before turning to follow him. More than anything, she feared being left alone again. If she let the man out of her sight, he might desert her.

That was unlikely, however. At least not right away. He was reeling with fatigue and on the verge of fainting. "Why don't you lie down and rest?" she suggested. Her strength had deserted her long ago. She was running only on adrenaline now.

"Because night's coming on fast," he said. "We've got to remove the seats of the plane so we'll have room to stretch out in there. Otherwise you might have to spend a night in the great outdoors for the first time in your life." He sarcastically added the last as an afterthought before reentering the airplane. Moments later, Rusty heard him cursing viciously. He came out, his brows drawn together in a fierce scowl.

"What's the matter?"

He held his hand up in front of her face. It was wet. "Fuel."

"Fuel?"

"*Flammable* fuel," he said, impatient with her ignorance. "We can't stay in there. One spark and we'll be blown to China."

"Then don't build a fire."

He glared at her. "Once it gets dark, you'll want a fire," he said scornfully. "Besides, all it would take is a spark from anything. One piece of metal could scrape against another and we'd be history."

"What do we do?"

"We take what we can and move."

"I thought it was always best to stay with the airplane. I heard or read that once. Search parties will be looking for a downed plane. How will they find us if we leave the crash site?"

He cocked his head arrogantly. "You want to stay? Fine, stay. I'm going. But I'd better warn you that I don't think there's any water near here. The first thing I'm going to do in the morning is look for water."

His know-it-all attitude was insufferable. "How do you know there's no water?"

"No animal tracks around. I suppose you could exist on rainwater for as long as it held out, but who knows how long that will be."

When and how had he noticed that there were no animal tracks around? She hadn't even thought to look. In fact, having no water was almost as frightening as having to cope with wild animals to get it. Search for water? How did one go about that? Wild animals? How would she defend herself if one attacked?

She'd die without him. After several moments of deliberation, that was the grim conclusion she reached. She had no choice but to go along with whatever survival tactics he knew and be grateful that he was there to implement them.

Swallowing her pride, she said, "All right, I'll go with you." He didn't even glance up or otherwise acknowledge her. She had no way of knowing whether he was glad or sorry over her decision. By all appearances, he was indifferent. He was already making a pile of things he'd salvaged from the wreckage. Determined not to be ignored, Rusty knelt down beside him. "What can I do to help?"

He nodded toward the luggage compartment of the aircraft. "Go through the luggage. Everybody's. Take whatever might come in handy later." He handed her several tiny suitcase keys, which he had obviously taken off the bodies before he buried them.

She glanced warily at the suitcases. Some had already popped open as a result of the crash. The victims' personal belongings lay strewn on the damp ground. "Isn't that...violating their privacy? Their families might resent—"

He spun around so suddenly that she nearly toppled over backward. "Will you grow up and face facts?" He grabbed her by the shoulders and shook her. "Look around. Do you know what our chances are of coming out of this alive? I'll tell you: Nil. But before I go down, I'm going to fight like hell to stay alive. It's a habit I have."

His face moved closer to hers. "This isn't a Girl Scout outing gone awry; this is survival, lady. Etiquette and propriety be damned. If you tag along with me, you'll do what I tell you to, when I tell you to. Got that? And there won't be any time to spend on sentiment. Don't waste tears on those who didn't make it. They're gone and there's not a damn thing we can do about it. Now, move your butt and get busy doing what I told you to do."

He shoved her away from him and began collecting pelts that the hunters had been taking home as trophies. There was mostly caribou, but also white wolf, beaver, and one small mink.

Holding back bitter tears of mortification and accumulated distress, Rusty bent over the suitcases and began sorting through their contents as she'd been instructed. She wanted to strike out at him. She wanted to collapse in a heap and bawl her eyes out. But she wouldn't give him the satisfaction of seeing her do either. Nor would she provide him with an excuse to leave her behind; he would probably grab at the flimsiest.

A half-hour later she carried her findings and added them to the pile of articles he had gathered. Apparently he approved of her selection, which included two flasks of liquor. She couldn't identify it by the smell, but Cooper wasn't particular. He seemed to enjoy the healthy drink he

took from one of the flasks. She watched his Adam's apple
bob up and down as he swallowed. He had a strong neck,
and a solid, square jaw. Typical, she thought peevishly, of
all stubborn mules.

He recapped the flask and tossed it down along with the
books of matches, a travel sewing kit, and the extra clothing she had accumulated. He didn't remark on how well
she'd done. Instead he nodded down at the small suitcase
she was carrying. "What's that?"

"That's mine."

"That's not what I asked."

He yanked the suitcase from her hand and opened it. His
large hands violated her neat stacks of pastel silk thermal
underwear, nightgowns, and assorted lingerie. He pulled
one set of leggings through the circle he made of his index
finger and thumb. His gray eyes met hers. "Silk?" Coldly,
she stared back at him without answering. His grin was
downright dirty. It insinuated things she didn't even want to
guess at. "Very nice."

Then his grin disappeared beneath his mustache and he
tossed the garment at her. "Take two sets of long johns. A
couple pairs of socks. A cap. Gloves. This coat," he added,
piling a ski jacket atop the other garments he'd selected.
"One extra pair of britches. A couple of sweaters." He
opened the zippered, plastic-lined travel bag she'd packed
her cosmetics and toiletries in.

"I need all of that," she said quickly.

"Not where we're going you don't." He rifled through her
cosmetics, heedlessly tossing a fortune's worth of beauty-
enhancing creams and makeup into the rotting, wet leaves.
"A hairbrush, toothpaste and toothbrush, soap. That's it.
And, just because I'm merciful, these." He handed her a
box of tampons.

She snatched it out of his hands and crammed it back into
the cosmetic bag along with the other few items he had allowed her.

Again he grinned. The juxtaposition of his white teeth and wide mustache made him look positively wicked. "You think I'm a real son of a bitch, don't you? You're just too nice to say so."

"No, I'm not." Her russet brown eyes flashed hotly. "I think you're a real son of a bitch."

His smile merely deepened. "It's only gonna get worse before it gets better." He stood up, glancing worriedly at the darkening sky. "Come on. We'd better get going."

As soon as he turned his back, Rusty slipped a colorless lip gloss, a bottle of shampoo and a razor into the bag. He might not need to shave before they reached civilization, but she was sure she would.

She jumped guiltily when he turned back and asked her, "Do you know how to shoot one of these?" He held up a hunting rifle.

Rusty shook her head no. Only yesterday she'd seen a beautiful Dall ram being brought down with a rifle just like that. It was a distasteful memory. Rather than celebrating the kill, her sympathies had been with the slain animal.

"I was afraid of that," Cooper muttered. "But you can carry it anyway." He hooked the heavy rifle over her shoulder by its leather strap and placed another, presumably his own, over his shoulder. He shoved a fearsome-looking pistol into his waistband. Catching her wary glance he said, "It's a flare gun. I found it in the cockpit. Keep your ears open for search planes."

By seaming up the neck of a sweater with a shoelace, he had fashioned a backpack out of it. He tied it around her neck by the sleeves. "Okay," he said, giving her a cursory inspection, "let's go."

Rusty cast one last sad, apprehensive look at the wreckage of the airplane, then struck out after him. His broad back made an easy target to follow. She found that by keeping her eyes trained on a spot directly between his shoulder blades, she was able to put herself into a semitrance and ward off her memory of the bodies they had left behind. She wanted to lapse into forgetfulness.

She plodded on, losing energy with each step. Her strength seemed to be seeping out of her with alarming rapidity. She didn't know how far they had gone, but it couldn't have been very far before it seemed impossible for her to put one foot in front of the other. Her legs were trembling with fatigue. She no longer swatted aside the branches that backlashed, but indifferently let them slap into her.

Cooper's image grew blurry, then began wavering in front of her like a ghost. The trees all seemed to have tentacles that tried to catch her clothes, tear at her hair, ensnare her ankles, impede her in any way possible. Stumbling, she glanced down at the ground and was amazed to see that it was rushing up to meet her. How extraordinary, she thought.

Instinctively, she grasped the nearest branch to break her fall and called out weakly, "Coo... Cooper."

She landed hard, but it was a blessed relief to lie on the cool ground, damp and soggy as it was. The leaf mold seemed like a compress against her cheek. It was a luxury to let her eyes close.

Cooper murmured a curse as he shrugged off his backpack and let the strap of the rifle slide down his arm. Roughly, he rolled her over onto her back and pried her eyelids open with his thumbs. She gazed up at him, having no idea that her face was as pale as death. Even her lips were as gray as the clouds overhead.

"I'm sorry to hold you back." She was vaguely surprised that her voice sounded so faint. She could feel her lips moving, but she wasn't sure she had actually spoken aloud. It seemed imperative to apologize for detaining him and being a nuisance in general. "I've got to rest for just a minute."

"Yeah, yeah, that's fine, uh, Rusty. You rest." He was working at the hook and eye buried deep in the fox-fur collar of her coat. "Do you hurt anywhere?"

"Hurt? No. Why?"

"Nothing." He shoved open her coat and plunged his hands inside. He slipped them beneath her sweater and began carefully pressing his fingers against her abdomen. Was this proper? she thought fuzzily. "You might be bleeding somewhere and don't know it."

His words served to clarify everything. "Internally?" Panicked, she struggled to sit up.

"I don't know. I don't—Hold it!" With a sudden flick of his hands, he flipped back the front panels of her full-length coat. His breath whistled through his teeth. Rusty levered herself up on her elbows to see what had caused him to frown so ferociously.

The right leg of her trousers was soaked with bright red blood. It had also made a sponge of her wool sock and run over her leather hiking boot.

"When did you do this?" His eyes, razor sharp, moved up to hers. "What happened?"

Dismayed, she looked at Cooper and wordlessly shook her head.

"Why didn't you tell me you were hurt?"

"I didn't know," she said weakly.

He slipped his knife from its scabbard. Pinching up the blood-soaked hem of her trousers, he slid the knife into the crease and jerked it upward. With one heart-stopping stroke, it cut straight up her pants leg, neatly slicing the fabric all the way from her hem to the elastic leg of her underpants. Shocked and fearful, she sucked in her breath.

Cooper, gazing down at her leg, expelled a long, defeated breath. "Hell."

Two

Rusty's head began to buzz. She felt nauseous. Her earlobes were throbbing and her throat was on fire. Each individual hair follicle on her head felt like a pinprick. The pads of her fingers and toes were tingling. She'd fainted once after having a root canal. She knew the symptoms.

But, damn, did they have to afflict her here? In front of him?

"Easy, easy." He grasped her shoulders and lowered her to the ground. "You don't remember hurting yourself?" She shook her head dumbly. "Must have happened when we crashed."

"I didn't feel any pain."

"You were too shocked. How does it feel now?"

Only then did she become aware of the pain. "Not bad." His eyes probed hers for the truth. "Really, it's not that bad. I've bled a lot, though, haven't I?"

"Yeah." Grim-faced, he rummaged through the first-aid kit. "I've got to sponge up the blood so I can see where it's coming from."

He tore into the backpack she'd been carrying and selected a soft cotton undershirt to swab up the blood. She felt the pressure of his hands, but little else as she gazed up through the branches of the trees overhead. Maybe she'd been premature to thank God for being alive. She might bleed to death lying here on the ground. And there wouldn't be anything Cooper or she could do about it. In fact, he would probably be glad to get rid of her.

His soft curse roused her from her macabre musings. She tilted her head up and looked down at her injured leg. Along her shinbone a gash ran from just below her knee to just above her sock. She could see flesh, muscle. It was sickening. She whimpered.

"Lie down, dammit."

Weakly, Rusty obeyed the emphatic order. "How could that happen without my feeling it?"

"Probably split like a tomato skin the moment of impact."

"Can you do anything?"

"Clean it with peroxide." He opened the brown opaque plastic bottle he'd found in the first-aid kit and soaked the sleeve of the T-shirt with the peroxide.

"Is it going to hurt?"

"Probably."

Ignoring her tearful, frightened eyes, he dabbed at the wound with the peroxide. Rusty clamped her lower lip with her teeth to keep from crying out, but her face twisted with anguish. Actually, the thought of the peroxide bubbling in the gash was as bad as the pain.

"Breathe through your mouth if you feel like vomiting," he told her tonelessly. "I'm almost finished."

She squeezed her eyes shut and didn't open them until she heard the sound of ripping cloth. He was tearing another T-shirt into strips. One by one he wrapped them around her calf, binding her lower leg tightly.

"That'll have to do for now," he said, more to himself than to her. Picking up his knife again, he said, "Raise your hips." She did, avoiding his eyes. He cut the leg of her trousers from around her upper thigh. His hands worked beneath her thighs and between them. His callused knuckles brushed against her smooth, warm skin, but she needn't have felt any embarrassment. He could have been cutting up a steak for all the emotion he showed.

"You damn sure can't walk."

"I can!" Rusty insisted frantically.

She was afraid that he would go off without her. He was standing over her, feet widespread, looking around. His brow was beetled and beneath his mustache she could tell that he was gnawing on the inside of his cheek as though giving something careful consideration.

Was he weighing his options? Deciding whether or not to desert her? Or maybe he was thinking of killing her quickly and mercifully instead of letting her die of her wound.

Finally he bent down and, cupping her armpits in his palms, lifted her into a sitting position. "Take off your coat and put on that ski jacket."

Without an argument, she let the fur coat slide from her shoulders. Using the hatchet he'd brought along, Cooper hacked down three saplings and stripped them of their branches. Silently Rusty watched as he fashioned them into an H, only placing the crossbar higher than normal. He bound the intersections with rawhide tongs, which he'd taken from the boots of the men they'd buried. Then he took her fur coat and ran a sleeve over each of the tops of the two longer poles. Rusty flinched when he stabbed through the fur and satin lining, gouging out a hole in the bottom of her precious fox coat.

He glanced up at her. "What's the matter?"

She swallowed, realizing that he was testing her. "Nothing. The coat was a gift, that's all."

He watched her for a few seconds more before making a similar hole in the other side. He then ran the poles through the holes. The finished product was a crude travois. No self-respecting American Indian would have claimed it, but Rusty was impressed with his ingenuity and skill. And vastly relieved that he obviously didn't plan to leave her behind or otherwise dispose of her.

He laid the rough contraption on the ground. Turning to her, he caught her under the knees and behind the back and lifted her. He laid her on the soft fur, then piled several pelts on top of her.

"I didn't see any animal up there with a hide that looked like this," she said, running her hand over a skin of short, fine wool.

"*Umingmak.*"

"Pardon?"

"That's what the Inuit called the musk-ox. Means 'the bearded one.' It wasn't my kill; I just bought the pelt. It's very warm." He tucked the wool around her and threw another pelt on top of that. "It's up to you to stay on and keep covered."

Standing, he wiped perspiration off his brow with the back of his hand. He winced when he grazed the bump on his temple. Rusty would have gone to bed for a week if she had sustained a blow like that; it must be killing him.

"Thank you, Cooper," she said softly.

He froze, glanced down at her, nodded quickly, then turned and began gathering up their paraphernalia. He tossed both backpacks onto her lap, along with both rifles. "Hang on to those, too, will you?"

"Where are we going?"

"Southeast," was his succinct reply.

"Why?"

"Sooner or later, we'll bump into an outpost of civilization."

"Oh." She dreaded moving, anticipating that the journey wasn't going to be a joyride. "May I have an aspirin please?"

He unpocketed the plastic bottle and shook two aspirin tablets into her hands.

"I can't take them without water."

He made an impatient scoffing sound. "It's either dry or with brandy."

"Brandy, please."

He passed her one of the flasks, watching her closely. She bravely put the spout to her mouth and took a hefty swallow to wash down the aspirin tablets. She choked and sputtered. Tears filled her eyes, but with dignity and poise she returned the flask to him. "Thank you."

His narrow lips twitched with the need to smile. "You might not have any common sense, but you've got guts, lady."

And that, she thought, was as close to a compliment as she was ever likely to get from Cooper Landry. He secured the trunks of the saplings beneath his arms and moved forward, dragging the travois behind him. After having gone only a few teeth-jarring, butt-bruising yards, Rusty realized that she wasn't going to be much better off in the travois than she would have been walking. It required all her concentration just to keep from sliding off. Her bottom would be black and blue with bruises—legacies of the rocks it encountered every grueling step of the way. She dared not even think of the satin lining of her coat being ripped to shreds by the forest debris as it was hauled over the rough ground.

It grew progressively darker and colder. A light precipitation began—snow grains she thought the meteorologists called the stuff, pellets of ice no larger than grains of salt. Her injured leg began to ache, but she would have bitten her tongue in two before she complained. She could hear Cooper's labored breathing. He wasn't having an easy time of it either. If it weren't for her, he could cover three times the distance in the same amount of time.

Darkness closed in suddenly, making it perilous for them to continue over the unfamiliar terrain. He stopped in the next clearing he came to and dropped the poles of the travois. "How're you doing?"

She didn't think about how hungry, thirsty, and uncomfortable she was. She said, "Fine."

"Yeah, sure. How are you really?" He knelt down and whipped off the covering of furs. Her bandage was soaked with fresh blood. He quickly replaced the furs. "We'd better stop for the night. Now that the sun has set, I can't tell which direction I'm going in."

He was lying, only saying that to make her feel better. Rusty knew that he would keep going if it weren't for her. It was doubtful that he was afraid of the dark or that inclement weather would faze him. Even though he'd been dragging her for hours, he appeared to have enough stamina to go at least another two.

He circled the clearing and began shoveling pine needles into a pile. He spread the pelts over them and came back for Rusty.

"Cooper?"

"Hmm?" He grunted with the effort of lifting her off the travois.

"I have to go to the bathroom."

She couldn't see him clearly in the darkness, but she could feel his shocked stare. Embarrassed beyond belief, she kept her head down. "Okay," he replied after a moment. "Will your leg support you while—"

"Yes, I think so," she said in a rush.

He carried her to the edge of the clearing and gently lowered her to stand on her left leg. "Brace yourself against the tree," he instructed gruffly. "Call me when you're done."

It was much more difficult than she had expected it to be. By the time she had refastened what was left of her trousers, she was shaking with weakness and her teeth were chattering with cold. "All right, I'm finished."

Cooper materialized out of the darkness and lifted her into his arms again. She would never have thought a bed of pine needles and animal pelts could have felt so good, but she sighed with relief when he laid her on it and she was able to relax.

Cooper packed the furs around her. "I'll build a fire. It won't be much of one. There's not enough dry wood. But it'll be better than nothing and might help ward off visitors."

Rusty shivered and pulled the furs over her head, as much to protect her from the thought of wild animals as the icy precipitation that continued to dust the ground. But the increasing pain in her leg wouldn't let her doze. She grew restless and finally peeped out from beneath the covering. Cooper had succeeded in building a sputtering, smoky fire. He'd lined the shallow bowl he'd scooped out of the ground with rocks to keep it from igniting her bed.

He glanced over at her and, unzipping one of the many pockets in his coat, took something out and tossed it to her. She caught it one-handed. "What is it?"

"Granola bar."

At the thought of food, her stomach rumbled noisily. She ripped open the foil wrapper, ready to stuff the whole bar into her mouth. Before she did, she got hold of herself and paused. "You...you don't have to share with me," she said in a small voice. "It's yours and you might need it later."

His gray eyes looked as hard and cold as gunmetal when he turned his head. "It isn't mine. I found it in a coat pocket that belonged to one of the others."

He seemed to take brutal delight in telling her that, implying that if the granola bar were his, he'd think twice before sharing it with her.

Whatever his intention, he had spoiled it for her. The bar tasted like sawdust in her mouth; she chewed and swallowed it mechanically. The tastelessness was partially due to her thirst. As though reading her mind, Cooper said, "If we don't find water tomorrow, we're in trouble."

"Do you think we will?"

"I don't know."

She lay amid the furs contemplatively. "Why do you think the plane crashed?"

"I don't know. A combination of things, I guess."

"Do you have any idea where we are?"

"No. I might have a general idea if it hadn't been for the storm."

"You think we were off course?"

"Yes. But I don't know how far."

She rested her cheek against her hand and stared into the feeble flame that was struggling for life. "Had you ever been to Great Bear Lake before?"

"Once."

"When?"

"Several years ago."

"Do you do a lot of hunting?"

"Some."

He wasn't exactly an orator, was he? She wanted to draw him into conversation to keep her mind off the pain in her leg. "Do you think they'll find us?"

"Maybe."

"When?"

"What do you think I am, a damned encyclopedia?" His shout bounced around the ring of trees surrounding them. He came to his feet abruptly. "Stop asking me so many questions. I don't have the answers."

"I just want to know," she cried tearfully.

"Well, so do I. But I don't. I'd say the chances of them finding us are extremely good if the plane was still on the flight plan and extremely remote if it was too far off, okay? Now, shut up about it."

Rusty lapsed into wounded silence. Cooper prowled the clearing in search of dry tinder. He added a few sticks to the fire before moving toward her. "Better let me tend to your leg."

He brusquely threw the covers back. The fire shed meager light onto the bloody bandage. Expertly wielding the hunting knife, he cut through the knots he'd tied earlier and began unwinding the stained cloth. "Does it hurt?"

"Yes."

"Well, it has every right to," he said grimly as he gazed down at the wound. His expression wasn't very encouraging.

While she held the flashlight for him, he soaked the gash with peroxide again and wrapped it in fresh bandaging. By the time he had finished, tears were stinging her eyes and her lips were blotchy from biting them, but she hadn't cried out once. "Where'd you learn to bandage so well?"

"Nam." His answer was curt, indicating that the subject was closed. "Here, take two more aspirin." He passed her the bottle after shaking out two for himself. He hadn't complained, but his head must have felt as though it were splitting in two. "And drink some more brandy. At least two swallows. I think that by morning, you're going to need it."

"Why?"

"Your leg. Tomorrow will probably be the worst day. After that, maybe it'll start to get better."

"What if it doesn't?"

He said nothing; he didn't have to.

With trembling hands, Rusty held the flask of brandy to her lips and took an occasional sip from it. Now that the dry kindling had caught, Cooper stacked more wood on the fire. But it wasn't burning hot enough for him to take off his coat, which he surprised her by doing. He took off his boots, too, and told her to do the same. Then, making a bundle of the coats and boots, he stuffed them down between the furs.

"What's that for?" Her feet were already getting cold.

"If we sweat in our boots and it turns colder, we'll get frostbite. Scoot over."

She stared up at him apprehensively. "Huh?"

Sighing impatiently, he crawled in with her, forcing her to move over and allow him room beneath the pile of furs. Alarmed, Rusty exclaimed, "What are you doing?"

"Going to sleep. If you'll shut up, that is."

"Here?"

"Accommodations with separate beds were unavailable."

"You can't—"

"Relax, Miss . . . What was it again?"

"Carlson."

"Yeah, Miss Carlson. Our combined body heat will help keep us warm." He snuggled close to her and pulled the furs up over their heads, effectively cocooning them inside. "Turn on your side, away from me."

"Go to hell."

She could almost hear him mentally counting to ten. "Look, I don't want to freeze. And I don't look forward to digging another grave to bury you in, either, so just do as I say. Now."

He must have been an officer in Vietnam, she thought petulantly as she rolled on to her side. He put his arm around her waist and drew her back against him, until they were lying together spoon fashion. She could scarcely breathe. "Is this really necessary?"

"Yes."

"I won't move away. There's nowhere to go. You don't have to keep your arm there."

"You surprise me. I thought you'd like this." He pressed against her stomach with the palm of his hand. "You're a real looker. Don't you expect men to get all hot and bothered when they're around you?"

"Let go of me."

"All that long hair, its unusual color."

"Shut up!"

"You're proud of your round little butt and perky tits, aren't you? I'm sure most men find you irresistible. That copilot sure did. He was salivating after you like a Doberman over a bitch in heat, almost stumbling over his tongue.''

''I don't know what you're talking about.''

He stroked her stomach. ''Oh, yes, you do. You must have enjoyed stunning all those men on the plane into speechlessness when you climbed aboard with your fur collar pulled up, brushing against your flushed cheeks and sexy mouth.''

''Why are you doing this?'' she sobbed.

He cursed and when he spoke again, his voice wasn't lilting and teasing. It was weary. ''So you'll rest assured that I'm not going to take advantage of you during the night. Redheads have never been my preference. Besides, your body is still warm from your sugar daddy's bed. All things considered, your virtue is safe with me.''

She sniffed back tears of humiliation. ''You're cruel and vulgar.''

He laughed. ''Now you sound offended that I'm not tempted to rape you. Make up your mind. If you have a hankering for sex tonight, I can oblige you. My body isn't as particular as my head. After all, it's awfully dark in here. And you know what they say about cats in the dark. But personally, I prefer safer, more comfortable surroundings to screw in. So just go to sleep, will you?''

Rusty grit her teeth in outrage. She held her body rigid and put a barrier between them, if not physically, then mentally. She tried to ignore his body heat, which permeated her clothing, and his breath that drifted over her neck each time he exhaled, and the latent power in the thighs that conformed to the backs of hers. Gradually, and with the help of the brandy she'd drunk, she relaxed. Eventually she dozed.

It was her own moan that woke her up. Her leg was throbbing painfully.

''What is it?''

Cooper's voice was gruff, but Rusty didn't think it was because he'd been roused from a deep sleep. Intuitively she knew that he had been lying there awake. "Nothing."

"Tell me. What's the matter? Your leg?"

"Yes."

"Is it bleeding again?"

"I don't think so. It's doesn't feel wet. It just hurts."

"Drink some more brandy." He angled himself away from her and reached for the flask of brandy, which he'd brought into the fur cocoon with them.

"I'm already woozy."

"Good. It's working." He poked her lips with the uncapped flask and tipped it forward. She either had to drink or drown.

The potent liquor burned a fiery path down her middle. At the very least, it took her mind off her painful wound for a few seconds. "Thanks."

"Open your legs."

"Pardon?"

"Open your legs."

"How much brandy have you had, Mr. Landry?"

"Do it."

"Why?"

"So I can get mine between them."

Without giving her another chance to argue, he slid his hand between her thighs and raised her injured leg. He wedged his knees between hers, then gently lowered her right leg to rest on top of his. "There. Keeping it elevated will help relieve the pressure. It'll also keep me from jostling it in the night."

She was too flabbergasted to fall back to sleep immediately; too uncomfortably aware of his nearness. And there was something else keeping her awake: a nagging guilt.

"Cooper, did you know any of the other men?"

"Those on board the plane? No."

"The men in the front two seats were brothers. While we were weighing our luggage, I heard them talking about getting their families together for Thanksgiving in a few weeks. They were going to show them the slides they'd taken this week."

"Don't think about it."

"I can't help it."

"Yes, you can."

"No, I can't. I keep asking myself why I'm alive. Why was I allowed to live? It doesn't make any sense."

"It doesn't have to make sense," he said bitterly. "That's just the way it *is*. It was their time, that's all. It's over, forgotten."

"Not forgotten."

"Force it out of your mind."

"Is that what you did?"

"Yes."

She shuddered. "How can you be so unfeeling about another human life?"

"Practice."

The word affected her like a hard slap on the cheek. It had been cruelly delivered to shut her up, and it did. But it didn't stop her from thinking. She wondered how many of his buddies Cooper had seen killed in Vietnam. Dozens? Scores? Hundreds? Still, she couldn't imagine ever becoming inured to death.

She'd had practice dealing with it, but not to the extent that he apparently had. It wasn't something she could block out, dismiss, by an act of will. When she thought about her losses, she still ached.

"My mother died of a stroke," she told him quietly. "Her death was almost a relief. She would have been severely incapacitated. I had a week to prepare myself for it. But my brother's death was sudden." Cooper wouldn't care to hear about any of this, but she wanted to talk about it.

"Brother?"

"Jeff. He was killed in a car wreck two years ago."

"No other family?"

"Only my father." She drew a gentle breath. "He was the man I was with at the lodge. The one I said goodbye to. Not a sugar daddy. Not a lover. My father."

She waited for an apology, but it never came. If his body hadn't been so tense, she might have thought he'd fallen asleep.

Finally he broke the silence by asking, "What is your father going to think when he's notified about the crash?"

"Oh, my God!" Reflexively, she clutched Cooper's hand where it still rested against her stomach. "I hadn't thought of that."

She could imagine her father's despair when he heard the news. He'd lost his wife. Then his son. Now his daughter. He would be disconsolate. Rusty couldn't bear to think of the suffering he would go through, the hell of uncertainty, of not knowing what had happened to her. Hopefully, as much for her father's sake as her own, they would be rescued soon.

"The guy looked like a real mover and shaker to me," Cooper said. "He'll ride the authorities until we're found."

"You're right. Father won't give up until he knows what happened to me."

Rusty was certain of that. Her father was a powerful man. He was dynamic and had both the talent and the means to get things done. His reputation and money could cut through miles of red tape. Knowing that he'd leave no stone unturned until she was rescued gave her an optimistic thread to cling to.

She was also surprised to discover that Cooper hadn't been as withdrawn and impervious as he had appeared to be. Before they boarded the plane, he had kept to himself. He hadn't mingled with the other passengers. But he'd noticed everything. Apparently her companion was an observant student of human nature.

Nature was having its way with him right now. While she'd been talking, Rusty became nervously aware of his sex snuggled solidly against her bottom. She blurted, "Are you married?"

"No."

"Ever?"

"No."

"Involved?"

"Look, I get my share of sex, okay? And I know why you're suddenly so curious. Believe me, I feel it too. But I can't do anything to help it. Well, actually I can, but as we discussed earlier, that isn't a very workable solution under the circumstances. The alternatives that come readily to mind would embarrass us both I'm afraid."

Rusty's cheeks grew hot and rosy. "I wish you wouldn't."

"What?"

"Talk like that."

"How?"

"You know. Dirty."

"You just left a big game hunting lodge. Didn't you intercept a few dirty jokes? Overhear some lewd comments? I thought you'd be used to bawdy language by now."

"Well, I'm not. And for your information, I went on that hunting trip for my father's sake. I didn't particularly enjoy myself."

"He forced you to go?"

"Of course not."

"Coerced you to? In exchange for that fur coat, maybe?"

"No," she grated with irritation. "The trip was my idea. I suggested that we take it together."

"And you randomly chose the Northwest Territories? Why not Hawaii? Or St. Moritz? I can think of a thousand other places on the globe where you would have fit in better."

Her sigh was an admission that he had her correctly pegged. On a big game hunt she was as out of place as a rusty nail in an operating room. "My father and brother always went hunting together. Four weeks every year. It was a family tradition." Filled with remorse, she closed her eyes. "Father hadn't been hunting since Jeff was killed. I thought the trip would be good for him. I insisted that he go. When he hesitated, I offered to go with him."

She expected murmurs of sympathy and understanding—perhaps even whispered praise for her unselfish and noble gesture. Instead all she heard from him was a grumpy "Be quiet, will you? I'm trying to get some sleep."

"Stop it, Rusty."

Her brother's voice echoed through her dream. They were wrestling, as only brothers and sisters who either hate each other intensely or love each other intensely can. With Jeff and her, the latter had been true. They were barely a year apart in age. From the time Rusty took her first steps, they had been bosom buddies and playmates. Much to their father's delight and their mother's aggravation, they had often engaged in rowdy hand-to-hand combat and always came up laughing.

But there was no levity in Jeff's voice now as he clasped her wrists and anchored them to the floor on either side of her head. "Stop it, now." He shook her slightly. "You're going to hurt yourself if you don't stop flailing around."

She came awake and opened her eyes. It wasn't Jeff's well-remembered, well-loved face she stared into, but the man's. The Loner's. She was glad he was alive, but she didn't like him very much. What was his name? Oh, yes, Cooper. Cooper...? Cooper something. Or something Cooper.

"Lie still," he commanded her.

She stopped thrashing. The air was cold on her exposed skin, and she realized that she'd kicked off all the furs he'd piled over them for the night. On his knees, he was straddling her chest and bending over her. Her wrists were stapled behind her head by his hard fingers.

"Get off me."

"Are you all right now?"

She nodded. She was as all right as a woman could be upon waking up to find a man the size and shape of Cooper Landry—that was it, Landry—straddling her with thighs that rose like columns above her, coming together... She averted her eyes from that mouth-drying juncture. "Please," she gasped. "I'm fine."

He eased himself off her. She sucked in frigidly cold air that hurt her lungs. But God, it felt good against her hot face. It felt good for only a second. Then she shivered with a chill and her teeth started clicking together. Cooper's brows were drawn together worriedly. Or crossly. She couldn't tell. He was either concerned or annoyed.

"You're burning up with fever," he told her bluntly. "I left the bed to build up the fire. You were delirious and started shouting for somebody called Jeff."

"My brother." Her shudders were convulsive. She pulled one of the furs around her.

It hadn't rained or drizzled anymore during the night. She could actually see flames and glowing coals beneath the sticks Cooper had added to the fire. The flames were so hot they burned her eyeballs until they hurt.

No, impossible. That must be the fever.

Leaving the fur covering her upper body alone, Cooper lifted the lower half of it off her leg. Once again he painstakingly unwrapped the bandage and stared down at the open wound. Rusty stared at him.

Finally he looked at her, his mouth set in a bleak line. "I won't try to fool you. It's bad. Infected. There's a bottle of antibiotics in the first-aid kit. I was saving them in case this happened, but I'm not sure they'll be adequate to take care of it."

She swallowed with difficulty. Even her feverish brain could assimilate what he was telling her. Raising herself to her elbows, she looked down at her leg. She wanted to gag. On either side of the deep gash, the skin was raised and puckered with infection. Flopping back down, she drew in shallow, rapid breaths. She wet her lips, ineffectually because the fever was making her mouth drier than it had been before. "I could get gangrene and die, couldn't I?"

He forced a half smile. "Not yet. We've got to do what we can to prevent that."

"Like cut it off?"

"God, you're morbid. What I had in mind was lancing out the pus and then closing the gash with stitches."

Her face turned ashen. "That sounds morbid enough."

"Not as bad as cauterizing it. Which it might come to." Her face went as colorless as chalk. "But, for right now, let's put some stitches in. Don't look relieved," he said, frowning deeply, "it's gonna hurt like hell."

She stared into the depths of his eyes. Strange as it was, rocky as their beginning had been, she trusted him. "Do whatever you have to do."

He nodded brusquely, then went to work. First he withdrew a pair of her silk long johns from the sweater cum backpack. "I'm glad you wear silk undies." She smiled waveringly at his mild joke as he began to unravel the casing of the waistband.

"We'll use these threads for the sutures." He nodded down toward the silver flask. "Better start on that brandy. Use it to swallow one of those penicillin tablets. You're not allergic to it, are you? Good," he said when she shook her head. "Sip the brandy steadily. Don't stop until you're good and drunk. But don't drink all of it. I'll have to sterilize the threads and bathe the gash with it."

She wasn't anesthetized nearly enough when he bent over her leg. The hunting knife, which he'd sterilized in the fire, was held poised in readiness over the infected wound. "Ready?" She nodded. "Try to keep still." She nodded again. "And don't fight unconsciousness. We'd both be better off if you passed out."

The first tiny puncture he made into the red, puffy skin caused her to cry out and yank her leg back. "No, Rusty! You've got to lie still."

It was an agonizing process and seemed to go on forever. He meticulously lanced the areas that needed it. When he doused the entire wound with brandy, Rusty screamed. After that, the stitches didn't seem so bad. He used the sewing needle from the matchbook kit they'd brought with them. After soaking individual threads in brandy, he drew them through her skin and tied them, firmly pulling the edges of the wound together.

Rusty stared at the spot where his tawny eyebrows grew together above the bridge of his nose. His forehead was sweating in spite of the cold. He never took his eyes off his work except to occasionally glance down at her face. He was sensitive to her pain. Even sympathetic toward it. His hands were amazingly tender for a man so large, and for one who had a cold, unfeeling stone where his heart should have been.

Eventually that spot between his eyebrows began to swim in and out of focus. Although she was lying still, her head was spinning, reeling with pain and trauma and the anesthetizing effects of the brandy. Despite Cooper's advice, she struggled to stay awake, afraid that if she went to sleep she might never wake up. Finally, she gave up the fight and let her eyes drift closed.

Her last conscious thought was that it was a shame her father would never know how brave she'd been right up to the moment of her death.

"Well," Cooper said, sitting back on his heels and wiping his perspiring forehead, "it's not pretty, but I think it will work."

He looked down at her with a satisfied and optimistic smile. But she didn't see his smile. She was unconscious.

Three

She came to, actually surprised that she was alive. At first she thought that darkness had fallen, but she inched her head upward. The small mink pelt slid off her head. It was still daylight—exactly what time was impossible to pinpoint. The sky was gloomily overcast.

With a sense of dread, she waited for the pain from her leg to penetrate her consciousness, but miraculously it didn't. Dizzy from the brandy she'd consumed, she eased herself into a sitting position. It took every ounce of strength she had left to lift the furs off her leg. For one horrid moment she thought it might not be hurting because Cooper had amputated it after all.

But when she moved aside the largest caribou pelt, she found that her leg was still intact and bandaged in strips of white cotton. No signs of fresh blood. She was by no means ready to run a marathon, but it felt much better.

Sitting up had exhausted her and she fell back amid the furs, pulling them to her chin. Her skin was hot and dry, but she was chilled. She still had a fever. Maybe she should take more aspirin. But where were they? Cooper would know. He—

Where was Cooper?

Her lethargy vanished and she sprang into a sitting position. Frantically her eyes scanned the clearing. Not a trace. He was gone. His rifle was missing, too. The other one lay on the ground within her reach. The fire still had glowing coals and was giving off heat.

But her protector had deserted her.

Forcibly tamping down hysteria, she reasoned that she was jumping to conclusions. He wouldn't do that. He wouldn't have nursed her so meticulously only to leave her stranded and helpless in the wilderness.

Would he?

Not unless he was an unfeeling bastard.

Hadn't she decided that was exactly what Cooper Landry was?

No. He was hard. Tough. Cynical, certainly. But not completely lacking in feelings. If he were, he'd have deserted her yesterday.

So where was he?

He'd left a rifle behind. Why? Maybe that was the extent of his human kindness. He'd tended to her wound, done all he could on that score. He'd provided her with the means to protect herself. Maybe now it was every man for himself. Survival of the fittest.

Well, she would die. If not of fever, then of thirst. She had no water. She had no food. She had no shelter to speak of. In just a little while the supply of firewood, which he'd cut and stacked nearby, would be used up. She'd die of exposure if the weather turned even marginally colder.

Like hell she would!

Suddenly she was furious with him for going off and leaving her. She'd show him; she'd show her father. Rusty Carlson was not an easily expendable, spineless wimp.

She threw off the covers and pulled on her ski jacket. For the time being she'd leave off her left boot because the pair of them were still stashed farther down in the pile of furs, too far for her to reach. Besides, if one foot was bare, the other might just as well be, too. And on top of that, putting on her coat had sapped her energy.

Food and water.

Those essentials were necessary. That's what she had to find first. But where? At best, her surroundings were intimidating. At worst, terrifying. For three hundred and sixty degrees, all she could see was virgin forest. Beyond the nearby trees—some so tall she couldn't even see the tops of them—there stretched endless miles of more just like them.

Before she could go in search of water, she had to get to her feet. It seemed like an impossible task, but she gritted her teeth with the determination to do it.

When they discovered her body, it wouldn't be hunkered under a pile of furs!

Reaching out as far as she could, she closed her hand around a stick of firewood and pulled it toward her. Using it as a prop, she came up on her good knee, keeping the injured one straight out in front of her. Then she paused to catch her breath, which was forming clouds of white vapor in front of her face.

Repeatedly she tried to stand up, but failed. She was as weak as a newborn kitten. And light-headed. Damn Cooper Landry! No wonder he'd urged her to drink so much brandy. He'd wanted her to pass out so she wouldn't know when he sneaked away like the miserable skunk that he was.

Making a Herculean final effort, she put all her weight on her left foot and stood up on it. The earth tilted precariously. Closing her eyes, she clasped her supporting stick of firewood and held on for dear life. When she felt it was safe to reopen her eyes, she did—and let out a thin squeak of astonishment. Cooper was standing on the other side of the clearing.

"Just what the hell do you think you're doing?" he bellowed.

Dropping what he was carrying, including his rifle, he bore down on her like a sorely provoked angel. Catching her under her arms, he kicked the stick of wood out from under her and lowered her back into her sickbed. He packed the covers around her shivering body.

"What the hell were you trying to do?"

"F...find water," she stuttered through chattering teeth.

His muttered expletive was so vivid it was almost tangible. He laid his open hand on her forehead to gauge her temperature. "You're so cold, you're blue. Don't try another damn stupid stunt like that again, understand? It's *my* job to find water. *Yours* is to stay put. Got that?"

Swearwords continued to pour out of him like the payoff of a slot machine. He turned toward the fire and began stoking it, angrily throwing firewood onto the smoldering coals and fanning them to life. When the fire was blazing, he crossed the clearing and picked up the limp rabbit carcass he'd dropped on the ground. He was also carrying a thermos, one of the things he'd brought with them from the wreckage. Uncapping it, he poured water into the lid/cup and knelt on one knee beside Rusty.

"Here. I'm sure your throat is dry and sore. But don't drink too much too fast."

She cupped her hands around his and raised the cup to her parched lips. The water was so cold it hurt her teeth, but she didn't mind. She took three deep swallows before Cooper withdrew the cup.

"Easy, I said. There's plenty."

"You found a source?" She licked drops of water off her lips.

Watching that motion closely, Cooper said, "Yeah. A stream about three hundred yards that way." He indicated the direction with his head. "Must be a tributary of the Mackenzie."

She looked at the lifeless carcass lying next to his boot. "Did you shoot the rabbit?"

"Killed it with a rock. I didn't want to waste any ammo unless I had to. I'll dress it and put it on to cook. We can . . . Oh, hell. What's the matter?"

Rusty, much to her dismay, burst into tears. The sobs racked her entire body. She covered her face with her hands, but even as dehydrated as she was, tears leaked through her fingers.

"Look, it was either him or us," Cooper said with agitation. "We've got to eat. You can't be so—"

"It's not the rabbit," she blubbered.

"Then what? Does your leg hurt?"

"I thought you had de . . . deserted me. Left me behind beca . . . cause of my leg. And maybe you should. I'm holding you up. You probably could have wa . . . walked to safety by now if it weren't for me and my leg."

She hiccuped around several attempts to go on. "But my leg really doesn't make much difference because I'm a washout in situations like this anyway. I loathe the great outdoors and think it's anything but great. I hate it. Even summer camp never appealed to me. I'm cold. And scared. And guilty for complaining when I'm alive and everybody else is dead."

She dissolved into another torrent, her shoulders shaking. Cooper let out a long-suffering sigh, several florid curses, and then walked forward on his knees to take her into his arms. He pressed her shoulders between his large hands. Rusty's initial reaction was to tense up and try to pull away. But he kept his hands there and drew her against him. The promise of comfort was too much for her to resist. She slumped against his broad chest, clutching handfuls of his thick hunting coat.

The clean, fresh essence of pine clung to his clothes and hair—and that appealing, musty smell of damp leaves and fog. In Rusty's weakened, woozy state, he seemed unnaturally large, as fantastic as the hero in a children's tale. Powerful. Strong. Fierce but benevolent. Able to slay any dragon.

When one of his capable hands cupped the back of her head, she burrowed her face deeper into the quilted cloth of his coat and luxuriated in the first feeling of security she'd known since the plane went down—even before that, since leaving the hunting lodge and her disappointed father.

Finally the tumult passed. Her tears dried up. There was no excuse for Cooper to go on holding her, so she eased away from him. Embarrassed now, she kept her head down. He seemed reluctant to let her go, but at last his hands slid away.

"Okay now?" he asked gruffly.

"Yes, fine, thank you." She wiped her moist nose on the back of her hand, as though she did that all the time.

"I'd better get that rabbit ready to cook. Lie back down."

"I'm tired of lying down."

"Then turn your head. I want you to be able to eat this and I'm afraid you won't if you watch me gut it."

Carrying the rabbit to the edge of the clearing, he laid it on a flat rock and proceeded to dress it. Rusty wisely kept her eyes averted. "That's what we had our argument over," she said quietly.

Cooper looked at her over his shoulder. "You and who?"

"My father. He had brought down a ram." She laughed without humor. "It was a beautiful animal. I felt sorry for it, but I pretended to be ecstatic over the kill. Father hired one of the guides to field-dress it. He wanted to supervise, to make sure the guide didn't damage the hide." Blinking tears out of her eyes, she continued. "I couldn't watch. It made me physically ill. Father—" she paused to draw in a deep breath "—I think I disgusted and disappointed him."

Cooper was cleaning his hands on a handkerchief he'd soaked with water from the thermos. "Because you couldn't stomach a field-dressing?"

"Not just that. That capped it off. I proved to be a terrible marksman, but I couldn't have shot anything if it had walked up and put its nose against the barrel of my rifle. I didn't like anything about that whole scene." Softly, she added almost to herself, "I wasn't as good an outdoorsman as my brother Jeff."

"Did your father expect you to be?" He had skewered the rabbit on a green twig and was now suspending it over the coals.

"I think he was hoping I would be."

"Then he's a fool. You're not physically equipped to be a hunter."

His eyes dropped to her chest. And lingered. Heat rushed into her breasts, filling them like mother's milk, making them heavy and achy. Her nipples drew tight.

The reaction startled Rusty enormously. Instinctively she wanted to cover and press her breasts back to normalcy, but he was still looking at her, so she couldn't. She didn't dare move at all. She was afraid that if she did, something terribly fragile would be broken—something that couldn't be replaced or repaired. Any reckless move would be disastrous and irrevocable. Something dreadful might happen as a result.

It was the first time he had made any sexual reference besides the vulgarities he'd spouted last night. He'd done that only to rile her. She realized that now. But this was something altogether different. This time, he was as much the victim as the perpetrator.

He yanked his eyes back toward the fire and the moment passed. But they didn't speak to each other for a long time. Rusty closed her eyes and pretended to doze, but she watched him as he busied himself around what was gradually coming to look like a bonafide camp. He sharpened the hatchet on a stone. He checked the roasting rabbit, turning it several times.

He moved with surprising agility for a man his size. She was sure that some women would consider him handsome, particularly now that his chin and jaw were deeply shadowed by a twenty-four-hour beard. The wide, curving mustache was sexy...if one liked facial hair. It sat directly on top of his lower lip, completely obscuring his upper one, making the thought of going in search of it intriguing.

She found herself staring at his mouth as he leaned down and spoke to her. "I...I beg your pardon?"

He looked at her strangely. "Your eyes are glassy. You're not going delirious again, are you?" He pressed his palm to her forehead.

Impatient with him and herself for her adolescent fantasies, she swatted his hand aside. "No, I feel fine. What did you say?"

"I asked if you were ready to eat."

"That's an understatement."

He assisted her into a sitting position. "This has been cooling for a minute or two. It should be about ready." He slid the rabbit off the spit and tore off a leg at the joint. He passed it to Rusty. Hesitantly she took it, staring at it dubiously.

"You're going to eat it if I have to force it down your throat." He tore off a bite of meat with his strong white teeth. "It's not half bad. Honest."

She pinched some of the meat off the bone and put it into her mouth, making herself chew and swallow it quickly. "Not so fast," he cautioned. "It'll make you sick."

She nodded and took another bite. With a little salt, it wouldn't have been bad at all. "There are some very nice restaurants in Los Angeles that have rabbit on the menu," she said conversationally. She instinctively reached for a napkin, remembered that she didn't have one, shrugged, and licked her fingers.

"Is that where you live, Los Angeles?"

"Beverly Hills, actually."

He studied her in the firelight. "Are you a movie star or something?"

Rusty got the impression that he wouldn't be impressed if she told him she was a three-time Oscar winner. She doubted if Cooper Landry put much stock in fame. "No, I'm not a movie star. My father owns a real-estate company. It has branches all over southern California. I work for him."

"Are you any good at it?"

"I've been very successful."

He chewed a mouthful and tossed the cleaned bone into the fire. "Being the boss's daughter, how could you miss?"

"I work hard, Mr. Landry." She took umbrage at his sly implication that her father was responsible for the success she had achieved. "I had the highest sales record of the agency last year."

"Bravo."

Miffed that he was so obviously unimpressed, she asked snidely, "What do you do?"

He silently offered her another piece of the meat, which she tore into as though she'd been eating fresh, unseasoned roasted rabbit cooked over an open fire every day of her life.

"I ranch," Cooper replied.

"Cattle?"

"Some. Horses mostly."

"Where?"

"Rogers Gap."

"Where's that?"

"In the Sierra Nevada."

"Never heard of it."

"I'm not surprised."

"Can you make a living at just ranching?"

"I do all right."

"Is Rogers Gap close to Bishop? Do people ski there?"

"We have a few runs. Serious skiers consider them a real challenge. Personally I think they're some of the most spectacular on the continent."

"Then why haven't I ever heard of this place?"

"We're a carefully guarded secret and want to remain that way. We don't advertise."

"Why?" Her interest was piqued. She never passed up an opportunity to locate new and interesting property for her clients to invest in. "With the right developer handling it, you could make something out of Rogers Gap. If it's as good for skiing as you say, it could become the next Aspen."

"God forbid," he said under his breath. "That's the point. We don't want to be put on the map. We don't want our mountains to be littered with concrete condos or the peaceful community to be overrun by a bunch of pushing, shoving, rude skiers from Beverly Hills who are more interested in modeling their Rodeo Drive duds than preserving our landscape."

"Does everyone in town hold to this philosophy?"

"Fortunately, yes, or they wouldn't be living there. We don't have much going for us except the scenery and the tranquillity."

She tossed her denuded bones into the fire. "You sound like a holdover from the sixties."

"I am."

Her eyes were teasing. "Were you a flower child, advocating universal harmony? Did you march for peace and participate in war protests?"

"No," he replied sharply. Rusty's goading grin collapsed. "I couldn't wait to join up. I wanted to go to war. I was too ignorant to realize that I would have to kill people or get killed myself. I hadn't bargained on getting captured and imprisoned. But I did. After seven months in that stinking hole, I escaped and came home a hero."

He practically snarled the last sentence. "The guys in that POW camp would have killed each other for a meal like the one you just ate." His gray eyes looked like glittering knife-blades as they sliced toward her. "So I'm not overwhelmed by your Beverly Hills glitz and glamour, Miss Carlson."

He stood up abruptly. "I'm going for more water. Don't wander off."

Don't wander off, she silently mimicked. All right, he had put her in her place, but she wasn't going to wear sackcloth and ashes for the rest of her life. Lots of men had fought in Vietnam and returned to lead happy, productive lives. It was Cooper's own fault if he was maladjusted. He thrived on his own bitterness. That's what fueled him. He nursed it. He cultivated his quarrel with society because he felt it owed him something.

Maybe it did. But it wasn't her fault. She wasn't responsible for whatever misfortune had befallen him. Just because he walked around with a chip on his shoulder the size of Mount Everest didn't make him a worthier human being than she was.

He returned, but they maintained a hostile silence while she drank her fill of water from the thermos. Just as wordlessly, he assisted her as she hobbled out of the clearing for a few minutes of privacy. When he eased her back down onto the thick pallet, which had become the nucleus of their world, he said, "I need to check your leg. Hold the flashlight for me."

She watched as he unbound the bandages and pulled them back to reveal a jagged, uneven row of stitches. She stared at it in horror, but he seemed pleased with his handiwork. With his hands around her calf muscles, he raised her leg to inspect it closer. "No signs of new infection. Swelling's gone down."

"The scar," she whispered roughly.

He looked up at her. "There wasn't much I could do about that." His lower lip thinned until it was hardly visible beneath his mustache. "Just be glad I didn't have to cauterize it."

"I am."

He sneered. "I'm sure a high-ticket plastic surgeon in Beverly Hills can fix the scar."

"Do you have to be so obnoxious?"

"Do you have to be so superficial?" He aimed a finger in the direction of the crashed plane. "I'm sure any of those guys we left up there would settle for a scar on their shin."

He was right, of course; but that didn't make his criticism any easier for her to swallow. She lapsed into sullen silence. He bathed her leg in peroxide and rebandaged it, then gave her one of the penicillin tablets and two aspirins. She washed them down with water. No more brandy for her, thank you.

Drunkenness, she had discovered, aroused her emotionally and sexually. She didn't want to think of Cooper Landry as anything but a wretched grouch. He was a short-tempered, surly ogre harboring a grudge against the world. If she didn't have to rely on him for her survival, she would have nothing to do with him.

She had already settled beneath the pile of furs when he slid in and embraced her as he had the night before.

"How much longer do we have to stay here?" she asked crossly.

"I'm not clairvoyant."

"I'm not asking you to predict when we'll be rescued; I was referring to this bed. Can't you rig up a shelter of some kind? Something we can move around in?"

"The accommodations aren't to m'lady's liking?"

She sighed her annoyance. "Oh, never mind."

After a moment, he said, "There's group of boulders near the stream. One side of the largest of them has been eroded out. I think with a little ingenuity and some elbow grease, I could make a lean-to out of it. It won't be much, but it will be better than this. And closer to the water."

"I'll help," she offered eagerly.

It wasn't that she didn't appreciate this shelter. It had saved her life last night. But it was disconcerting to sleep this close to him. Since he had taken off his coat as he had the night before, Rusty was keenly aware of his muscled chest against her back. She could therefore assume that he was keenly aware of her body because she wasn't wearing her coat, either.

She could think of little else as his hand found a comfortable spot midway between her breasts and her waist. He even wedged his knees between hers, elevating her injured leg again. She started to ask him if that was necessary, but since it felt so much better that way, she let it pass without comment.

"Rusty?"

"Hmm?" His warm breath drifted into her ear and caused goose bumps to break out over her arms. She snuggled closer to him.

"Wake up. We've got to get up."

"Get up?" she groaned. "Why? Pull the covers back up. I'm freezing."

"That's the point. We're soaking wet. Your fever broke and you sweated all over both of us. If we don't get up and dry off, we stand a good chance of getting frostbite."

She came fully awake and rolled to her back. He was serious. Already he was tossing off the furs. "What do you mean, dry off?"

"Strip and dry off." He began unbuttoning his flannel shirt.

"Are you crazy? It's freezing!" Recalcitrantly, she pulled the pelt back over herself. Cooper jerked it off her.

"Take off all your clothes. Now!"

He shrugged off his flannel shirt and draped it over the nearest bush. With one fluid motion, he crossed his arms at his waist and peeled the turtleneck T-shirt over his head. It made his hair stick up funnily, but Rusty didn't feel like laughing. Laughter—in fact any sound at all—got trapped inside her closed throat. Her first glimpse of the finest chest she'd ever seen rendered her speechless.

Hard as rocks those muscles were. Beautifully sculpted, too, beneath taut skin. His nipples were dark and pebbly from the cold, their areolae shriveled around them. It was all tantalizingly covered with a blanket of crisp hair that swirled and whorled, tipped and tapered beguilingly.

He was so trim she could count every single rib. His stomach was as flat and tight as a drum. She couldn't see his navel very well. It was deeply nestled in a sexy tuft of hair.

"Get started, Rusty, or I'll do it for you."

His threat plucked her out of her trance. Mechanically, she peeled off her sweater. Beneath it she was wearing a cotton turtleneck much like his. She fiddled with the hem while she watched him stand up and work his jeans down his legs. The long johns weren't the most alluring sight she'd ever seen.

But Cooper Landry unclothed had to be.

In seconds he was standing there, silhouetted against the dim glow of the fire, stark naked. He was beautifully shaped and generously endowed—so marvelously made that she couldn't help her gaping stare. He quite literally took her breath away.

He draped the articles of discarded clothing on the bush, then pulled a pair of socks over his hands and ran them over his body, drying it thoroughly—everything—before removing the socks from his hands.

Kneeling, he tore into one of the backpacks looking for underwear. He pulled on a pair of briefs, all with a supreme lack of self-consciousness, much less modesty.

When he turned toward her and noticed that she hadn't moved, he frowned with irritation. "Come on, Rusty. Hurry up. It's damn cold out here."

He reached for her sweater, which, so far, was the only thing she'd taken off. She handed it to him and he hung it up to dry. Holding out his hand for more clothes, he snapped his fingers quickly and repeatedly to hurry her along. "Come on, come on." Casting one anxious glance up at him, she pulled the T-shirt over her head and passed it to him.

The cold air was a breathtaking shock to her system. Immediately she was chilled and started trembling so violently she couldn't handle the button on her one-legged trousers.

"Here, let me do that, dammit. Or I'll be standing out here all night." Cooper dropped to his knees and straddled her thighs. Impatiently he pushed her hands out of the way so he could unfasten the button and pull down the zipper. With a detached air he eased the trousers down her legs and tossed them haphazardly toward the nearest bush.

But he was brought up short by what he obviously hadn't expected. A pair of extremely feminine, extremely scanty bikini panties. He'd seen the lace-edged leg, but that was all. For what seemed like an eternity, he stared at them before saying gruffly, "Take them off."

Rusty shook her head. "No."

His face became fierce. "Take them off." Rusty shook her head emphatically. Before she could brace herself for it, he pressed his open hand directly over the triangular scrap of silk and lace. "They're wet. Take them off."

Their eyes, like their wills, clashed. It was as much the chill in his stare as the chill in the air that prompted Rusty to slide the damp garment down her legs.

"Now dry off."

He handed her a cotton sock like the ones he'd used. She ran it over her lower body and her legs. Keeping her head bowed, she groped blindly for the underwear Cooper handed her. He hadn't chosen long johns because they would chafe her injury. She pulled on a pair of panties similar to the ones she'd just taken off and which were now dangling from the lower branches of the bush, fluttering like a victory banner the morning after a fraternity beer bust.

"Now the top."

Her brassiere was just as frivolous as the panties that matched them. The morning she left the lodge, she had dressed in clothes befitting her return to civilization. After having to wear thermal underwear for several days, she had been good and sick of it.

Leaning forward, she grappled with the hook at her back, but her fingers were so numb from the cold she couldn't get it to open. Muttering curses, Cooper reached around her and all but ripped the hook from its mooring. The brassiere fell forward. She peeled the straps down her arms, flung it away and faced him defiantly.

Beneath his mustache, his mouth was set in a hard, unyielding line. He paused for only a heartbeat before he began roughly rubbing the cotton sock over her throat, chest, breasts, and stomach. Then, reaching around her again, he blotted the sweat off her back. They were so close that her breath stirred his chest hair. Her lips came perilously close to touching one of his distended nipples. Hers, hard and peaked from the cold, grazed his skin.

He pulled back quickly and angrily dragged a thermal top over her head. While she was working her arms into the sleeves, he ripped the damp fur they'd been lying on off the pallet and replaced it with another one. "It's not as soft, but it's dry."

"It'll be fine," Rusty said hoarsely.

Finally they were cocooned again. She didn't resist when he pulled her close to him. She was shivering uncontrollably and her teeth were chattering. But it wasn't long before they began to warm up. Their bodies were in chaos because of what their eyes had seen. Erotic impressions lingered in their minds.

Lying in his embrace fully dressed had been unnerving enough. Lying there with him wearing only underwear wreaked havoc on Rusty's senses. Her fever had broken, but her body was burning like a furnace now.

His bare thighs felt delicious against hers. She liked their hair-smattered texture. Because she was braless, she was sharply aware of his hand resting just beneath her breasts, almost but not quite touching them.

He wasn't immune to the enforced intimacy. He'd exerted himself by switching out the pelts and changing clothes so quickly, but that wasn't the only reason he was breathing heavily. His chest swelled and receded against her back rhythmically but rapidly.

And then there was that other inexorable evidence of his arousal.

It prompted her to whisper, "I don't think I need to... uh... prop my leg on top of yours."

A low moan vibrated through his chest. "Don't even talk about it. And for God's sake, don't move." His distress was obvious.

"I'm sorry."

"For what? You can't help being beautiful any more than I can help being a man. I guess we'll just have to tolerate that from each other."

She honored his request and didn't move so much as a muscle. She didn't even reopen her eyes once they were closed. But she did fall asleep with a tiny smile on her lips. Inadvertently, perhaps, but he had told her that he thought she was beautiful.

Four

It made a difference in their relationship.

The forced intimacy of the night before didn't draw them closer together. Rather, it created a schism of uneasiness between them. Their conversation the following morning was stilted. They avoided making eye contact. They dressed with their backs to each other. They moved awkwardly. Their motions were jerky and unsure, like those of invalids who had just regained the use of their limbs.

Taciturn and withdrawn, Cooper whittled her a pair of crutches out of two stout tree branches. Aesthetically, they weren't much to rave about, but Rusty was immensely grateful for them. They allowed her mobility. She would no longer be confined to the bed.

When she thanked him, he only grunted an acknowledgement and stamped off through the underbrush toward the stream to get water. By the time he returned, she was accustomed to the crutches and was hobbling around the clearing on them.

"How does your leg feel?"

"Okay. I cleaned it with peroxide myself and took another pill. I think it's going to be okay." She had even managed to dress in her one remaining pair of slacks and put her boots on. Enough of the soreness was gone that the additional pressure of clothing didn't irritate the wound.

They drank from the thermos in turn. That passed for breakfast. Cooper said, "I'd better start building that shelter today."

They had awakened to find their cocoon dusted with snow. This time the flakes weren't merely grains; they were real and ominous, harbingers of the first winter storm. Both knew how harsh the winters in this area could be. It was imperative that they have a shelter to use until they were rescued. If they weren't rescued, a temporary shelter would be of little consequence, but neither wanted to think about that.

"What can I do to help?" she asked.

"You can cut up that suede jacket into strips." He nodded toward a jacket that had belonged to one of the crash victims and handed her an extra knife. "I'll need plenty of thongs to tie the poles together. While you're doing that, I'd better see if we've got food for dinner." She looked at him quizzically. "I set some snares yesterday."

She glanced around her apprehensively. "You won't go far, will you?"

"Not too far." He shouldered his rifle and checked to see that he had pocketed a box of ammunition. "I'll be back before the fire needs to be refueled. Keep the knife and rifle handy, though. I haven't seen any bear tracks, but you never know."

Without another word he turned and dissolved into the dense screen of trees. Rusty stood leaning on her crutches, her heart thumping fearfully.

Bears?

After several moments, she shook off her paralyzing fright. "This is silly," she muttered to herself. "Nothing's going to get me."

She wished she had a radio, a television set, anything to relieve the oppressive silence. It was only occasionally broken by the cracking of twigs and the rustling of leaves as unseen forest animals scurried about on their daily forages. Rusty's eyes searched out these silence-breakers, but they remained hidden and thereby more intimidating. She couldn't put Cooper's mention of bears out of her mind.

"He probably said that on purpose just to frighten me," she said out loud as she viciously sliced through the tough suede with the knife he'd left behind for her use. It was smaller than the one that constantly rode in the scabbard attached to his belt.

Her stomach growled. She thought about fresh, hot and buttery breakfast croissants, toasted bagels and cream cheese, warmed glazed donuts, pancakes and bacon, ham and eggs. That only made her hungrier. The only thing she could do was to fill her empty stomach with water.

Soon, however, drinking so much water created another problem. She put it off as long as possible, but finally had no choice but to set aside her handiwork. Painstakingly, and without a smidgen of grace or coordination, she stood up and propped her arms on her crutches. Going in the direction opposite to that Cooper had taken, she found a spot in which to relieve herself.

As she struggled with her crutches and her clothes, at the same time checking for creepy crawlies on the ground, she marveled that this was really Rusty Carlson, real-estate princess of Beverly Hills, seeking a place in the woods to pee!

Her friends would never have guessed she could come this far without going stark, staring mad. Her father would never believe it. But if she lived to tell about it, he would be so proud of her.

She was in the process of refastening her pants when she heard the nearby movement. Swiveling her head in that direction, she listened. Nothing.

"Probably just the wind." Her voice sounded unnaturally loud and cheerful. "Or a bird. Or Cooper coming back. If he's creeping up on me as a joke, I'll never forgive him.''

She ignored the next rustling noise, which was louder and nearer than the last one, and moved as fast as she could back toward the camp. Determined not to do anything so cowardly as to whimper or cry out, she clenched her jaw in fear as she stumbled along over the uneven ground.

All her bravery deserted her when the form materialized from between the trunks of two pines and loomed directly in her path. Her head snapped up, she looked into the beady eyes, the hairy, leering face, and let out a bloodcurdling scream.

Cooper was in a hurry to get back, but he decided to dress the two rabbits before he returned. He had told himself that he wasn't testing her fortitude when he'd gutted the rabbit where she could see it.

But he knew deep down inside that's exactly what he'd been doing. Perversely, he had wanted her to cringe, to retch, to get hysterical, to demonstrate some feminine weakness.

She hadn't. She'd borne up well. Far better than he'd expected her to.

He tossed away the entrails and began scraping the insides of the pelts. They would come in handy later. The fur was warm and he could always use it to make Rusty—

Rusty. Her again. Couldn't he think of anything else? Did his every single thought have to come full circle back to her? At what point had they become a pair as inseparable as Adam and Eve? Couldn't he think of one without thinking immediately of the other?

He remembered the first thought that had registered when he regained consciousness. Her face, alluringly framed in that tumble of russet curls, had been bending over him, and he'd thought of the vilest obscenity the marine corps had ever coined and came just short of saying it out loud.

He'd been glad to be alive—but barely. He had thought he'd be better off dead rather than having to put up with this airhead swathed in expensive fur and sexy perfume. In the wilderness she wouldn't stand a marshmallow's chance at a bonfire. He'd figured that before it was over, he'd probably have to kill her to put them both out of their misery.

That was an unsettling and unappetizing thought, but he had been forced to do worse in order to save his own life in Nam. The plane crash had caused him to automatically revert to the law of the jungle, to slip back into the role of survivor.

Rule number one: You either killed or got killed. You stayed alive no matter what it cost. The survival tactics taught to the army's special services knew no conscience. You did whatever was necessary to live one more day, one more hour, one more minute. He had been steeped in that doctrine and had practiced it more times than he wanted to remember—but too many times to let him forget.

But the woman had surprised him. That leg injury had caused her a great deal of pain, but she hadn't whined about it. She hadn't nagged him about being hungry and thirsty and cold and scared, although God knew she must have been. She'd been a tough little nut and she hadn't cracked yet. Unless things got drastically worse, he doubted now that she would.

Of course that left him with a whole new set of problems. Few people had ever won his admiration. He didn't want to admire Rusty Carlson, but found himself doing so.

He was also coming to acknowledge that he was stranded in the middle of nowhere with a tempting piece of womanhood, and that they might be alone and dependent on each other for a long time.

The demons who had guided his fate were having a huge laugh at his expense this time. They'd run amok many times in the past, but this was the clincher. This was the big punch line that had made his whole life a joke.

Traditionally, he despised women like Rusty Carlson. He had no use for wealthy, silly, superficial society broads who'd been born with silver spoons in their mouths. They didn't know, or want to know, about anything outside their gilded cages. Wasn't it just his luck to draw one who had earned his grudging respect by bearing up under the worst of circumstances?

But even that wasn't enough for the malicious gods. She could have been a silly society broad who wouldn't have given a warthog any competition in the looks department. She could have had a voice that would shatter glass.

Instead, the fates had forced on him a woman who looked like a dream. Surely the devil had designed her. Temptation incarnate. With cinnamon-colored hair a man could wrap himself in and nipples that looked so sweet they must taste like candy. Her voice would melt butter. That's what he thought about every time she spoke.

What a cruel joke. Because he would not touch her. Never. He'd been down that road. Women like her followed vogue. Not only in clothes; in everything. When he'd met Melody it had been fashionable to love a veteran. She had, until it became convenient not to.

Scratch the silky surface of Rusty Carlson and you'd find another Melody. Rusty was only sucking up to him now because she depended on him for her survival. She looked like a tasty morsel, but inside she was probably as rotten and devious as Melody had been.

Slinging the rabbit pelts over his shoulder and folding the meat in a cloth, he headed back toward their camp. She wasn't going to get to him. He couldn't afford to start feeling soft toward her. Last night he'd let her cry because he felt that she deserved one good, cleansing cry. But no more. He'd held her during the night because it was necessary for them to keep warm. But he would keep his distance from now on. Once the shelter was built, they wouldn't have to sleep together like that. He wouldn't have to endure any more nights with her curled against his front and her bottom cushioning his involuntary reaction to her.

Stop thinking about it, he told himself. Forget how smooth her belly felt beneath your hand. Forget the shape of her breasts and the color of the hair between her thighs.

Groaning, he thrashed through the woods, viciously determined to keep his thoughts on track. As soon as he built the shelter, such close proximity wouldn't be necessary. He would keep his eyes and his hands—

The piercing scream brought him up short.

If he'd walked into an invisible wall, he couldn't have stopped more abruptly. When Rusty's next scream rent the stillness, he instinctively slipped into the role of jungle fighter as easily as well-greased gears fitting into their notches. Silently, he slithered through the trees in the direction of her scream, knife drawn and teeth bared.

"Who...who are you?" Rusty's hand was gripping her own throat, where her pulse was beating wildly.

The man's bearded face split into a wide grin. He turned his head and said, "Hey, Pa, *she* wants to know who *I* am."

Chuckling, another man, an older version of the first, stepped out from between the trees. The two gaped at Rusty. Both had small, dark eyes embedded in deep sockets.

"We could ask you the same question," the older one said. "Who are you, little girl?"

"I...I...I survived the airplane crash." They gazed back at her with perplexity. "You didn't know about the crash?"

"Can't say that we did."

She pointed with a shaking finger. "Back there. Two days ago. Five men were killed. My leg was injured." She indicated the crutches.

"Any more women?"

Before she could answer, Cooper lunged up behind the older of the two men and laid the gleaming blade of his knife against the whiskered throat. He grasped the man's arm, twisted it behind him and shoved his hand up between his shoulder blades. The man's hunting rifle clattered to the ground at his feet.

"Move away from her or I'll kill him," he said to the stunned younger man.

He was staring at Cooper as though he were Satan himself, who had sprung up out of the ground straight from hell. Even Rusty was quelled by the evil threat in Cooper's eyes. But she was trembling with relief to see him.

"I said to move away from her." Cooper's voice seemed as deadly as his knife. It was void of inflection, emotionless. The younger man took two exaggerated steps away from Rusty. "Now, drop the rifle," Cooper told him.

Since it appeared that the attacker was human after all, the younger man's face puckered with rebellion. He whined, "Pa, do I have to do—"

"Do as he says, Reuben."

Reluctantly the younger man tossed down his hunting rifle. Cooper kicked the two rifles now on the ground out of reach and gradually released his stranglehold on the man. He stepped around him and stood beside Rusty, facing the two. "Rusty?" She jumped. "Are you okay?"

"Fine."

"Did they hurt you?"

"They scared me, that's all. I don't think they meant to."

Cooper didn't take his eyes off the two men, but regarded them warily. "Who are you?"

His bark carried more authority than Rusty's feeble question. The older man answered him at once. "Quinn Gawrylow and my son, Reuben. We live here." Cooper didn't even blink. The man went on. "Across the deep ravine." He hitched his chin in that direction.

Cooper had discovered the ravine the day before. The stream where he'd been getting water lay at the bottom of it. He hadn't crossed it to explore because he hadn't wanted to leave Rusty alone that long. He thanked God now that he hadn't. These men might be perfectly harmless. Then again, they might not be. His suspicious nature had served him well on more than one occasion. Until they proved to be otherwise, he'd consider this duo the enemy. They hadn't done anything harmful so far, but he didn't like the way the younger one was staring at Rusty as though she were a celestial vision.

"What brought you across the ravine?" Cooper asked.

"We smelled your wood smoke last night and this morning came to investigate. We don't usually see other people in our woods."

"Our plane crashed."

"That's what the young lady said."

She'd been elevated from a little girl to a young lady. Rusty silently thanked Cooper for that. She, too, was unnerved by the younger man's stare and inched closer to Cooper, taking shelter behind his arm. "How far are we from the nearest town?" she asked.

"A hundred miles." Her hopes plummeted. The man obviously noticed. "But the river isn't too far."

"The Mackenzie?"

"Right. If you reach that before it freezes closed, you'll catch a boat on its way down to Yellowknife."

"How far to the river?" Cooper asked.

The man scratched his head beneath his wool stocking cap. "Ten, fifteen miles, wouldn't you say, Reuben?"

The younger man bobbed his head, never taking his lustful eyes off Rusty. Cooper squinted at him, his stare malevolent and dangerous. "Could you direct us to the river?"

"Yes," the elder Gawrylow said. "Tomorrow. Today we'll feed you. Let you rest up." He glanced down at the fresh meat Cooper had dropped. "Would you like to follow us to our cabin?"

Rusty glanced up at Cooper expectantly. His face remained a mask as he studied the two men cautiously. At last he said, "Thanks. Rusty could use the food and rest before we strike out. You go on ahead." Using his rifle, he pointed them toward their camp.

The two men bent to pick up their rifles. Rusty felt Cooper's muscles tense with precaution. But the father and son shouldered their rifles and turned in the direction Cooper had indicated. Cooper glanced down at her and spoke from the side of his mouth. "Stay close. Where's the knife I gave you?"

"I left it behind when I went—"

"Keep it with you."

"What's the matter with you?"

"Nothing."

"You don't act very glad to see them. I'm delighted. They can lead us out of here."

His only comment was a thin-lipped "Yeah."

The Gawrylows were impressed with Cooper's improvisations. They helped gather up the pelts and the belongings Cooper and Rusty had salvaged from the crash. Nothing in the wilderness was ever wasted. Reuben kicked stones into the fire to make certain it was out.

The band, under Quinn's guidance, with his son following closely, set out for their cabin. Cooper brought up the rear so he could keep an eye on both Gawrylows and on Rusty, who was making admirable if awkward progress on her crutches.

The men seemed to be well-meaning, but Cooper had learned the hard way never to trust anyone. He'd seen too many soldiers blown to bits by hand grenades handed to them by smiling children.

At the stream they paused to rest. Rusty's lungs felt as though collapse were imminent; her heart was beating double time; and the crutches were chafing her armpits, even though Cooper had tried to prevent that by padding the tops of them with articles of extra clothing.

"How are you doing?" he asked her, uncapping the thermos and passing it to her.

"Fine." She forced a smile.

"Does your leg hurt?"

"No, it just feels like it weighs a ton."

"It can't be much farther. Then you can lie down for the rest of the day."

The Gawrylows waited patiently nearby until she had regained her breath and was ready to start again. "We'll cross at the easiest point," the elder one informed Cooper.

They walked along the streambed for several hundred yards. At any other time, Rusty would have been entranced with the landscape. The stream was crystal clear. It gurgled over rocks that had been polished as smooth as mirrors by the gallons of water that had rushed across them. Towering trees interlaced and formed canopies overhead. The evergreens were so deeply green that they appeared blue. The leaves of the deciduous trees ranged from vivid red to vibrant yellow. Encroaching winter had already caused many leaves to fall. They provided a crunchy carpet beneath their feet.

Rusty's chest was burning with exertion by the time the Gawrylows drew to a halt. She laid her crutches on the ground and gratefully sank down onto a rock beside the stream, which ran shallow at this point. The side of the ravine rising up on the other side of the brook looked as high as the Himalayas.

"This is it," Quinn said. "I'll lead the way. Reuben can carry the woman. You can bring your gear."

"Reuben can bring the gear. I'll carry the woman," Cooper amended in a steely voice.

The older man shrugged and ordered his son to take the bundles from Cooper. Reuben did so, but not without shooting Cooper a sour look. Cooper stared back at him unmoved. He didn't care whether Reuben liked it or not; he wasn't going to let those grubby hands get anywhere near Rusty.

When the father and son had moved out of earshot, he bent over her and whispered, "Don't be shy of using that knife." She looked up at him with alarm. "Just in case these Good Samaritans turn on us." He laid the crutches across her lap and picked her up in his arms.

The Gawrylows were already well up the side of the ravine. He started after them, keeping one eye on them and the other on the treacherously steep incline. If he fell, Rusty would go with him. She had put up a brave front, but he knew her leg must be causing her considerable discomfort.

"Do you really think we'll be rescued tomorrow, Cooper?"

"Looks like there's a good chance. If we make it to the river and if a boat of some kind happens by." He was breathing with difficulty. Sweat had popped out on his forehead. His jaw was set with determination.

"You need a shave." The remark came from nowhere, but it indicated to them both how carefully she'd been studying his face. Without moving his head, he cast his eyes down toward her. Embarrassed, she looked away and murmured, "Sorry I'm so heavy."

"Hardly. Your clothes weigh more than you do."

That comment reminded them that he knew just how much of her was clothing and how much was flesh and bone. He'd seen her without any clothes, hadn't he? Rusty decided that if all their conversations were going to result in awkwardness, it was safer not to engage in conversation at all.

Besides, by this time they had reached the top of the ravine. Quinn was biting off a chaw of tobacco. Reuben had removed his stocking cap and was fanning himself with it. His dark hair was greasily plastered to his head.

Cooper set Rusty down. Wordlessly Quinn offered him the brick of tobacco. Rusty was grateful when, with a shake of his head, Cooper turned it down.

"We'll wait until you're rested," Quinn said.

Cooper looked down at Rusty. Her face was pale with fatigue. Her leg was probably hurting. The moist wind had picked up, making the temperature noticeably colder. No doubt she needed to take it slow and easy, but all things considered, the sooner he got her under a roof, fed, and lying down, the better.

"No need to wait. Let's go," he said tersely.

He pulled Rusty to her feet and propped her up on her crutches. He noticed her wince with pain, but steeled himself against compassion and indicated to their hosts that they were ready to proceed.

At least the remaining distance to the cabin was level ground. By the time they reached it, however, Rusty's strength was totally spent. She collapsed on the sagging porch like a rag doll.

"Let's get the woman inside," Quinn said as he pushed open the door.

The rickety door was attached to its frame by leather hinges. The interior of the cabin looked as uninviting as an animal's lair. Rusty eyed the opening with trepidation and a sense of dread. Then and there she decided that there were worse things than being exposed to the outdoors.

Cooper remained expressionless as he scooped her into his arms and carried her into the gloomy interior. The small windows were so blackened by grime that they let in little light. A dim, smoky fire gave off meager illumination, but what Rusty and Cooper saw would have been better left hidden in darkness.

The cabin was filthy. It stank of wet wool, rancid grease, and unwashed men. The only merit it had was that it was warm. Cooper carried Rusty toward the stone hearth and set her down in a cushionless, straight-backed chair. He upended an aluminum bucket and propped the foot of her injured leg on it. He stirred the fire with an iron poker. The desultory flames showed new life when he added sticks of firewood from the wooden box on the hearth.

The Gawrylows stamped in. Reuben closed the door behind them, deepening the darkness inside. In spite of the warmth the fire was now giving off, Rusty shivered and shrank deeper into her coat.

"You must be hungry." Quinn went to the wood-burning stove in one corner. He lifted the lid on a simmering pot and peered inside. "Stew smells done. Want some?"

Rusty was on the verge of refusing but Cooper answered for both of them. "Yes, please. Got any coffee?"

"Sure. Reuben, start a pot of coffee to boiling."

The younger man hadn't stopped staring at Rusty since he'd slunk in and dropped Cooper's and her belongings just inside the door.

Cooper followed Reuben's gawking stare back to Rusty. He wished to hell the firelight didn't shine through her hair, making it shimmer. Pale and drawn as her face was, her eyes looked huge, vulnerable, female. To the young man, who apparently lived alone in this wilderness with his father, a woman wouldn't even have to be pretty to be enticing. Rusty must have embodied his wildest fantasies.

With his bare hand, Reuben reached into a metal canister of coffee and tossed a handful into an enamel pot. He filled the pot with water from the pump in the dry sink and set it on the stove to boil. Within a few minutes Rusty and Cooper were handed plates filled with an unidentifiable stew. She was sure she was better off not knowing what meat was in it, so she refrained from asking. She chewed and swallowed quickly. It was at least hot and filling. The coffee was so strong that she grimaced as she swallowed, but she drank most of it.

While they ate, Cooper and she had a captivated audience. The older man's stare was more subtle than his son's, but possibly more observant. His deep-set eyes didn't miss a single move they made.

He broke a long silence by asking, "You married?"

"Yes," Cooper lied easily. "Five years."

Rusty swallowed the last bite she'd taken, hoping that the Gawrylows didn't notice how difficult it was to get down. She was glad Cooper had taken the initiative to answer. She didn't think she could have uttered a word.

"Kids?"

This time Cooper got tongue-tied, so it was left to Rusty to say "No," hoping that that answer was satisfactory to her "husband." She planned on asking him later why he had lied, but for now she would play along. His wariness was out of proportion, she thought; but she would still rather ally herself with him than with the Gawrylows.

Cooper finished eating and set his plate and cup aside. He glanced around the cabin. "You don't have a transmitter, do you? A ham radio?"

"No."

"Have you heard any airplanes flying over lately?"

"I haven't. Reuben?" Gawrylow nudged his gawking son in the knee. The younger man dragged his eyes away from Rusty.

"Planes?" he asked stupidly.

"We crashed two days ago," Cooper explained. "They're bound to have figured that out by now. I thought there might have been search planes out looking for survivors."

"I haven't heard any planes," Reuben said abruptly and returned his unwavering attention to Rusty.

"How can you stand to live so far away from everything?" she asked. Such self-imposed isolation dismayed her. She couldn't imagine doing without the amenities a city had to offer, particularly by choice. Even rural living would be tolerable if one could get to a city every now and then. But to deliberately sever all contact with civilization—

"We walk to the river and hitch a ride to Yellowknife twice a year," Quinn told them. "Once in April and once in October. We stay for a few days, sell a few pelts, buy what supplies we'll need, and hitch a ride back. That's all the dealings we want with the outside world."

"But why?" Rusty asked.

"I got a bellyful of towns and people. I lived in Edmonton, worked on a freight dock. One day the boss accused me of stealing."

"Were you?"

Rusty was amazed at Cooper's audacity, but the old man didn't seem to take offense at the blunt question. He merely cackled and spat a stringy wad of tobacco juice into the fireplace.

"It was easier to disappear than to go to court and prove my innocence," he said evasively. "Reuben's mother was dead. He and I just up and left. Took nothing with us but what money we had and the clothes on our backs."

"How long ago was this?"

"Ten years. We drifted for a while, then gradually migrated here. We liked it. We stayed." He shrugged. "We've never felt the urge to go back."

He concluded his story. Rusty had finished eating, but the Gawrylows seemed content to continue staring at Cooper and her.

"If you'll excuse us," Cooper said after an awkward silence, "I'd like to check my wife's injury."

Those two words, *my wife's,* seemed to come easily to his lips, but they jangled with falsehood in Rusty's ears. She wondered if the Gawrylows were convinced that they were a couple.

Quinn carried their plates to the sink where he pumped water over them. "Reuben, do your chores."

The young man seemed inclined to argue, but his father shot him a baleful, challenging glance. He shuffled toward the door, pulling on his coat and cap as he went. Quinn went out onto the porch and began stacking firewood against the wall of the cabin.

Rusty leaned close to Cooper where he knelt in front of her. "What do you think?"

"About what?"

"About them," she replied with asperity. He pinched the hem of her slacks between his fingers and sliced a knee-high tear in them with his knife. She reacted angrily. "Why'd you do that? This is my last pair of slacks. I won't have any clothes left by the time you get through cutting them to shreds."

He raised his head. His eyes were hard. "Would you rather take them off and give Reuben an eyeful of those nothing-to-them panties you wear?"

She opened her mouth, but discovered that she had no proper comeback, so she fell silent while he unwrapped her bandages and checked her stitched wound. It seemed to have suffered no ill effects as a result of her hike. But it was sore again. Lying to him about it was useless since she was grimacing by the time he finished rewrapping it.

"Hurt?"

"A little, yes," she admitted.

"Stay off it for the rest of the day. Either sit here or lie on the pallet I'm about to make."

"Pallet? What about the beds?" She glanced across the room to where two beds stood against adjacent walls. "Don't you think they'll offer me one?"

He laughed. "I'm sure Reuben would love for you to join him in his. But unless you want lice, I'd advise you to stay out of it."

She jerked her leg back. Cooper just couldn't be nice, could he? They were comrades because they had to be, but they were not—no, definitely not—friends.

Five

It seemed to take forever for bedtime to arrive. Early in the evening they shared another meal with the Gawrylows. Their discussion about the extensive hike to the Mackenzie River carried over long after they were finished eating.

"There's no path to follow. It's rugged terrain, so it's a full day's walk," Quinn told them.

"We'll leave as soon as it's light enough." Cooper hadn't let Rusty out of his sight. He'd kept an eagle eye on her all afternoon. Now, as she sat in the straight-backed chair, he sat beside her on the floor, a proprietary arm draped over her thigh. "We won't need to pack much. I don't plan to take everything—only what's absolutely necessary."

Quinn asked, "What about the woman?"

Rusty felt Cooper's biceps contract against her leg. "What about her?"

"She'll slow us down."

"I'll stay here with her, Pa," Reuben offered gallantly.

"No." Cooper's response was as sharp as a jab made with a hat pin. "She goes. I don't care how slow we have to travel."

"It's all the same to us," Quinn said with his characteristic shrug, "but I thought you were in a hurry to contact your friends and family. They must be worried about you."

Rusty glanced down at the top of Cooper's head. "Cooper?" He looked up at her. "I don't mind staying here alone. If you can cover more ground without me hobbling along, it only makes sense, doesn't it? You could call my father as soon as you get to a telephone. He'll send someone to pick me up. This could all be over by tomorrow night."

He regarded her wistful expression. She'd go along and bear up under the hardships stoically if he insisted. But it wouldn't be easy for her to cover fifteen miles of forested ground even if she weren't injured. Through no fault of her own, she would cause them endless delays that might necessitate making camp for a night.

Still, he didn't like the idea of being separated from her. No matter how feisty she was, she couldn't effectively defend herself. In this environment she was as helpless as a butterfly. He wasn't being sentimental, he assured himself. It was just that she had survived this long against incredible odds; he would hate for something to happen to her now that rescue was a probability instead of a pipe dream.

His hand folded around her knee protectively. "Let's wait and see how you feel in the morning."

The next several hours crawled by. Rusty didn't know how the Gawrylows maintained their sanity. There was nothing to do, nothing to read, nothing to listen to or to look at—except each other. And when that became boring, they all stared at the sputtering kerosene lamp that put out more smelly black smoke than light.

One would expect these hermits to ply them with a million questions about the outside world, but the Gawrylows showed a marked absence of interest in anything that was going on beyond their boundaries.

Feeling grimy and unwashed, Rusty timidly asked for a bowl of water. Reuben stumbled over his own long feet while fetching it for her and slopped some of it in her lap before successfully setting it down.

She pushed the sleeves of her sweater up to her elbows and washed her face and hands with the bar of soap Cooper had permitted her to bring along. She would have liked to savor the luxurious feeling of cupping handful after handful of water over her face, but three pairs of eyes were focused on her. When Cooper thrust one of his own T-shirts into her wet hands, she accepted it regretfully and dried her face.

Picking up her hairbrush, she began pulling it through her hair, which was not only dirtier than it had been in her life, but also matted and tangled. She was just beginning to work all the snarls out when Cooper jerked the brush out of her hands and said bossily, "That's enough."

She rounded on him, ready to protest, but his stony face stopped her. He'd been behaving strangely all day—more so than usual. She wanted to ask what the hell was wrong with him, why he was so edgy, but wisely decided that now wasn't an opportune time for an argument.

She did, however, show her irritation by angrily snatching her hairbrush back and repacking it in her precious bag of toiletries. They were her only reminders that somewhere in the world hot water, cream rinse, perfume, bubble bath and hand lotion were still realities.

At last, they all settled down for the night. She slept with Cooper as she had the past two nights. Lying curled on her side, her injured leg the uppermost, she faced the fire. Beneath her was the pallet Cooper had made using the pelts they'd carried with them. He had tactfully declined to use the bedding Quinn had offered them.

Cooper didn't curve his body around hers as he had been doing. He lay on his back tensely, never completely relaxed, and ever watchful.

"Stop twitching," she whispered after about half an hour. "What's your problem?"

"Shut up and go to sleep."

"Why don't you?"

"I can't."

"Why?"

"When we get out of here I'll explain it to you."

"Explain it to me now."

"I shouldn't have to. Read the signs."

"Does it have anything to do with why you told them we were married?"

"It has everything to do with that."

She pondered that for a moment. "I'll admit that they're kinda spooky, the way they keep staring at us. But I'm sure they're only curious. Besides, they're sound asleep now." The chorus of loud snores should have been his assurance that the Gawrylows were harmlessly asleep.

"Right," he said dryly, "and so should you be. Nighty-night."

Exasperated with him, she rolled back onto her side. Eventually she sank into a deep sleep. It was mercilessly short-lived. It seemed only minutes after her eyes closed that Cooper was nudging her awake. She groaned in protest, but remembering that today was the day her ordeal would come to an end, she sat up.

The cabin was still in total darkness, although she could see the shadowy outlines of Cooper and the Gawrylows moving about. Quinn was at the stove brewing coffee and stirring the pot of stew. It must never run out but he continually added to, she thought, hoping that she didn't return home with a case of ptomaine poisoning.

Cooper knelt beside her. "How do you feel?"

"Cold," she replied, rubbing her hands up and down her arms. Even though she hadn't slept in his embrace, his body heat had kept her warm throughout the night. He was better than any electric blanket she'd ever slept with.

"I meant health-wise. How does your leg feel?"

"Stiff, but not as sore as yesterday."

"You sure?"

"Positive."

"Get up and move around on it. Let's give it a test run."

He helped her to her feet. Once she had slipped her coat on and propped herself on her crutches, they went outside so she could have some privacy; the Gawrylows cabin didn't have indoor plumbing.

When she emerged from the outhouse, the rising sun had turned the overcast sky a watery gray. That light only emphasized her wanness. Cooper could tell that the effort of leaving the cabin to go to the bathroom had taxed her. Her hard breathing created clouds of vapor around her head.

He cursed beneath his breath. "What?" she asked him anxiously.

"You'll never make it, Rusty. Not in days." Hands on hips, he expelled his frustration in a gust of ghostly white breath and said, "What the hell am I going to do with you?"

He didn't soften the question with any degree of tenderness or compassion. His inflection intimated that he'd far rather not be bothered with her at all.

"Well, I'm sorry to inconvenience you further, Mr. Landry. Why don't you bait a bear trap with me? Then you can jog all the way to that damn river."

He stepped forward and put his face close to hers. "Look, Pollyanna, you're apparently too naive to see it, but there's a lot more at stake here than just getting to the river."

"Not as far as I'm concerned," she shot back. "If you sprouted wings and flew there, it couldn't be fast enough for me. I want to get out of here, away from you, and back home where I belong."

His stern lip all but disappeared beneath his mustache. "All right, then." He spun around and stamped back toward the cabin. "I'll get there much faster without having you tagging along. You'll stay here."

"Fine," she called after him.

Then, setting her own chin as stubbornly as his, she made her halting progress up the incline toward the cabin. The men were in the midst of an argument by the time she reached the door, which Cooper, in his haste or anger, had left ajar. Turning sideways and using her elbows, she maneuvered her way inside.

"Be reasonable, Gawrylow," Cooper was saying. "Reuben is twenty or so years younger than you. I want to move fast. He goes with me. You stay with my... my wife. I can't leave her here alone."

"But, Pa—" Reuben whined.

"He's right, Reuben. You'll move much faster than I could. If you're lucky, you might reach the river by midafternoon."

The plan wasn't to Reuben's liking at all. He gave Rusty one last, hungry glance, then ambled out, muttering under his breath. Cooper didn't appear much happier. He drew Rusty aside and handed her the flare gun, curtly instructing her on how to use it.

"Think you can manage that?"

"I'm not an idiot."

He seemed prone to argue, but changed his mind. "If you hear an airplane, get outside as fast as you can and fire the flare straight up."

"Why aren't you taking it with you?"

The flare gun had been within Cooper's reach since they left the wreckage. "Because the roof of the cabin would be easier to spot than two men on foot. Keep this with you, too." Before she knew what he was about, he pulled the waistband of her slacks away from her body and slid the sheathed skinning knife inside. The smooth leather was cold against the naked skin of her abdomen. She gasped and sucked in her breath. He smiled at her startled reaction. "That should keep you mindful of where it is at all times."

"Why should I be mindful of that?"

He stared into her eyes for a long moment. "Hopefully you'll never have to know why."

She returned his stare. Up until that moment, she hadn't realized how much she hated the thought of his leaving her behind. She had put up a courageous front, but the idea of covering miles of wilderness on crutches had been overwhelming. In a way she was glad he had opted to go without her. But now that he was actually leaving, she wanted to cling to him and beg him not to.

She didn't, of course. He had little enough respect for her as it was. He thought she was a petted, pampered, city girl. Obviously he was right, because at that moment, she was sorely dreading the hours she would have to spend until he came back for her.

Cooper broke the telling stare and, with an impatient curse, turned away.

"Cooper!"

He spun back around. "What?"

"Be . . . be careful."

Within a heartbeat, she was anchored against his chest and his mouth was above hers, taking from it a scorching kiss that burned her soul. It surprised her so that she slumped against him. His arms tightened around her waist and drew her up so close and high that her toes dangled inches above his boots. She sought to regain her balance by clutching handfuls of his coat.

His lips ground against hers. They were possessive and hard. But his tongue was soft and warm and wet. It filled her mouth, explored, stroked. A desire that had been building for forty-eight hours overcame his iron control. His self-discipline snapped, but he was still masterful. This was a no-nonsense kiss that had nothing to do with romance. It was a kiss of passion. Raw. Carnal. Selfish.

Dizzily Rusty threw one of her arms around his neck and tilted her head back to give him deeper access, which he took. His stubbled jaw scraped her skin, but she didn't care. His mustache was surprisingly silky. It tickled and tantalized.

All too soon for her, he broke the kiss, pulling his head back abruptly and leaving her lips parted and damp and wanting more. "I'll be back as soon as possible. Goodbye, honey."

Honey? *Honey?*

He released her and turned toward the door. That's when she noticed Quinn Gawrylow sitting at the table, mindlessly chewing his perpetual wad of tobacco and watching them with the still, silent concentration of a cougar.

Rusty's heart sank like lead. Cooper had kissed her for the old man's benefit—not for his own. And certainly not for hers.

She shot his broad back a venomous look as he went through the door. It slapped closed behind him. Good riddance, she thought. How dare he—

Then, realizing that the old man's eyes were still on her, she looked at him with a vapid good-little-wife smile. "Do you think he'll be all right?"

"Reuben knows what he's doing. He'll take care of Mr. Landry." He waved down at the pallet still spread out in front of the hearth. "It's early yet. Why don't you go back to sleep?"

"No, I, uh—" she cleared her throat noisily. "—I'm too keyed up to sleep. I think I'll just sit here for a while."

"Coffee?" He moved toward the stove.

"Please."

She didn't want any, but it would give her something to do and help pass the time. She set her crutches and the flare gun on the hearth within easy reach and lowered herself into the chair. The knife's scabbard poked her lower abdomen. Why it hadn't plunged right into her when Cooper had pulled her against his—

Her heart fluttered with the memory. It hadn't been only the knife's hardness she'd felt against her middle. He'd probably derived a lot of joy out of humiliating her like that.

Feeling rebellious, she defiantly took the knife out of her waistband and laid it on the hearth. Accepting the cup of steaming coffee from Quinn, she settled down to wait through what would probably be the longest day of her life.

Cooper calculated that they'd gone no farther than a mile when Reuben commenced to talk. Cooper could have gone the whole fifteen miles without a conversation, but maybe talking would make the time pass more quickly and help take his mind off Rusty.

"How come you don't have any kids?" Reuben asked him.

Cooper's instincts slipped into overdrive. Each of his senses was on the alert. That prickle at the back of his neck, which could always be relied upon to warn him that something wasn't quite right, hadn't gone away. Ever since he'd heard Rusty's scream and found her in a standoff with the Gawrylows, he had been suspicious of the two men. He might be doing them a grave injustice. They were probably on the level. But probabilities weren't worth a damn. Until he had Rusty safely turned over to the authorities, he wasn't giving either of the recluses the benefit of the doubt. If they proved to be reliable, then they would have earned his undying gratitude. Until then—

"Huh?" Reuben probed. "How come you—"

"I heard you." Cooper was following Reuben's lead. He didn't let the man get too far ahead of him, nor did he crowd up too close behind him. "Rusty has a career. We're both busy. We'll get around to having kids one of these days."

He hoped that would end the discussion. Children and families were topics Cooper always avoided talking about. Now, he didn't want to talk at all. He wanted to pour every ounce of energy into reaching that river as soon as possible.

"If I'd been married to her for five years, we'd have five kids by now," Reuben bragged rashly.

"But you're not."

"Maybe you ain't doing it right."

"What?"

Reuben gave him a sly wink over his shoulder. "You know, screwing."

The word crawled over Cooper like a loathsome insect. It wasn't that he was offended by the word. He used far worse on a daily basis. It was that he was offended by the word in connection with Rusty. It didn't occur to him that only the night before last he'd used it himself. He was too busy hoping that before the day was out, he wouldn't have to pound Reuben's face to mush; but if he made many more references to Rusty in that context, he just might.

"If she was my woman—"

"But she isn't." Cooper's voice cracked like a bullwhip.

"She will be, though."

With that, Reuben, wearing the grin of a madman, spun around and aimed his rifle at Cooper's chest. Cooper had subconsciously been bracing himself all morning for such an attack. He raised his rifle a split second after Reuben, but Reuben got off the first shot.

"What was that?" Rusty jumped, realizing that she'd been drowsing in her chair.

Quinn was sitting where she'd last seen him, at the table. "Hmm?"

"I thought I heard something."

"I didn't hear anything."

"I could swear—"

"The logs in the fireplace shifted. That's all."

"Oh." Chagrined by her nervousness, she relaxed again in her chair. "I must have dozed off. How long ago since they left?"

"Not long."

He got up and moved toward her, kneeling down on the hearth to add logs to the fire. The warmth seeped into Rusty's skin and her eyes drifted closed again. Sad and dirty as this cabin was, at least it provided a roof over her head

and protection from the cold west wind. She was grateful for
that. After spending days—

Her eyes popped open at his touch. Quinn, still kneeling
in front of her, had his hand folded around her calf. "I
thought you might want to prop up your leg again," he said.

His voice was as gentle as a saint's, but his eyes were Lu-
cifer's own as they stared up at her from within their cave-
like sockets. Terror gripped her, but common sense warned
her not to show it.

"No, thank you. In fact," she said in a thin voice, "I
think I'll walk around a bit to exercise it."

She reached for her crutches, but he grabbed them up
first. "Let me help you."

Before she could protest, he caught her arm and pulled
her out of the chair. He had caught her off guard and the
momentum caused the front of her body to bump against
his. She backed away instantly, but found that she couldn't
go far because his other hand was at the small of her back,
urging her forward.

"No!"

"I'm only trying to help you," he said smoothly, obviously enjoying her mounting distress.

"Then please let me go, Mr. Gawrylow. I can manage."

"Not without help. I'll take your husband's place. He
told me to take care of you, didn't he?" He ran his hand
over her hip and Rusty went cold with fear.

"Don't touch me like that." She tried to squirm away
from him but his hands were everywhere. "Get your hands
off me."

"What's wrong with my hands?" His expression suddenly turned mean. "Aren't they clean enough for you?"

"No...yes...I...I just meant that Cooper will—"

"Cooper won't do anything," he said with a sinister
smile. "And from now on I'll touch you however I want."

He yanked her against him. This time there was no doubt
about his intention. Rusty funneled all her strength into

getting away from him. She placed the heels of her hands on his shoulders and arched her back, trying to push herself away and at the same time to dodge his kiss.

The crutches slid out from under her arms and fell to the floor. She had to support herself on her sore leg and a pain shot up the jagged scar. She cried out.

"Go ahead, scream. I won't mind." His breath was foul and hot against her face. She turned her head away, but he caught her jaw between iron fingers and pulled it back around. Just before his mouth made contact with hers, they heard thudding footsteps outside.

"Help me," Rusty screamed.

"Reuben?" the old man shouted. "Get in here."

Quinn turned his head toward the door, but it wasn't Reuben who came crashing through. Cooper's sweating face was a fierce mask of hatred and rage. His hair was littered with twigs and leaves. There were bleeding scratches on his cheeks and hands. His shirt was specked with blood. To Rusty, no one had ever looked better.

Feet wide apart, Cooper barked, "Let her go, you filthy animal."

Rusty collapsed to the floor when Gawrylow released her. He spun around. As he did so, he reached behind his back. Before Rusty fully realized what had happened, she heard a solid thunk. Then she saw the handle of Cooper's knife in the center of Quinn's chest. The blade was fully buried between his ribs.

The old man was wearing a startled expression. He groped for the handle of the knife. His searching fingers closed around it as he dropped to his knees. Then he fell face down onto the floor and was still.

Rusty gathered her arms and legs against her body, forming herself into a ball. She clapped her hands over her mouth and stared at the still form with wide, unfocusing eyes. Her breath was trapped in her lungs.

Cooper, knocking furniture aside, rushed across the room and crouched in front of her. "Are you all right?" He laid a hand on her shoulder. She recoiled in fright.

He froze. His eyes went as hard as slate as he said, "No need to thank me."

Gradually Rusty lowered her hands and released her breath. She gazed up at Cooper, her lips white with fear. "You killed him." The words had no sound; she mouthed them.

"Before he killed me, you little fool. Look!" He pointed down at the dead man's back. There was a small handgun tucked into the waistband of his pants. "Don't you get it yet?" he roared. "They were going to waste me and keep you. They planned to share you between them."

She shuddered with revulsion. "No!"

"Oh, yeah," Cooper said, nodding his head. Apparently exasperated with her, he stood up and rolled the body over. Squeezing her eyes shut, Rusty averted her head. She heard the body being dragged across the floor and out the door. She heard Quinn's boots thump on the steps as Cooper dragged him down them.

She wasn't sure how long she stayed curled up in that fetal position on the floor. But she still hadn't moved when Cooper returned. He loomed over her. "Did he hurt you?"

Miserably she shook her head.

"Answer me, dammit! Did he hurt you?"

She raised her head and glared up at him. "*No!*"

"He was about to rape you. You *do* realize that, don't you? Or are the stars in your eyes still keeping you from seeing the light?"

Not stars, but tears filled her eyes. She was experiencing a delayed reaction to her horror. "What are you doing here? Why did you come back? Where's Reuben? What are you going to say to him when he gets back?"

"Nothing. Reuben won't be coming back."

She clamped her teeth over her quivering lower lip and closed her eyes. Tears rolled down her cheeks. "You killed him, too, didn't you? That's his blood on you."

"Yes, dammit," he hissed, bending over her. "I shot him in self-defense. He walked me into the woods just far enough to separate us, then he turned a gun on me with every intention of killing me and making you his 'woman.'" Staring up at him, she shook her head in disbelief, which seemed to infuriate him. "And don't you dare pretend to be surprised. You had whipped them into a sexual froth and you know it."

"Me? How? What did I do?"

"Brushing your hair for God's sake!"

"'Brushing'—"

"Just being you. Just looking the way you do."

"Stop yelling at me!" she sobbed. "I didn't do anything."

"Except cause me to kill two men!" he shouted. "Think about that while I'm out burying them."

He stalked out. The fire in the fireplace burned out and the cabin grew cold. But Rusty didn't care.

She was still sitting in a heap on the floor and crying hard when he came back. She was tired. There wasn't a place on her body that didn't ache either from sleeping on the ground or walking on crutches or suffering Quinn Gawrylow's squeezing caresses.

She wanted good, honest food. She'd gladly trade her Maserati for a glass of milk. Her clothes had been ripped by tree branches or ravaged by this barbaric hoodlum she was marooned with. The fur coat she had prized so highly had been used as a litter.

And she had seen men die.

Five in the plane crash. Two at the hands of the man who now threw himself down beside her. He roughly raised her head by placing his callused fingers beneath her chin.

"Get up," he ordered. "Dry your face. You're not going to spend the rest of the day sitting around crying like a baby."

"Go to hell," she spat, lifting her chin out of his grasp.

He was so furious, his lips hardly moved when he spoke. "Look, if you had a good thing going with Reuben and his pa, you should have told me. I'm sorry I ruined it for you."

"You bastard."

"I would have been all too glad to leave you in this paradise and strike out for the river by myself. But I think I should tell you that Reuben had a lot of children in mind. Of course you might not have ever known if the kids you hatched were his or his daddy's."

"Shut up!" She raised her hand to slap him.

He caught it in midair and they stared at each other for several tense seconds. Finally Cooper relaxed his fingers from around her wrist. Snarling angrily, he stood up and kicked a chair as far across the cabin as he could.

"It was either them or me," he said in a voice that vibrated with rage. "Reuben fired first. I got lucky and deflected his rifle just in time. I had no choice."

"You didn't have to kill them."

"No?"

An alternative didn't leap into her mind, but she was sure that if she thought about it long enough she would come up with one. Temporarily conceding, she lowered her eyes. "Why didn't you just keep going?"

His eyes narrowed to slits as he looked down at her. "Don't think I didn't consider it."

"Oh," she ground out. "I can't wait until I'm rid of you."

"Believe me, the feeling is mutual. But in the meantime we've got to tolerate each other. First thing on the agenda is to get this place cleaned up. I'm not spending another night in this stink hole."

Her jaw went slack with disbelief. Slowly her eyes roamed the grimy interior of the cabin. "Clean this place up? Is that what you said?"

"Yeah. We'd better get started, too. The day's getting away."

He righted the chair he'd just kicked over and made his way toward the pile of dingy bedding where Reuben had slept the night before. Rusty started laughing and her laughter was tinged with impending hysteria.

"You're not serious?"

"Like hell I'm not."

"We're spending the night here?"

"And every night from now on until we're rescued."

She came to her feet, propping herself up on one crutch while she watched him strip both beds and pile the bedding in the middle of the floor. "What about the river?"

"That might have all been a lie."

"The Mackenzie River is real, Cooper."

"But where is it from here?"

"You could keep walking in the direction they said until you found it."

"I could. I could also get terribly lost. Or injured and stranded. If you went with me, we might not make it out before the first real snow, in which case we'd probably die of exposure. If you stayed here and something happened to me, you'd die of starvation before the winter was over. And I'm not even sure the direction Reuben led me in was the right one. I've got 359 other choices from this cabin, and getting around to them all would take over a year."

Hands braced on his hips, he faced her. "None of those alternatives sounds very appealing to me. On the other hand if we clean this place up, we can survive. It's not the Beverly Hills Hotel, but it's shelter and there's a constant supply of fresh water."

She didn't appreciate his sarcasm and her mutinous expression let him know it. His whole demeanor suggested that she was foolish not to see all that without his having to explain it, and issued a challenge she wasn't about to back down from. She had been weak this morning, but she never would be again. Pushing up the sleeves of her sweater, she said, "What do you want me to do?"

He hitched his head backward. "Start with the stove."

Without another word, he gathered up the foul bedding and carried it outside.

Rusty attacked the black iron stove with a vengeance, scouring it from top to bottom, using more elbow grease than soap, since she had more of that. It was hard work, especially since she had to keep herself propped up on one crutch. She moved from the stove to the sink, then to the windows, then every stick of furniture got washed down.

After he had boiled the bedding in a caldron outside and hung it up to dry—or freeze, if the temperature turned much colder—Cooper came inside and washed the stones of the hearth. He found a colony of dead insects beneath the woodpile. They had no doubt died of old age since it was almost a certainty that the hearth had never been swept. Keeping the door and windows open to air the place out, he shored up the front porch and stacked firewood on the cabin's south side to protect it from the weather's brunt.

Rusty couldn't sweep the floor, so he did. But when he was finished, she got down on hands and knees and scrubbed it. Her sculptured nails broke off one by one. Where a mere chip would have sent her into a tizzy not long ago, she merely shrugged and went on with her scrubbing, taking satisfaction in the results of her labor.

Cooper brought in two beheaded and plucked birds—she didn't recognize the species—for their dinner. She had made an inventory of the Gawrylows' hoard and was pleased to find a fair amount of canned goods. They had apparently made their October trip to Yellowknife and were well stocked for the winter. A gourmet cook she wasn't, but it didn't take much talent to boil the fowl together with two cans of vegetables and a sprinkling of salt. By the time the stew was done, the aroma was making her mouth water. Darkness was settling in before Cooper carried in the bedding.

"Is it deloused?" she asked, turning from the stove.

"I think so. I boiled the hell out of it. I'm not sure it's quite dry, but if I leave it out any longer, it's going to freeze. We'll check it after dinner and if it's not dry, we'll hang it up in front of the fire."

He washed his hands at the sink, which was sparkling compared to what it had been.

They sat down to eat at the table Rusty had sanded clean. Cooper smiled when he unfolded what had once been a sock and was now acting as a napkin and placed it in his lap, but he didn't comment on her ingenuity. If he noticed the jar with the arrangement of autumn leaves serving as a centerpiece, he said nothing to indicate it. He ate two portions of the stew but didn't say a word about it.

Rusty was crushed. He could have said something nice—one single word of encouragement. Even a puppy needs to be patted on the head now and then.

She dejectedly carried their tin dishes to the sink. While she was pumping water over them, he moved up behind her. "You worked hard today."

His voice was soft and low and came from directly above her head. He was standing very close. His sheer physicality overwhelmed her. She felt tremulous. "So did you."

"I think we deserve a treat, don't you?"

Her stomach rose and fell as weightlessly as a balloon. Memory of the kiss he had given her that morning filled her mind, while a potent desire to repeat it flooded her veins. Slowly she turned around and gazed up at him. Breathlessly she asked, "What did you have in mind, Cooper?"

"A bath."

Six

━━━∽◦∾━━━

"A...bath?" Dorothy couldn't have said "Oz?" with any more awe and wistfulness.

"A real one. The works. Hot water, soap." He went to the door, opened it, and came back in rolling a large washtub. "I found this behind the cabin and cleaned it out."

She didn't remember feeling this grateful when she opened the present from her father and found her full-length, red fox coat folded amid tissue paper. She clasped her hands beneath her chin. "Oh, Cooper, thank you."

"Don't get gushy," he said querulously. "We'll get as disgusting as the Gawrylows if we don't bathe. Not every day, though."

Rusty didn't let him spoil her good mood. He didn't allow people to get even close enough to thank him. Well, that was his problem. He'd done something very thoughtful for her. She had thanked him. Beyond that, what else could she do? He must know how much this meant to her, even if he chose to act like a heel about it now.

She filled several pots and kettles with water from the pump. He carried them to the stove to heat them up, refueling the fire to hurry them along. He then dragged the tub across the wooden floor and placed it directly in front of the fireplace. The metal was icy cold, but in a few minutes the fire would warm it up.

Rusty watched him making all these preparations with expectation, then a growing concern. "What do I do about, uh..."

Saying nothing, expressionless, Cooper unfurled one of the rough muslin bed-sheets he'd boiled and aired that day. The ceiling of the cabin had bare beams. Apparently the Gawrylows had hung meat from it because there were several metal hooks screwed into the dark wood.

Cooper stood on a chair and pushed one of the sharp hooks through a corner of the sheet. Repositioning the chair several times, he soon had the sheet hanging like a curtain behind the tub.

"Thank you," Rusty said. She was glad to have the sheet there but couldn't help but notice that with the fireplace behind it, it was translucent. The tub was silhouetted against it. Anybody in the tub would be, too.

Cooper must have noticed that at the same time, because he shifted his eyes away from it and ran his hands nervously up and down his pants legs. "I think the water's just about ready."

Rusty assembled her precious cache of toiletries—a bar of scented soap, a small plastic bottle of shampoo, her razor—on the seat of the chair near the tub.

Earlier in the day, she had separated the meager clothing they had left and neatly folded and stacked it on separate shelves, one for her, one for Cooper. She took a fresh pair of long johns and a tank top from her stack now and draped them over the back of the chair.

When everything was ready, she stood awkwardly by while Cooper carefully carried the heavy pots of boiling water across the room and poured them into the tub. Steam rose out of it, but as far as Rusty was concerned it couldn't be too hot. She had four days' accumulation of grime and fatigue to soak away. Besides, she was accustomed to spending several minutes each day in her hot tub at home.

"What do I dry with?" she asked.

Cooper tossed her a coarse, dingy towel from the pile of bedding he'd carried in earlier. "I found a couple of these hanging from nails outside the cabin. I boiled them, too. They've never known fabric softener, but they're better than nothing."

The towel did feel more like sandpaper than terry cloth, but Rusty accepted it without comment.

"There, that should do it," Cooper said brusquely, emptying the contents of the last kettle into the tub. "Ease into it carefully. Don't scald yourself."

"Okay."

Standing at opposite sides of the tub, they faced each other. Their eyes met through the rising steam. The humidity was already curling Rusty's hair and making her complexion look dewy and rosy.

Cooper turned his back abruptly and impatiently swatted aside the curtain. It fell back into place. Rusty could hear his stamping, booted footsteps against the uneven flooring. He went outside and slammed the door closed behind him.

She sighed with resignation. He had a sour disposition and that's all there was to it. And while she was lolling in her first bath in four days, she certainly wasn't going to dwell on his personality flaws. She wouldn't let him spoil this for her, no matter how disagreeable he became.

Because she still avoided putting any weight on her leg, it was a challenge to get out of her clothes. When she had managed that, it was an even greater challenge to ease herself into the bathtub. She was finally able to do so by supporting herself on her arms and sitting down slowly, pulling her sore leg in behind her.

It felt more heavenly than she had allowed herself to anticipate. Cooper had been right to caution her; the water was hot, but deliciously so. The corrugated bottom of the tub felt odd against her buttocks and took some getting used to, but before long the luxury of being submerged in hot, soothing water took her mind off that one minor discomfort.

She immersed as much of herself as possible and rested her head against the rim. Her eyes slid closed. She was so relaxed that she didn't even flinch when she heard Cooper come back inside. She only frowned slightly when a breath of cold air reached her before he shut the door behind him.

Eventually she extended one dripping arm and took the bar of soap off the seat of the chair. She was tempted to lather herself liberally, wantonly, wastefully. But she thought better of it. This bar of soap might have to last a long time. Better not squander it, she decided, as she worked up an adequate lather and soaped herself all over.

Propping her feet one at a time on the rim of the tub, she shaved her legs, carefully maneuvering the razor around Cooper's stitching. With anguish she realized what an unsightly scar she was going to have but was ashamed of her vanity. She was lucky to be alive. As soon as she got back to Beverly Hills, she would have a plastic surgeon repair Cooper's well-intentioned, but unattractive, handiwork.

It struck her then that he was being awfully noisy. "Cooper, what are you doing?"

"Making up the beds," he said, grunting with the effort. "These frames are made of solid oak and weigh a ton."

"I can't wait to lie down on one."

"Don't expect it to be much better than the ground. There're no mattresses. Just canvas platforms like cots. But mattresses would have had lice, so it's just as well."

Laying aside her razor, she picked up the bottle of shampoo and after dunking her head beneath the water, squeezed out a dollop. The shampoo would have to be rationed even more sparingly than the soap. She worked it through her thick hair, scrubbing ruthlessly from her scalp to the ends.

She dunked her head to rinse it, then wrung out as much water as she could.

Laying her head against the tub's rim again, she fanned her hair out behind her so it could begin to dry. It would drip on the floor, but water was probably the least offensive substance to ever be dripped on it.

Again, her eyes closed as she luxuriated in the warmth of the water, the floral fragrance of shampoo and soap, and the deliciousness of feeling clean again.

Eventually the water began to cool and she knew it was time to get out. Anyway, she doubted that Cooper would go to bed before she did. He must be exhausted after all he'd done since getting up before daybreak that morning. She had no idea what time it was. The crash had stopped both their watches. Time was measured by the sun coming up and going down. The days were short, but today had been long—emotionally as well as physically taxing.

She braced her arms on the rim of the tub and tried to push herself up. To her dismay, her arms collapsed like wet noodles. She had stayed in the hot water too long; her muscles were useless. Several times she tried, but to no avail. Her arms simply wouldn't support her. She devised other plans, but none of them worked because of her sore leg, which she couldn't put any weight on.

Finally, growing chilled and knowing that the inevitable couldn't be postponed indefinitely, she bashfully called his name.

"What?"

His irritable response wasn't too encouraging, but she had no choice. "I can't get out."

After a silence long enough for a telephone pole to stretch out in, he said, "Huh?"

Rusty squeezed her eyes shut and repeated, "I can't get out of the tub."

"Get out the same way you got in."

"I'm too weak from the hot water. My arms won't hold me up long enough to step out."

His curses were so scorching, she didn't know why the bed-sheet curtain didn't combust. When she heard his approaching footsteps, she crossed her arms over her breasts. Cool air fanned across her wet, bare back as he moved the curtain aside. She stared straight ahead into the fireplace, feeling his eyes on her as he moved toward the tub.

For a long time he just stood there, saying nothing. Rusty's lungs were almost ready to burst from internal tension by the time he said, "I'll slide my hands under your arms. Come up on your left leg. Then while I'm holding you up, lift it out of the tub and set it on the floor. Okay?"

His voice was low and of the same texture as the towel he'd given her to use—as rough as sandpaper. "Okay." She eased her arms slightly away from her body. Even though she'd been expecting it, the first touch of his fingertips against her slippery, wet skin, came as a shock. Not because it felt awful, but because it didn't.

And it only got better from there. Confident and strong, his hands slid into the notches of her armpits and cupped them supportively. He braced his legs wide apart, almost straddling the tub, and lifted her. She sucked in her breath sharply.

"What's the matter?"

"My...my underarms are sore," she told him breathlessly. "Because of the crutches." He muttered a curse. It was so vile she hoped she hadn't heard it correctly.

His hands slipped over her wet skin and encased her ribs. "Let's try it this way. Ready?"

Rusty, according to his instructions, supported herself on her left leg, letting the injured one dangle uselessly as he raised her out of the water.

"Okay so far?" She nodded. "Ready?" She replied in the same soundless way. He took all her weight on his hands as she lifted her left foot over the edge of the tub and set it on the floor.

"Oh!"

"What now?"

He was just about to release her when she made the exclamation and tipped forward slightly. With lightning reflexes, his arm slid around her, clasping her just below her breasts.

"The floor is cold."

"Christ, don't scare me like that."

"Sorry. It was a shock."

Each was thinking, "You can say that again."

Rusty groped for the back of the chair to lend her support and hastily clutched the towel to the front of her body. Of course that still left her back naked to his eyes, but she trusted that he was being a gentleman and wasn't taking advantage.

"All right?"

"Yes."

His hands moved from her front to her sides, but he didn't release her entirely. "Sure?"

"Yes," she answered thickly, "I'm fine."

He withdrew his hands. Rusty sighed with relief—as it turned out, prematurely.

"What the hell is this?" She gasped when his hand cupped the side of her hip. His thumb made a long, slow sweep across her buttock, sluicing off water. Then the other buttock was similarly examined. "What the devil happened to you? I thought you said he didn't hurt you?"

"I don't know what you mean." Breathless and dizzy, she turned her head and looked up at him over her shoulder. His brows were pulled together into a deep V and his mustache was curved downward with displeasure.

"You're black-and-blue."

Rusty looked over her shoulder and down the length of her back. The first thing that registered with her was that

Cooper's dark hands against her pale flesh made a very sensuous picture. Only when he made another solicitous movement with his thumb did she see the bruises.

"Oh, those. They're from the ride in the travois."

His eyes swung up to hers and penetrated her with their heat. He kept his hands against her flesh. His voice was as soft as his touch. "You should have said something."

She became entranced with the movements of his mustache as his mouth formed words. Perhaps that's why she whispered, "Would saying something have changed anything?"

A strand of her hair got caught in the stubble on his chin. It connected them like a filament of light. Not that they needed it. Their stare was almost palpable. It lasted forever and wasn't broken until a log in the fireplace popped loudly. They both jumped guiltily.

Cooper resumed his broody expression and growled. "No. It wouldn't have changed anything."

Seconds later the drape fluttered back into place behind him. Rusty was trembling. *From the cold*, she averred. He had kept her standing here long enough to get chilled. She wrapped the towel around her and dried quickly. The cloth was so coarse it left her skin tingling. It chafed the delicate areas of her body, especially her nipples. When she finished drying, they were abnormally rosy and pointed. Achy. And throbbing. And hot.

"It's the *towel*," she muttered as she pulled on her silk long johns.

"What is it this time?" The cantankerous question came from the other side of the drape.

"What?"

"I heard you say something."

"I said this towel would make a great scouring pad."

"It was the best I could come up with."

"I wasn't being critical."

"That'd be a first."

She muttered something else beneath her breath, making sure he didn't overhear it this time, since it was an epithet grossly unflattering to his lineage and personality.

Aggravated, she ungracefully pulled the tank top over her head. Her nipples poked darkly against the clinging fabric. The silkiness, which should have felt soothing after the towel, only seemed to irritate them more.

She repacked her toiletries in their carrying case and dropped down into the chair. Bending at the waist, she flipped all her hair forward and rubbed it vigorously with the towel, alternately brushing it. Five minutes later, she flung her head back and her semidried hair settled against her shoulders in russet waves. It wasn't styled, but it was clean, and that was a definite improvement.

It was when she was replacing her hairbrush in the cosmetic kit that she noticed the condition of her nails. They had been jaggedly broken or torn away. She groaned audibly.

Within a heartbeat, the curtain was thrown back and Cooper was standing there. "What's the matter? Is it your leg? Is it—"

He broke off when he realized that Rusty wasn't in any pain. But even if that realization hadn't shut him up, the sight of her sitting silhouetted against the golden firelight, a halo of wavy cinnamon-colored hair wreathing her head like an aura would have. She was wearing a top that was more alluring than concealing. The shadows of her nipples drew his eyes like magnets. Even now, he could feel the heaviness of her breasts where they had rested on his forearms minutes ago.

His blood turned to molten lava, hot and thick and rampant. It surged toward his sex where it collected and produced the normal, but currently unwanted, reaction. It was painful in its intensity.

And since he couldn't alleviate it, he released his sexual tension by another means: fury. His face grew dark with menace. His heavy brows, more gold than brown in the firelight, were intimidatingly drawn into a frown over his eyes. Since he couldn't taste her with his tongue—as he was dying to do—he'd use it to verbally lash her.

"You were groaning over your damn fingernails?" he shouted.

"They're all chipped and broken," Rusty yelled back at him.

"Better them than your neck, you little fool."

"Stop calling me that, Cooper. I'm not a fool."

"You couldn't even figure out that those two hillbillies wanted to rape you."

Her mouth drew up into a sullen pout that only inflamed him further because he wanted to kiss it so badly. His unquenchable desire prompted him to say ugly, hurtful things. "You did all you could to entice them, didn't you? Sitting near the fire when you know what it does to your eyes and complexion. Brushing your hair until it crackled. You know what that kind of thing does to a man, don't you? You know it drives him crazy with lust." Then, realizing that his tirade was as good as a confession, he sneered, "I'm surprised you didn't come out in that getup last night and flaunt yourself in front of Reuben, the poor jerk."

Rusty's eyes smarted with tears. His estimation of her was far lower than she had thought. Not only did he think she was useless, he thought she was no better than a whore.

"I didn't do anything on purpose. You know that, no matter what you say." Instinctively, in self-defense, she crossed her arms over her chest.

Suddenly he dropped to his knees in front of her and jerked her arms away. In the same motion, he whipped the lethal knife from its scabbard at his waist. Rusty squealed in fright when he clasped her left hand tightly and raised the glittering blade to it. He made a short, efficient job of paring her nails down even with the tops of her fingers. When he dropped that hand, she looked at it remorsefully.

"That looks awful."

"Well, I'm the only one here to see them and I don't give a damn. Give me your other hand."

She complied. She had no choice. In an arm-wrestling match, she could hardly win against him. And now her breasts were fair game for his condemning gaze again. But when his eyes glanced up from the bizarre manicure he was giving her, they weren't condemning. Nor were they cold with contempt. They were warm with masculine interest. A lot of interest. So much interest that Rusty's stomach took another of those elevator rides that never quite took it to the top or the bottom but kept it bobbing up and down somewhere in between.

Cooper took his time trimming the nails on her right hand, as if they needed more care and attention than those on her left. His face was on a level with her chest. In spite of the awful things he'd said to her just moments ago, she wanted to run her fingers through his long, unruly hair.

As she watched his lips, set firmly in a scowl, she couldn't help but remember how soft they could become in a kiss—how warm and damp—and how marvelous his mustache had felt. If it had felt that good against her upper lip, how good would it feel against other parts of her body? Her neck? Her ear? Her areola—while his lips tugged at her nipple with the gentle fervency of a baby hungry for milk?

He finished cutting her nails and sheathed his knife. But he didn't release her hand. He held it, staring down at it, then laid it on her thigh, pressing it there with his own hand. Rusty thought her heart would explode from the pressure inside her chest.

He kept his head down, staring at the spot where his hand covered hers high on her thigh. His eyes looked closed from Rusty's angle. The lashes were thick and crescent shaped. She noticed that they, like his mustache and eyebrows, were tipped with gold. In the summertime his hair would be naturally streaked, bleached from the sun.

"Rusty."

He said her name. There was a slight creak in his voice, a groaning protest of the raw emotion behind his saying it. Rusty didn't move, but her heart was beating so fast and wildly that it stirred the silk that wasn't doing a very adequate job of covering her.

He removed his hand from hers and placed each of his on either side of the chair seat, bracketing her hips. His knuckles pressed into their flaring shape. He remained staring fixedly at her hand, which still lay on her thigh. He looked ready to lower his head and wearily rest his cheek against it, or to bend down and tenderly kiss it, or to nibble on the very fingers he'd just cut the nails from.

If he wanted to, Rusty wouldn't stop him. She knew that positively. Her body was warm and moist and receptive to the idea. She was ready for whatever happened.

No, she wasn't.

Because what happened was that Cooper came to his feet hastily. "You'd better get to bed."

Rusty was stunned by his about-face. The mood had been shattered, the intimacy dispelled. She felt like arguing, but didn't. What could she say? "Kiss me again, Cooper," "Touch me,"? That would only confirm his low opinion of her.

Feeling rejected, she gathered her belongings, including the pile of dirty clothes she'd left beside the tub, and walked around the curtain. Each of the two beds had been spread with sheets and blankets. A fur pelt had been left at the foot of each. At home her bed was covered in designer sheets and piled with downy pillows, but it had never looked more inviting than this one.

She put her things away and sat down on the bed. In the meantime, Cooper had made several trips outside with buckets of bathwater. When the water level was low enough, he dragged the tub to the door and out onto the porch, then tipped it over the edge and emptied the rest of it. He brought the tub back into the room, replaced it behind the curtain, and from the pump in the sink began filling the pots and kettles again.

"Are you going to take a bath, too?"

"Any objections?"

"No."

"It's been a while since I chopped firewood and my back is sore. Besides that, I think I'm beginning to stink."

"I didn't notice."

He looked at her sharply, but when he could see that she was being honest, he came close to smiling. "You will now that you're clean."

The kettles had begun to boil. He lifted two of them off the stove and headed toward the tub.

"Do you want me to massage it?" Rusty asked guilelessly.

He stumbled, sloshed boiling water on his legs, and cursed. "*What*?"

"Massage it?" He gazed at her as though he'd been hit between the eyes with a two-by-four. "Your back."

"Oh, uh..." His eyes moved over her. The tank top left her throat and shoulders bare, cloaked only with a mass of reddish-brown curls. "No—" he refused curtly "—I told you to go to sleep. We've got more work to do tomorrow." He rudely returned to his task.

Not only was human courtesy impossible for him, he wouldn't let anybody be nice to him. Well he could rot, for all she cared!

Rusty angrily thrust her feet between the chilly sheets and lay down, but she didn't close her eyes. Instead she watched Cooper sit down on the edge of his bed and unlace his boots while he was waiting for more water to boil. He tossed his socks onto the pile of dirty clothing she had made and began unbuttoning his shirt. He was wearing only one today because he'd been working so hard outside. He pulled the tails of it from his jeans and took it off.

Rusty sprang to a sitting position. "What happened to you?"

He flung his shirt down onto the pile of clothes to be washed. He didn't have to ask what she was referring to. If it looked as bad as it felt, the bruise was noticeable even in the dim light.

"My shoulder came into contact with the barrel of Reuben's rifle. I had to deflect it that way, so my hands would be free to get my own rifle up."

Rusty winced. The fist-size bruise at the outer edge of his collarbone was black-and-blue and looked extremely painful. "Does it hurt?"

"Like hell."

"Did you take an aspirin?"

"No. We need to conserve them."

"But if you're hurting—"

"You aren't taking them for the bruises on your butt."

That remark shocked her speechless. But it didn't last long. After a moment she said stubbornly, "I still think two aspirin would help."

"I want to save them. You might have fever again."

"Oh, I see. You don't have any aspirin to take for your shoulder because I wasted them on my fever."

"I didn't say you wasted them. I said, oh—" Then he said a word that described something neither was in the mood to do, a word that should never be spoken aloud in polite company. "Go to sleep, will you?"

Wearing only his jeans, he went to the stove, apparently decided that the water was hot enough even though it wasn't quite boiling, and emptied it all into the tub. Rusty had lain back down, but she watched his shadow moving on the curtain as he shucked off his jeans and stepped naked into the tub. Her imagination got the night off because his shadow left nothing up to it, especially in profile.

She heard cursing as he lowered himself into the water. The tub didn't accommodate him as easily as it had her.

How he expected her to go to sleep with all that splashing going on, she didn't know. He had splashed more water on the floor than was left in the bottom of the tub by the time he stood up to rinse off.

Rusty's throat went dry as she watched his shadow. He bent at the waist, repeatedly scooping handfuls of water over himself to rinse off the soap. When he stepped out, he dried with masculine carelessness. The only attention he gave his hair was to make one pass over it with the towel, then to comb his fingers through it. He finished by wrapping the towel around his waist.

He went through the laborious procedure of emptying the tub again. After the last trip to the porch, he left the tub outside. Rusty could tell he was shivering when he moved back to the fire and added several logs. Using the chair as his ladder, he took down the screen the same way he'd put it up. He folded the sheet, placed it on one of the several shelves against the wall, and blew out the lantern on the table. The last thing he did before sliding into his bed was yank the towel from around his waist.

During all that time, he never looked at Rusty. She was hurt that he hadn't even said good-night. But then, she might not have been able to answer him.

Her mouth was still dry.

Counting sheep didn't help.

Reciting poetry didn't help, especially since the only poems he knew by heart were limericks of a licentious nature.

So Cooper lay there on his back, with his hands stacked beneath his head, staring at the ceiling, and wondering when his stiff manhood was going to stop tenting the covers and relax enough to let him fall asleep. He was exhausted. His overexerted muscles cried out for rest. But his sex wasn't listening.

Unlike the rest of him, it was feeling great. He felt like taps all over, but it felt like reveille: alert and alive and well. Too well.

In desperation, he put one hand beneath the covers. Maybe... He yanked his hand back. Nope. Uh-uh. Don't do that. Trying to press it down only made the problem worse.

Furious with Rusty for doing this to him, he rolled to his side. Even that movement created unwanted friction. He uttered an involuntary groaning sound, which he hastily turned into a cough.

What could he do? Nothing that wouldn't be humiliating. So he'd just have to think about something else.

But dammit, he'd tried. For hours, he'd tried. His thoughts eventually meandered back to her.

Her lips: soft.

Her mouth: vulnerable but curious; then hungry, opening to him.

He clenched his teeth, thinking of the way her mouth had closed around his seeking tongue. God, she tasted good. He'd wanted to go on and on, thrusting his tongue inside her, sending it a little farther into her mouth each time, until he decided exactly what it was she tasted like. It would be an impossible task and therefore endless—because she had her own unique taste.

He should have known better than to kiss her—not even for the sake of fooling the old man. Who had been fooling whom? he asked himself derisively. He had kissed her because he'd wanted to and he *had* known better. He had suspected that one kiss wouldn't satisfy him and now he knew that for sure.

What the hell? Why was he being so hard on himself? He was sleeplessly randy because she was the only woman around. Yeah, that was it.

Probably. Possibly. Maybe.

But the fact still remained that she had a knockout face. Sexy-as-hell hair. A body that begged to be mated. Breasts that were created for a man's enjoyment. A cute, squeezable derriere. Thighs that inspired instant arousal. And what lay nestled between them—

No! his mind warned him. Don't think about that or you'll have to do what you have miraculously, and with considerable self-discipline, refrained from doing tonight.

All right, that's enough. *Finis. No mas.* The end. Stop thinking like a sex-crazed kid at worst and a redneck sexist at best, and go to sleep.

He closed his eyes and concentrated so hard on keeping them closed that at first he thought the whimpering sound that issued from the other bed was his imagination. Then Rusty sprang up out of the covers like a jack-in-the-box. That wasn't his imagination. Nor was it something he could ignore by playing possum.

"Rusty?"

"What is that?"

Even with no more to light the room than the dying fire, he could see that her eyes were round and huge with fear. He thought she was having a nightmare. "Lie back down. Everything's okay."

She was breathing erratically and clutching the covers to her chest. "What is that noise?"

Had he made a noise? Had he failed to camouflage his groans? "Wha—"

But just as he was about to ask, the mourning, wailing sound came again. Rusty covered her ears and bent double. "I can't stand it," she cried.

Cooper tossed back the covers on his bed and reached hers in seconds. "Wolves, Rusty. Timber wolves. That's all. They're not as close as they sound and they can't hurt us."

Gently he unfolded her and eased her back until she was lying down again. But her face was far from restful. Her eyes apprehensively darted around the dark interior of the cabin as though it had been invaded by demons of the night.

"Wolves?"

"They smell the—"

"Bodies."

"Yes," he replied with regret.

"Oh, God." She covered her face with her hands.

"Shh, shh. They can't get to them because I covered the graves with rocks. They'll eventually go away. Hush, now, and go to sleep."

He'd been so miserable with his own problem that he'd paid scant attention to the barking of the pack that lurked in the woods surrounding the cabin. But he could see that Rusty's fear was genuine. She clasped his hand and drew it up under her chin as a child might hold his teddy bear to help ward off the terrors of a recent nightmare.

"I hate this place," she whispered.

"I know."

"I've tried to be brave."

"You have been."

She shook her head adamantly. "No, I'm a coward. My father saw it. He was the one who suggested that I return home ahead of schedule."

"Lots of people can't stand seeing animals killed."

"I broke down and cried today in front of you. You've known all along that I'm useless. I'm no good at this. And I don't want to be good at it." Her voice was defiant, incongruous with the tears that washed her cheeks. "You think I'm a terrible person."

"No, I don't."

"Yes, you do."

"No, honest."

"Then why did you accuse me of enticing those men?"

"I was angry."

"Why?"

Because you entice me, too, and I don't want to be enticed. He didn't tell her that. Instead he muttered, "Never mind."

"I want to go home. Where everything is safe and warm and *clean*."

He could argue that the streets of Los Angeles couldn't always been considered safe, but knew that now wasn't the time for teasing—even gentle teasing.

It went against his grain to compliment her, but he felt she'd earned it. "You've done exceptionally well."

She lifted watery eyes to his. "No, I haven't."

"Far better than I ever expected."

"Really?" she asked hopefully.

The breathlessness of her voice and the feminine appeal on her face was almost too much for him. "Really. Now, ignore the wolves and go back to sleep." He pulled his hand from her grasp and turned away. Before he could move, however, another wolf howled. She cried out and reached for him again, throwing herself against him when he turned back to her.

"I don't care if I am a coward. Hold me, Cooper. Please hold me."

Reflexively his arms went around her. Like that other time he had held her while she wept, he felt the same sense of helplessness steal over him. It was lunacy to hold her for any reason, but it would be abominably cruel to turn away. So even though it was as much agony as ecstasy, he drew her close and buried his lips in her wealth of hair.

As he spoke them, his words were sincere. He was sorry this had happened to her. He wished they would be rescued. He wanted her to be returned safely home. He was sorry she was frightened. If there was something he could do to get them out of their predicament, he would.

"You've done everything possible. But just hold me a minute longer," she begged.

"I will."

He continued to hold her. His arms remained around her. But he didn't move his hands. He didn't trust himself to rub them over her back and stop with that. He wanted to touch her all over. He wanted to knead her breasts and investigate the warm, soft place between her thighs. Desire made him shiver.

"You're freezing." Rusty ran her hands over the gooseflesh on his upper arms.

"I'm fine."

"Get under the covers."

"No."

"Don't be silly. You'll catch a cold. What's the big deal? We've slept together for the past three nights. Come on." She pulled back the covers.

"Uh-uh. I'm going back to my own bed."

"You said you'd hold me. Please. Just until I fall asleep."

"But, I'm—"

"Please, Cooper."

He swore, but slid beneath the covers with her. She cuddled against him, nuzzling her face against the fuzzy security of his chest. Her body became pliant against his. He gritted his teeth.

Seconds after she had relaxed against him, she pushed herself away. "Oh!" she exclaimed softly. "I forgot that you were—"

"Naked. That's right. But it's too late now, baby."

Seven

Masculine urges governed him now. His mouth moved over hers in a deep, long, questing kiss while his body settled heavily against hers. Angling his head first to one side, then the other, he made heated love to her mouth with his greedy tongue.

Shock was Rusty's initial reaction. His wonderful nakedness was a stunning surprise. Then, before she could recover from that, she was swept up into his tempestuous kiss.

Her next reaction was spontaneous longing. It surged up through her middle, overwhelming her heart and mind, obliterating all else but the man who was ravishing her mouth so expertly. Her arms encircled his neck and drew him closer. Reflexively she arched against him, bringing her body in contact with his hard, rigid flesh.

Groaning in near pain, he buried his face in her neck. "God, it's so full it's about to burst."

"What do you want, Cooper?"

He laughed harshly. "That's obvious, isn't it?"

"I know; but, what do you want me to do?"

"Either touch me all over or don't touch me at all." His breath struck her face in hot, rapid gusts. "But whatever you decide, decide now."

Rusty hesitated only half a heartbeat before she ran the fingers of one hand up through his hair and settled them against his scalp. She used the other to comb through the crisp hair on his chest, massaging the muscles that had beguiled her.

Their lips met in another rapacious kiss. He ran his tongue over her lower lip, then drew it between his lips and sucked it lightly. The sheer sexuality of it electrified her. He took her moaning whimper as encouragement and began kissing his way down her throat and chest. He wasn't a man to ask permission. Boldly he lowered his hand to her breast, cupped it, and pushed it up.

"I've been going out of my mind wanting you," he rasped. "I thought I'd go insane before I touched you, tasted you."

He opened his mouth over the smooth flesh that swelled above her tank top. He kissed it fervently, applying enough suction to draw it up against his teeth. He tickled it with his tongue at the same time he unhurriedly whisked his thumb back and forth across her nipple. When it began to respond and grow hard, he accelerated that fanning caress until Rusty was almost delirious.

"Stop, Cooper," she gasped. "I can't breathe."

"I don't want you to be able to breathe."

He lowered his head and, through the cloth of her tank top, flicked his tongue against her raised nipple, playfully nudging it. Rusty's heels ground into the bed beneath her and her back came off it. But even that revealing response didn't satisfy him.

"Say you want me," he said in a low, vibrating voice.

"Yes, I want you. Yes, yes."

Driven by a wild, uncontrollable hunger, heedless of the consequences, she pushed him back and became the aggressor. Her lips moved down his throat and over his chest and stomach, striking as randomly as raindrops on parched earth. Each time her mouth touched his hair-smattered skin, she whispered his name. It became like a prayer, growing in fervency with each kiss.

"You're beautiful, beautiful," she whispered over his navel. Then, moving her head lower and rubbing her cheek in the hair that grew dense and dark, she said with a sigh, "Cooper."

The passion she'd unleashed stunned him. He tilted his head up and gazed down at her. Her hair was sweeping across his belly. Her breath was disturbing his body hair. The love words she was chanting had more erotic rhythm than any he'd ever heard. Her lips... God, her lips... were leaving dewy patches on his skin.

Her head moving over him was the most erotic, most beautiful sight he'd ever seen. And it scared the hell out of him. He pushed her away from him and rolled off the bed. Standing at the side of it, he trembled visibly, swearing beneath his breath.

Hard, passionate, mindless coupling he could handle, but not this. Not this. He didn't want any real yearning and feeling and emotion to be involved, thank you. He'd done every sensual thing that was physically possible to do with a woman. But no woman had ever expressed such honest longing. What Rusty had done suggested an intimacy between them that went beyond the physical.

He didn't need that. No romance. No love. No thanks.

He was temporarily responsible for Rusty Carlson's survival, but he damned sure wasn't going to assume responsibility for her emotional stability. If she wanted to mate, fine, but he didn't want her fooling herself into thinking that it meant something more than physical gratification. She could do whatever she wanted to with his body. He would permit, even welcome her, to indulge her most carnal desires. But that's where it stopped. No one was allowed to trespass on his emotions.

Rusty stared up at him, bewildered and hurt. "What's wrong?" Self-conscious now, she raised the sheet up to her chin.

"Nothing."

He crossed the room and tossed another log on the fire. It sent up a shower of sparks that threw a brief, but bright, glow into the room. In that light, she saw that he was still fully aroused.

He saw that her eyes were inquiring and disillusioned. "Go to sleep," he said crossly. "The wolves are gone. Besides, I told you they can't hurt you. Now stop being a crybaby and don't bother me again."

Returning to his own bed, he pulled the covers up around his ears. In seconds he was drenched with sweat. Damn her. His body was still on fire.

Damn her, why had she responded that way? So honestly. With no coyness. No affectation. Her mouth had been so receptive. Her kisses so generous. Her breasts so soft and her nipples so hard.

He clenched his teeth against the memories. Was he a fool? A damn fool for not taking what she had offered so unconditionally?

But that was the hitch. It wasn't unconditional. Otherwise he'd be lying between her silky thighs now instead of in a pool of his own sweat. That dazed expression on her face had told him that it meant more to her than simple rutting. She was reading things into it that he would never be able to deliver.

Oh, he could imbed himself deeply into that sweet feminine body and succeed in pleasing both of them physically. But he couldn't *feel*, and that's what she wanted. Maybe even what she deserved. He didn't have it to give. His heart was the Sahara of emotional wastelands.

No, better to hurt her now and get it over with. Better to be a bastard now than to take advantage of the situation. He didn't engage in long-term affairs. Certainly not in anything more. A relationship between them could go nowhere once they were rescued.

Until then, he'd live. Contrary to popular myth, a man couldn't die from being perpetually hard. It wouldn't be comfortable, but he'd live.

The following morning, Rusty's eyes were so swollen from crying that she could barely open them. With an effort, she pried them apart and noticed that the cabin's other bed was empty. The covers had already been neatly smoothed into place.

Good. He wouldn't notice her puffy eyes until she had had a chance to bathe them in cold water. The weakness she'd exhibited last night made her furious with herself. Unreasonably, the crying wolves had frightened her. They personified all the threats surrounding her and made the precariousness of her situation very real.

For some inexplicable reason, her terror had manifested itself in desire. Cooper had responded. Then she had. Thank heaven he'd come to his senses before something drastic had happened.

Rusty only wished that she had been the one to come to her senses first. He might erroneously think that she'd wanted *him*—when in fact, what she had wanted was *someone*. He was just the only one around. And if he thought anything else, he was sorely mistaken.

Imitating him by making her bed—never let it be said that he was a superior survivor—she went to the sink and pumped enough water to bathe her face and brush her teeth. She dressed in the same pair of slacks she'd worn yesterday—air conditioning provided by Jack the Ripper, she thought peevishly—but put on a fresh flannel shirt. She brushed her hair and tied it back with a shoelace. It was when she was pulling on her socks that she realized she had been moving about without the aid of her crutches. There was very little soreness left in her leg. They might not be pretty, but Cooper's stitches had worked to heal her injury.

Not wanting to feel any kindness toward him, she moved to the stove and fed short sticks of firewood into it. She filled a kettle with water and spooned coffee into it, sadly thinking about the automatic coffee maker with the built-in digital timer that she had in her kitchen at home.

Forcibly tamping down a wave of homesickness, she began making a breakfast of oatmeal. Reading the directions on the side of the cylindrical box that she'd found among the food supplies, she was glad to discover that oatmeal didn't require any cooking skills beyond boiling water and pouring in the correct portion of oats.

Unfortunately her guess was off a trifle.

Cooper came stamping in and without preamble demanded, "Have you got breakfast ready yet?"

None too charitably, she answered, "Yes. Sit down."

She wanted to serve him a steaming bowl of creamy oatmeal like the ones in the commercials on TV. Instead, when she lifted the lid on the pot, she gazed down into a gooey mess about the color and consistency of setting concrete, except lumpier.

Dismayed, but determined not to show it, she squared her shoulders and dug out two spoonfuls. When she dumped them into the tin bowls, they landed in the bottom of them like lead. She carried the bowls to the table, set them on the rough wood plank with forceful disdain, and took her chair across from him.

"Coffee?" he said.

She bit her lip in consternation, but got up, poured their coffee and returned to the table without saying a single word. She let her body language convey her dislike for his lord-of-the-manor attitude.

He scooped up a bite of the oatmeal and weighed it in his spoon, eyeing her skeptically. Silently, she challenged him to say anything derogatory about her oatmeal. He put the bite in his mouth.

As though instructing him on what to do with it once it was there, Rusty took a bite of hers. She almost spat it out immediately. Instead, knowing he was watching her with his eagle eyes, she chewed it. It seemed to expand instead of get smaller. Finally she had no recourse but to swallow it to get rid of it. Her stomach must have thought she was eating golf balls. She swilled down a scalding gulp of coffee.

Cooper's spoon clattered against his bowl. "Is this the best you can do?"

Rusty wanted to come back with, "Was last night the best *you* could do?" But she reasoned that aiming such an insult at a man's lovemaking abilities might be justifiable grounds for homicide, so she judiciously said, "I don't cook that much at home."

"Too busy flitting from one expensive, fancy restaurant to another, I guess."

"Yes."

Making a terrible face, he forced down another swallow of the foul stuff. "This isn't that presalted, presweetened oatmeal that comes in the cute little packages with teddy bears and bunnies on them; this is the real stuff. Add salt to the water next time. Use only about half as much oatmeal, and then sprinkle sugar over it. But not too much. We've got to ration our supplies."

"If you know so much about cooking, Scoutmaster, why don't you do it?" she asked sweetly.

He shoved his bowl aside and propped his forearms on the table. "Because I've got to do the hunting and fishing and firewood cutting. But, now that I think about it, cooking is a whole lot easier. Want to swap? Or do you plan to make me do *all* the work while you lounge around and watch your fingernails grow back?"

In a flash and a scraping sound of wood on wood, Rusty was out of her chair and leaning across the table. "I don't mind doing my share of the work and you know it. What I *do* mind is having my best efforts criticized by you."

"If this is any indication of your best efforts, we'll be dead of starvation inside a week."

"I'll learn to do better," she shouted.

"It can't be soon enough for me."

"Oh!"

She spun away and when she did, the flannel shirt, which she'd left unbuttoned, flared open. Cooper's arm shot out and grabbed her arm.

"What's that?" Reaching inside the open shirt, he pulled down the strap of her tank top.

Rusty followed the direction of his gaze down to the slight discoloration on the upper curve of her breast. She looked at the round bruise, then lifted her eyes up to his. "That's where you . . . kissed . . ." Unable to go on, she made a helpless gesture with her hands. "Last night," she added huskily.

Cooper snatched his hand back, as guilty as Adam when caught sampling the forbidden fruit. Rusty could feel the blush rising in her neck. It spread as evenly and thoroughly as his eyes were moving over her. He noticed the rosy abrasions that his whiskered jaw had made around her mouth and against her face and throat. He grimaced with regret and raised his hand to his chin. When he rubbed it, the scratching noise filled the silence.

"Sorry."

"It's okay."

"Does it . . . do they hurt?"

"Not really."

"Did it, you know, when . . . ?"

She shook her head. "I didn't notice then."

They quickly glanced away from each other. He moved to the window. It was drizzling outside. Occasionally a pellet of sleet would ping against the glass.

"I guess I should explain about last night," he said in a low, deep voice.

"No. No explanation is necessary, really."

"I don't want you to think I'm impotent or anything like that."

"I know you're not impotent."

His head snapped around and their gazes locked. "I don't guess I could keep it a secret that I was ready and able."

Rusty swallowed with difficulty and lowered her head. "No."

"That leaves willing." She kept her head bowed. "Well, aren't you even curious as to why I didn't go through with it?" he asked after a lengthy moment.

"I didn't say I wasn't curious. I only said that you didn't have to explain. We're strangers, after all. We owe each other no explanations."

"But you wondered." He pointed an accusing finger at her. "Don't deny that you wondered why I didn't finish it."

"I assumed that there is someone back home. A woman."

"No woman," he barked. At her shocked expression, he smiled crookedly. "No man, either."

She laughed uneasily. "That never occurred to me."

The injection of humor didn't last. His smile inverted itself into a frown. "I don't make sexual commitments."

Her chin went up a notch. "I don't remember asking for one."

"You didn't have to. If we... If I... With just the two of us here, for God knows how long, that's what it would amount to. We're already dependent on each other for everything else. We don't need to make the situation any more complicated than it already is."

"I couldn't agree with you more," she said breezily. She had never taken rejection very well, but neither had she ever let her hurt feelings show. "I lost my head last night. I was frightened. More exhausted than I realized. You were there, you did the humane thing and rendered comfort. As a result, things got out of hand. That's all there was to it."

The lines running down either side of his mouth pulled in tighter. "Exactly. If we'd met anywhere else, we wouldn't have looked at each other twice."

"Hardly," she said, forcing a laugh. "You wouldn't exactly fit in with my cosmopolitan crowd. You'd stick out like a sore thumb."

"And you in your fancy clothes would be laughed off my mountain."

"So, fine," she said testily.

"Fine."

"It's settled."

"Right."

"We've got no problem."

One might wonder, then, why they were facing each other like pugilists squaring off. The air was redolent with animosity. They'd reached an agreement. They'd figuratively signed a peace treaty. But by all appearances they were still at war.

Cooper was the first to turn away and he did so with an angry jerk of his shoulders. He pulled on his coat and picked up his rifle. "I'm going to see what the stream has to offer in the way of fish."

"Are you planning to shoot them?" She nodded at his rifle.

He frowned at her sarcasm. "I rigged up a trotline while you were languishing in bed this morning." He didn't give her time to offer a rebuttal before he added, "I also started a fire under that caldron outside. Do the laundry."

Rusty followed his gaze down to the tall pile of dirty clothes and looked at it with unconcealed astonishment. When she turned back to him, the spot he'd been standing in was empty. She hurried to the door as quickly as her limp would allow.

"I was going to do the laundry without you telling me to," she shouted at his retreating back. If he heard her, he gave no indication of it.

Cursing, Rusty slammed the door shut. She cleared the table. It took her almost half an hour to scrub clean the pot she'd cooked the oatmeal in. Next time she would remember to pour hot water in it as soon as she'd spooned the oatmeal out.

She then attacked their pile of dirty clothes with a vengeance. By the time he came back, she wanted to be finished with the chore she'd been summarily assigned. It was mandatory that she prove to him that last night's breakdown was a fluke.

After putting on her coat, she carried the first load of clothes outside and dropped it into the caldron. Previously, she had thought that such black iron pots suspended over smoldering coals existed only in movies. She used a smooth stick to swish the clothes around. When they were as clean as she thought they'd get, she lifted them out of the water with the stick and tossed them into a basket that Cooper had washed out the day before.

By the time she'd finished washing all the clothes using this archaic method, her arms were rubbery with fatigue. And by the time she had wrung them out and hung them up to dry on the wire that stretched from the corner of the house to the nearest tree, her arms felt as if they were about to fall off. Not only that, her wet hands were nearly frozen, as was her nose, which dripped constantly. Her leg, too, had begun to ache again.

A rewarding sense of accomplishment helped relieve some of her miseries. She took comfort in the thought of having done her job well. Once again inside the cabin, she warmed her hands by the fire. When circulation returned to them, she tugged off her boots and wearily climbed onto her bed. If anyone deserved a nap before dinner, it was she.

* * *

Apparently she'd been in a much deeper sleep than she had planned on. When Cooper came barging through the door shouting her name, she sprang up so suddenly that her head reeled dizzily and yellow dots exploded in front of her eyes.

"Rusty!" he shouted. "Rusty, did you— Dammit, what are you doing in bed?" His coat was open, his hair wild. His cheeks were ruddy. He was breathing hard, as though he'd been running.

"What am I doing in bed?" she asked around a huge yawn. "I was sleeping."

"Sleeping! *Sleeping!* Didn't you hear the plane?"

"Plane?"

"Stop repeating every damn word I say! Where's the flare gun?"

"The flare gun?"

He was all but foaming at the mouth. "Where's the flare gun? There's a plane buzzing overhead."

Her feet hit the floor. "Is it looking for us?"

"How the hell should I know?" He tore through the cabin, uprighting everything he laid his hands on in his frantic search for the flare gun. "Where is that...here!" Brandishing the gun, he raced outside, leaped over the porch, and scanned the sky. In stocking feet, Rusty hobbled after him.

"Do you see it?"

"Shut up!" He cocked his head to one side while he listened carefully. The unmistakable hum of the engine reached them at the same time. They turned simultaneously and were met with a dismal sight.

It was an airplane, all right. Obviously a search plane, because it was flying low. But it was flying in the opposite direction. Firing the flares now would serve no purpose except to waste them. Two pairs of eyes remained on the diminishing speck until it grew too small to see and the whine of the engine could no longer be heard. It left a deafening silence in its wake. As the noise had died, so had their chances for a probable rescue.

Cooper came around slowly. His eyes looked cold and colorless and so laden with murderous intent that Rusty took a step backward.

"Just what the *hell* were you doing asleep?"

Rusty preferred him shouting. Ranting and raving she knew how to deal with and respond to. This soft, hissing, sinister-as-a-serpent voice terrified her. "I . . . I finished the wash," she said hastily. The words tripped over themselves. "I was exhausted. I had to lift—"

It suddenly occurred to her that she owed him no stuttering apologies. From the beginning, he'd assumed charge of the flare gun. It hadn't been out of his possession since they'd left the wrecked aircraft.

Belligerently, she placed her hands on her hips. "How dare you blame this on *me*! Why did you go off without the flare gun?"

"Because I was mad as hell this morning when I left. I forgot it."

"So it's your fault the flare wasn't fired, not mine!"

"It was your fault that I was so damn mad when I left."

"If you can't control your short temper, how can you expect me to?"

His eyes turned dark. "Even if I'd had the gun and fired it, they could have missed it. But they damn sure could have seen smoke from our chimney. But, no. You needed a beauty rest. So you went to sleep and let the fire burn out."

"Why haven't you built a signal fire, a big one, one a potential rescuer couldn't miss?"

"I didn't think I'd need one. Not with a chimney. Of course I didn't count on you taking afternoon naps."

She faltered, then said defensively, "Chimney smoke wouldn't have attracted their attention anyway. That's nothing out of the ordinary."

"This far off the beaten track it is. They would have at least circled around to investigate."

Rusty groped for another valid alibi. "The wind is too strong for a column of smoke to form. Even if the fire had been going, they wouldn't have spotted our smoke."

"There was a *chance*."

"Not as good a chance as seeing a flare, if you had had the gun with you."

It would have been prudent not to point out his dereliction of duty at that particular moment. His lower lip disappeared beneath his mustache and he took a menacing step forward. "I could easily murder you for letting that plane go by."

She tossed her head back. "Why don't you? I'd rather you do that than keep harping about my shortcomings."

"But you provide me with such a wealth of material. You've got so many shortcomings that if we were stranded here for years I would never get around to harping on all of them."

Her cheeks grew pink with indignation. "I admit it! I'm not qualified to live in a rustic cabin in the middle of nowhere. It wasn't a life-style I chose for myself."

His chin jutted out. "You can't even cook."

"I've never wanted to or needed to. I'm a career woman," she said with fierce pride.

"Well, a helluva lot of good your career is doing me now."

"Me, me, me," Rusty shouted. "You've thought only of yourself through this whole ordeal."

"Ha! I should be so lucky. Instead I've had you to think about. You've been nothing but an albatross."

"It was not my fault that my leg got hurt."

"And I suppose you're going to say it wasn't your fault that those two men went dotty over you."

"It *wasn't*."

"No?" he sneered nastily. "Well, you haven't stopped putting out signals that you'd like to have me in your pants."

Later, Rusty couldn't believe she'd actually done it. She'd never guessed that she had a latent violent streak. Even as a child, she'd always given in to other children to avoid a confrontation. By nature she was a pacifist. She'd never been physically aggressive.

But at Cooper's intentionally hurtful words, she launched herself at him, fingers curled into claws aimed for his smirking face. She never reached him. She came down hard on her injured leg. It buckled beneath her. Screaming with pain, she fell to the frozen ground.

Cooper was beside her instantly. He picked her up. She fought him so strenuously that he restrained her in an armlock. "Stop that or I'll knock you unconscious."

"You would, wouldn't you?" she asked, breathless from her efforts.

"Damn right. And I'd enjoy it."

Her struggles subsided, more out of weakness and pain than capitulation. He carried her indoors and set her down in the chair near the fire. Casting her a reproachful look, he knelt on the cold hearth and painstakingly coaxed the fire back to life.

"Does your leg still hurt?"

She shook her head no. It hurt like hell, but she'd have her tongue cut out before admitting it. She wasn't going to speak to him, not after what he'd said, which was patently untrue. Her refusal to speak was childish, but she clung to her resolution not to, even as he separated her torn pants leg, rolled down her sock, and examined the zigzagging incision on her shin.

"Stay off it for the rest of the day. Use your crutches if you move around." He patted her clothes into place, then stood up. "I'm going back to get the fish. I dropped them in my pell-mell rush to the cabin. I hope a bear hasn't al-

ready made them his dinner." At the door he turned back.
"And I'll cook them if it's all the same to you. They look
like good fish and you'd probably ruin them."

He slammed the door behind him.

They were good fish. Delicious, in fact. He'd cooked
them in a skillet until they were falling-off-the-bones tender,
crusty on the outside and flaky on the inside. Rusty regret-
ted passing up the second one, but she wasn't about to de-
vour it ravenously, as she had done the first. Cooper added
insult to injury by eating it when she refused it. She wished
he would choke on a bone and die. Instead, he compla-
cently licked his fingers, smacking noisily, and patted his
stomach.

"I'm stuffed."

Oh, boy, did she have some excellent comebacks for that
leading line. But she maintained her stony silence.

"Clean up this mess," he said curtly, leaving the dirty table and stove to her.

She did as she was told. But not without making a terrible racket that echoed off the rafters. When she had finished, she threw herself down on her bed and gazed at the
ceiling overhead. She didn't know if she were more hurt or
angry. But whichever, Cooper Landry had coaxed more
emotion from her than any other man ever had. Those
emotions had run the gamut from gratitude to disgust.

He was the meanest, most spiteful human being she'd ever
had the misfortune to meet, and she hated him with a passion that appalled her.

True, she had begged him to get into bed with her last
night. But for comfort, not sex! She hadn't asked for it; she
hadn't wanted it. It had just happened. He was bound to
realize that. His puffed-up, colossal ego just kept him from
admitting it.

Well, one thing was for certain: from now on she was going to be as modest as a nun. He'd see the skin of her face,

possibly her neck, surely her hands, but that was it. It wasn't going to be easy. Not living together in this—

Her thoughts came to an abrupt halt as she spied something overhead that provided the solution to her problem. There were hooks over her bed, exactly like the ones Cooper had used to drape the curtain in front of the bathtub.

Filled with sudden inspiration, she left the bed quickly and retrieved an extra blanket from the shelf against the wall. Completely ignoring Cooper, who she knew was watching her covertly, she dragged a chair across the floor and placed it beneath one of the hooks.

Standing on the chair, she had to stretch her calf muscles—more than they'd ever been stretched in aerobics class—in order to reach the hook, but eventually she managed it. Moving the chair directly beneath another hook, she repeated the procedure. When she was done, she was left with a curtain of sorts around her bed, which would give her privacy.

She shot her cabin mate a smug glance before she ducked behind the blanket and let it fall into place behind her. There! Let him accuse her of asking for "it."

She shuddered at the memory of the crude thing he'd said to her. Add *uncouth* to all his other disagreeable traits. She undressed and slid into bed. Because of her nap, she couldn't fall asleep right away. Even after she heard Cooper go to bed and his steady breathing indicated that he was fast asleep, she lay there awake, watching the myriad flickering patterns the fire cast on the ceiling.

When the wolves began to howl, she rolled to her side, covered her head with the blanket, and tried not to listen. She clamped her finger between her teeth and bit down hard to keep from crying, to keep from feeling lost and alone, and to keep herself from begging Cooper to hold her while she slept.

Eight

⟡⟡⟡

Cooper sat as perfectly still as a hunter in a deer stand. Motionless, feet planted far apart, elbows propped on widespread knees, fingers cupped around his chin. Above them, his eyes stared at her unblinkingly.

That was the first sight Rusty saw when she woke up the following morning. She registered surprise, but managed to keep from jumping out of her skin. Immediately she noticed that the screen she had so ingeniously devised and hung around her bed the night before had been torn down. The blanket was lying at the foot of her bed.

She levered herself up on one elbow and irritably pushed her hair out of her eyes. "What are you doing?"

"I need to talk to you."

"About what?"

"It snowed several inches last night."

She studied his expressionless face for a moment, then said with a great deal of pique. "If you're wanting to build a snowman, I'm not in the mood."

His eyes didn't waver, although she could tell that he was willfully restraining himself when he was sorely tempted to strangle her.

"The snowfall is important," he said calmly. "Once winter gets here our chances of being rescued are greatly reduced."

"I understand that," she replied in a serious tone befitting his observation. "What I don't understand is why it has such grave implications at this very minute."

"Because before we spend another day together, we've got to get some things straight, lay down some ground rules. If we're going to be marooned up here together all winter—which looks like a very real possibility—then we must reach an understanding on several points."

She sat up but kept the blanket raised to her chin. "Such as?"

"Such as no more pouting spells." His brows were drawn together in a straight, stern line of admonition. "I won't put up with that kind of brattiness from you."

"Oh, you won't?" she asked sweetly.

"No, I won't. You're not a child. Don't act like one."

"It's all right for you to insult me, but I'm supposed to turn the other cheek, is that it?"

For the first time, he looked away, apparently chagrined. "I probably shouldn't have said what I did yesterday."

"No, you shouldn't have. I don't know what evil thoughts you've cultivated in your dirty little mind, but don't blame me for them."

He gnawed on the corner of his mustache. "I was mad as hell at you."

"Why?"

"Mainly because I...I don't like you very much. But I still want to sleep with you. And by 'sleep' I don't mean just sleep." If he had slapped her, she couldn't have been more astounded. Her lips parted with a sudden intake of breath, but he didn't give her a chance to say anything. "Now isn't the time to beat around the bush or to mince words, right?"

"Right," she repeated hoarsely.

"I hope you can appreciate my honesty."

"I can."

"Okay, concede this point. We're physically attracted to each other. Bluntly stated, we want to get off together. It doesn't make any sense, but it's a fact." Rusty's gaze dropped to her lap. He waited until his patience gave out. "Well?"

"Well, what?"

"Say something for God's sake."

"I'll concede both points."

He let out a long breath. "All right then, knowing that, and knowing that it's unreasonable to do anything about it, and knowing, too, that's it's going to be a helluva long winter, we've got some things to iron out. Agreed?"

"Agreed."

"First, we'll stop the mudslinging." Her russet eyes treated him to a frosty stare. Grudgingly he added, "I'll admit to being guilty of that more than you. Let's just promise not to be verbally abusive to each other from here on."

"I promise."

He nodded. "The weather will be our enemy. A fearsome one. It will require all our attention and energy. We can't afford the luxury of fighting each other. Our survival depends on living together. Our sanity depends on doing it peaceably."

"I'm listening."

He paused to collect his thoughts. "As I see it, our roles should be traditional."

"You Tarzan, me Jane."

"Sort of. I'll provide the food. You'll cook it."

"As you've so untactfully pointed out, I'm not a very good cook."

"You'll get better."

"I'll try."

"Don't get defensive if I offer you advice."

"Then don't make snide remarks about my lack of talent. I'm good at other things."

His eyes lowered to her lips. "I can't argue that." After a long, silent moment, he roused himself. "I don't expect you to wait on me hand and foot."

"I don't expect that from you, either. I want to pull my weight."

"I'll help you keep the cabin and our clothes clean."

"Thank you."

"I'll teach you to shoot more accurately so you can protect yourself when I'm gone."

"Gone?" she asked faintly, feeling that the rug had just been pulled out from under her.

He shrugged. "If the game gives out, if the stream freezes over, I might have to go in search of food."

She would face with fear and dread the times she might have to stay in the cabin alone, perhaps for days. Even a vulgar and insulting Cooper was better than no Cooper at all.

"And this is the most important point." He waited until he had her full attention, until her dazed eyes had refocused on him. "I'm the boss," he said, tapping his chest. "Don't let's kid ourselves. This is a life-or-death situation. You might know all there is to know about residential real estate and California chic and the life-styles of the rich and famous. But up here, all that knowledge isn't worth a damn. On your turf you can do whatever the hell you please and I say, more power to you, 'You've come a long way, Baby,' and all that. But up here, you obey me."

She was stung by his implication that her field of expertise wasn't much use outside Beverly Hills. "As I recall, I haven't tried to usurp your position as the macho provider."

"Just see that you don't. In the wilderness there's no such thing as equality between the sexes."

He stood up and happened to catch sight of the blanket lying on the foot of the bed. "One more thing: No more silly screens. The cabin is too small and we're living too close together to play coy games like that. We've seen each other naked. We've touched each other naked. There're no more secrets. Besides," he said, raking his eyes over her, "if I wanted you bad enough, no damn blanket would keep me from you. And if rape was what I had in mind, I would have done it a long time ago."

Their eyes locked and held. Finally, he turned his back. "It's time you got up. I've already started the coffee."

That morning the oatmeal was considerably better than it had been the day before. At least it didn't stick to the palate like a day-old peanut-butter sandwich. It had been frugally seasoned with salt and sugar. Cooper ate every bite of his, but didn't offer her a compliment.

She didn't take umbrage as she once would have done. His failure to criticize was tantamount to a compliment. They had only promised not to be verbally abusive; they hadn't promised to shower each other with flattery.

He went outside after breakfast and by the time he came in for a lunch of biscuits and canned soup, he had made himself a pair of snowshoes out of bent greenwood and woven dead vines. He strapped them to his boots and clumped around the cabin, modeling them for her. "These will make it a lot easier to navigate the ravine between here and the river."

He spent the afternoon away from the cabin. She straightened it, but the housekeeping didn't take more than half an hour. That left her with nothing to do but fret until she saw him through the window at dusk, making awkward progress toward the cabin in the homemade snowshoes.

She rushed out on the porch to greet him with a cup of hot coffee and a tentative smile, feeling slightly foolish for being so pleased to see him return safe and sound.

Unstrapping the snowshoes and propping them against the cabin's outside wall, he looked at her strangely and took the proffered coffee. "Thanks." He stared at her through the cloud of rising steam as he took a sip.

She noticed, as he held the cup to his lips, that they were chapped and that his hands were raw and red despite the shearling gloves he always wore when he was outdoors. She wanted to commiserate, but decided against it. His lecture that morning discouraged anything except mutual tolerance.

"Any luck at the stream?" she asked.

He nodded down toward the creel, which had belonged to the Gawrylows. "It's full. We'll leave some out to freeze and save them for days when I can't get down the ravine. And we should start filling containers with water in case the pump freezes up."

Nodding, she carried the basket of fish inside, proud of the appetizing aroma of her stew. She had made it with dried beef found among the hermits' stock of canned food. Its aroma filled the cabin. Cooper ate two full bowls of it and made her day by saying, "Pretty good," at the conclusion of the meal.

The days followed that basic pattern. He did his chores. She did hers. He helped her with hers. She helped him with his. They were scrupulously polite, if politely distant.

But while they could fill the short days with activity, the evenings seemed endless. They came early. First the sun sank below the tree line and cast the area surrounding the cabin in deep shadow, making outdoor chores hazardous and forcing them indoors.

The instant the sun was swallowed by the horizon, it was dark, even though it was still officially afternoon. Once dinner was eaten and the dishes were washed, there was little to do. There weren't enough inside chores to keep them occupied and separated. They had nothing to do except stare into the fire and avoid staring at each other—something that required supreme concentration on both their parts.

That first snowfall melted the next day, but the night following that, it snowed again and continued into the day. Because of the steadily dropping temperature and blowing snow, Cooper returned to the cabin earlier than usual, which made the evening stretch out unbearably long.

Rusty, her eyes swinging back and forth like twin pendulums, watched him as he paced the length of the cabin like a caged panther. The four walls were making her claustrophobic, and his restlessness only irritated her further. When she caught him scratching his chin, something she'd noticed him doing repeatedly, she asked with asperity, "What's the matter?"

He spun around as though spoiling for a fight and delighted that someone had finally picked one with him. "With what?"

"With you?"

"What do you mean?"

"Why do you keep scratching your chin?"

"Because it itches."

"Itches?"

"The beard. It's at the itchy stage."

"Well, that scratching is driving me crazy."

"Tough."

"Why don't you shave it off if it itches?"

"Because I don't have a razor, that's why."

"I—" She broke off when she realized that she was about to make a confession. Then, noticing that his eyes had narrowed suspiciously, she said haughtily. "I do. I have one. I brought it along and now I'll bet you're glad I did."

Leaving her chair near the fireplace, she went to the shelf where she had stored her toiletries. She treasured them as a miser did his bag of gold coins. She brought the plastic, disposable razor back to Cooper. And something else besides. "Put this on your lips." She passed him the tube of lip gloss. "I noticed that your lips are chapped."

He took the tube from her and rolled the stick of lip balm out. He seemed pressed to make several comments, but said none of them. She laughed at the awkward way he applied the gloss. When he was done, he handed the capped tube back to her. She gave him the razor. "Be my guest."

"Thanks." He turned the razor over in his hand, studying it from every angle. "You didn't by chance sneak some hand lotion, too, did you?"

She held up her hands. Like his, they had been ravaged by water, wind and cold. "Do these look like they've seen any lotion lately?"

His smiles were so rare that her heart melted beneath the one he flashed her now. Then, in what seemed like a reflexive gesture, he captured one of her hands and lightly kissed the backs of her fingers with lips made soft by shiny gloss.

His mustache tickled her fingers. And in a bizarre correlation that made absolutely no sense, it tickled the back of her throat as well. Her stomach executed a series of somersaults.

Suddenly realizing what he'd done, he dropped her hand. "I'll use the razor in the morning."

Rusty hadn't wanted him to let go of her hand. In fact, she'd been tempted to turn it and cover his mustache and lips with her palm. She wanted to feel their caress in that vulnerable spot. Her heart was pounding so hard she had difficulty speaking. "Why not shave now?"

"There's no mirror. With this much stubble, I'd lacerate myself."

"I could shave you."

For a moment neither of them said anything, only filled the narrow space between them with leaping arcs of sexual electricity. Rusty didn't know where the impulse had sprung from. It had just popped up from nowhere and she'd acted on it before thinking—maybe because it had been days since they'd touched each other for any reason. She was feeling deprived. As the body gets hungry for a certain food when it needs the vitamins and minerals it contains, she'd unconsciously expressed her desire to touch him.

"All right." Cooper's permission was granted in a ragged voice.

Nervous, now that he had agreed to her suggestion, she clasped her hands at her waist. "Why... why don't you sit over there by the fire. I'll bring the stuff."

"Okay."

"Roll the collar of your shirt in and tuck a towel inside," she said over her shoulder as she poured water from the kettle on the stove into a shallow bowl. She pulled a chair up close to his and set the bowl and razor on the seat. She also got her bar of soap from the shelf, and a spare towel.

"I'd better soak it first." He dipped the extra towel into the bowl of hot water. "Ouch, damn," he cursed when he tried to wring it out.

"It's hot."

"No foolin'?"

He juggled the scalding towel from one hand to the other before finally slapping it against the lower portion of his face, letting out a yelp when he did so. He held it there, although Rusty didn't know how he could stand it.

"Doesn't that burn?" Without removing the towel, he nodded solemnly. "You do it to soften the whiskers, right?" Again, he nodded. "I'll try to work up a good lather."

Tentatively she wet her hands in the bowl of hot water and picked up the cake of soap. Cooper watched her every move as she rubbed the soap between her hands until they were covered with honeysuckle-scented suds. The foam looked rich and creamy as she slid it between her palms. It oozed between her fingers, looking intensely sexy, although exactly why, he didn't know.

"Whenever you're ready," she said, moving behind him.

Gradually Cooper lowered the towel. Just as gradually, Rusty raised her hands to his face. Gazing down at him from her position above and behind him, the planes and ridges of his face looked even more harsh, more pronounced. But there was a vulnerability to his eyelashes that gave her enough courage to lay her palms against his prickly cheeks.

She felt him tense up in reaction to her touch. She didn't move her hands at first, but kept them still, resting lightly against his cheeks, while she waited to see if he was going to tell her that this wasn't a good idea.

It was a given that it wasn't a good idea.

She just wondered which one of them was going to admit it first and call a halt to the proceedings. But Cooper said nothing, and she didn't want to stop, so she began to rotate her hands over his cheeks.

The sensation of that scratchy surface against her palms was enticing. She moved her hands to encompass more area and found that the bones of his jaw were just as chiseled and rigid to the touch as they looked. His square chin had a shallow indentation in its center. She slipped the edge of her fingernail into it, but didn't investigate it nearly as long as she wanted to.

She ran her hands simultaneously down his throat, smoothing on the lather as she went. Her fingers glided over his Adam's apple and toward the base of his neck, where she felt his pulse pounding. Dragging her fingers back up his neck and over his chin again, she encountered his lower lip and, beyond it, the brush of his mustache.

She froze and drew in a quick, hopefully inaudible breath. "Sorry," she murmured. Removing her hands, she dipped them in the water to rinse them off. She leaned forward and inspected her handiwork from another angle. There was a speck of soap on his lower lip and some bubbles clinging to several of the blond hairs in his mustache.

With her wet finger, she whisked away that speck from his lip, then rubbed her finger over his mustache until the bubbles disappeared.

A low sound emanated from him. Rusty froze, but her eyes flew to his. "Get on with it," he growled.

With his face partially obscured by white foam, he shouldn't have posed any threat. But his eyes were alight. They glittered in the firelight. She could see the flames dancing in their depths and sensed a coiled violence over which he exercised tenuous control. It prompted her to step behind him again and out of harm's way.

"Don't cut me," he warned as she lifted the razor to his jaw.

"I won't if you'll be still and shut up."

"Have you ever done this before?"

"No."

"That's what I was afraid of."

He stopped talking as she drew the first swipe up his cheek. "So far so good," she said softly as she dipped the razor in the bowl. He mumbled something, trying to keep his mouth still, but Rusty didn't catch what he said. She was concentrating too hard on giving him a clean shave without nicking his skin. When the lower part of his face was clean, she let out a deep sigh of relief and satisfaction. "Smooth as a baby's bottom."

A laugh rolled up from the depths of his chest. Rusty had never heard him actually laugh with pure humor before. His infrequent laughs were usually tinged with cynicism. "Don't start bragging yet. You're not finished. Don't forget my neck. And for God sake, be careful with that blade."

"It's not that sharp."

"That's the worst kind."

She swished the razor in the water to dampen it, then placed one hand beneath his chin. "Tilt your head back."

He did. It rested heavily against her breasts. Rusty, unable to move for a moment, kept the razor poised above his throat. His Adam's apple bobbed with a hard, involuntary swallow. To take her mind off their position, she turned her attention to the task at hand, which only made matters worse. She had to come up on her toes and lean forward to see well. By the time she'd shaved his neck clean, his head was cushioned between her breasts and they were both keenly aware of it.

"There." She stepped back and dropped the razor as though it were the single piece of incriminating evidence in a murder trial.

He yanked the towel out of his collar and buried his face in it. For what seemed like hours he didn't move or lower the towel.

"How does it feel?" she asked.

"Great. It feels great."

Then, he stood up abruptly and tossed the towel onto the chair. Tearing his coat from the peg near the door, he pulled it on, ruthlessly shoving his arms into the sleeves.

"Where are you going?" Rusty asked anxiously.

"Outside."

"What for?"

He shot her a sizzling glance that wasn't in keeping with the blizzard blowing beyond the open door. "Believe me, you don't want to know."

He continued to behave in that volatile manner until noon the next day. All morning the weather had been prohibitive to beast and man, so they'd been snowbound in the cabin. For the most part, Cooper ignored her. She responded in kind. After several unsuccessful attempts to make conversation with him, she gave up and lapsed into a moody silence that matched his.

It was a relief when the snowy wind stopped its incessant howling and he announced that he was going out to take a look around. She was concerned for his safety, but refrained from persuading him to stay indoors. They needed the breathing space away from each other.

Besides, she needed some privacy. Cooper wasn't the only one who'd been itching lately. The incision on her leg was giving her fits. As the skin began to knit, it had become tight and dry. Her clothing only aggravated it further. She decided that the stitches had to come out. She also decided that she was going to pull them out herself rather than involve Cooper, especially since their relationship was so rocky and his mood shifts so unpredictable.

He'd been gone only a few minutes when she stripped off all her clothes, having decided to use this opportunity to give herself a thorough sponge bath. When she finished washing, she sat down in front of the fire, wrapped in a blanket for warmth. She propped her injured leg over the knee of the other and examined it. How hard could it be to clip those stitches and pull them out?

Where before, the thought would have given her qualms the size of goose eggs, she approached the chore pragmatically. The first obstacle was to find something to clip the silk stitches with. The knife Cooper had given her was too cumbersome. The only thing in the cabin sharp enough and delicate enough was her razor.

It had seemed like a good idea, but when she held the razor lengthwise over the first stitch, poised and ready to saw into it, she realized that her hand was perspiring with apprehension. Drawing a deep breath, she touched the silk thread with the razor.

The door burst open and Cooper tramped through it, snowshoes and all. He'd covered his head with a fur pelt and was bundled up from his neck to his boots. His own breath had frozen on his mustache, making it appear ghostly white. Rusty emitted a squeak of alarm and momentary fright.

But her surprise couldn't compare to his. She was just as supernatural a vision as he, in an entirely different way. Silhouetted as she was against the fireplace, the flames shone through her hair. One leg was propped up, exposing a tantalizing length of naked thigh. The blanket she'd wrapped herself in after her sponge bath had slipped off her shoulder, revealing most of one breast. As his eyes fastened on it, the nipple grew taut with the chilly air he was letting in.

He closed the door. "What the hell are you doing sitting there like that?"

"I thought you'd be gone longer."

"I could have been anybody," he roared.

"Like who?"

"Like . . . like . . ."

Hell, he couldn't think of a single other person who might have barged in the way he just had, never guessing that he'd find a breathtaking sight like this one in a rude cabin in the Canadian wilds. He felt the front of his pants strain with his instant erection. Either she genuinely had no idea what effect she had on him, or she did know and was maliciously using it to slowly drive him crazy. Whichever, the result was the same.

Frustrated, he tore the pelt from his head and shook snow out of it. Gloves went flying. He tore at the tongs tying on his snowshoes. "Back to my original question, what the hell are you doing?"

"Taking my stitches out."

The peg in the wall caught the coat he tossed in that general direction. "*What?*"

His stance—that know-it-all, arrogant, condescending, masculine stance—grated on her like a pumice stone. Not to mention his superior tone of voice. She looked him directly in the eye. "They're itching. The wound has closed. It's time they came out."

"And you're using a razor?"

"What do you suggest?"

He crossed the floor in three angry strides, pulling his hunting knife from its scabbard as he came. When he dropped to his knees in front of her, she recoiled and drew the blanket tightly around herself. "You can't use *that*!"

His expression was forbearing as he unscrewed the handle of his knife and shook out several implements that Rusty hadn't known until now were in there. Among them was a tiny pair of scissors. Instead of being pleased, she was furious: "If you had those all along, why did you cut my fingernails with that bowie knife?"

"I felt like it. Now, give me your leg." He extended his hand.

"I'll do it."

"Give me your leg." He enunciated each word as he glared up at her from beneath his brows. "If you don't, I'll reach into that blanket and bring it out myself." His voice dropped to a seductive pitch. "No telling what I might encounter before I find it."

Mutinously she thrust her bare leg out from under the blanket. "Thank you," he said sarcastically.

"Your mustache is dripping on me."

The frost was beginning to melt. He wiped it dry on his shirt sleeve, but he didn't release her bare foot. It looked small and pale in his large hand. Rusty loved the feeling, but she fought against enjoying it. She waged a war within when he tucked her heel into the notch of his thighs. She gasped over the firm, solid bulge that filled her arch.

He raised sardonic eyes up to hers. "What's the matter?"

He was daring her to tell him. She would die before she even let him know she had noticed. "Nothing," she said nonchalantly. "Your hands are cold, that's all."

The glint in his eyes told her that he knew she was lying. Grinning, he bent his head to his task. Clipping the silk threads presented no problems to either of them. Rusty was thinking that she could just as easily have done it herself. But when he picked up a small pair of tweezers and pinched the first clipped thread between them, she realized that the worst was yet to come.

"This won't hurt, but it might sting a little," he cautioned. He gave one swift tug to pull the stitch out. Reflexively Rusty's foot made a braking motion against him.

"Ah, God," he groaned. "Don't do that."

No, she wouldn't. She definitely would not. She would keep her foot as still as stone from now on, even if he had to tear the stitches out with his teeth.

By the time the tweezers had picked the last thread out, tears of tension and anxiety had filled her eyes. He'd been as gentle as he could be, and Rusty was grateful, but it hadn't been pleasant. She laid her hand on his shoulder. "Thanks, Cooper."

He shrugged her hand off. "Get dressed. And hurry up with dinner," he ordered with the graciousness of a caveman. "I'm starving."

Soon after that, he started drinking.

Nine

The jugs of whiskey had been among the Gawrylows' supplies. Cooper had discovered them the day they cleaned out the cabin. He had smacked his lips with anticipation. That was before he tasted the whiskey. He had tossed back a healthy gulp and swallowed it without chewing—the stuff had looked viscous enough to chew. It was white lightning, moonshine, rotgut, and it had crashed and burned inside his stomach like a meteor.

Rusty had laughed at his coughing/wheezing spasm. He wasn't amused. After he'd recovered the use of his vocal cords, he had darkly informed her that it wasn't funny, that his esophagus had been seared.

Until now, he hadn't touched the jugs of whiskey. This time, there was nothing funny about his drinking it.

After he had built up the fire, he uncorked a jug of the smelly stuff. Rusty was surprised, but said nothing as he took a tentative swig. Then another. At first she thought he was drinking it in order to get warm. His expedition outside had been brief, but long enough to freeze his mustache. He was no doubt chilled to the marrow.

That excuse didn't serve for long, however. Cooper didn't stop with those first two drinks. He carried the jug with him to the chair in front of the fireplace and drank what must have equaled several cocktails before Rusty called him to the table. To her irritation, he brought the jug with him and poured an intemperate amount of the whiskey into his coffee mug. He sipped from it between bites of the rabbit stew she had cooked.

She weighed the advisability of cautioning him not to drink too much, but after a time, she felt constrained to say something; the regularity with which he drank from the tin mug was making her uneasy.

What if he passed out? He'd have to lie where he fell because she'd never be able to lift him. She remembered how much effort it had taken to drag him out of the crashed fuselage of the airplane. A great deal of her strength then had come from adrenaline. What if he ventured outside and got lost? A thousand dreadful possibilities elbowed their way through her mind.

Finally she said, "I thought you couldn't drink that."

He didn't take her concern at face value. He took it as a reprimand. "You don't think I'm man enough?"

"What?" she asked with bewilderment. "No. I mean yes, I think you're man enough. I thought you didn't like the taste of it."

"I'm not drinking it because I like the taste. I'm drinking it because we're out of the good stuff and this is all I've got."

He was itching for a fight. She could see the invitation to one in his eyes, hear it in his snarling inflection. Rusty was too smart to pull a lion's tail even if it was dangling outside the bars of the cage. And she was too smart to wave a red flag at Cooper when his face was as blatant a warning of trouble as a danger sign.

In his present mood he was better left alone and unprovoked, although it was an effort for her to keep silent. She longed to point out how stupid it was to drink something that you didn't like just for the sake of getting drunk.

Which was apparently what he intended to do. He nearly overturned his chair as he pushed himself away from the table. Only trained reflexes that were as quick and sure as a striking rattler's kept the chair from landing on the floor. He moved back to the hearth. There he sipped and sulked while Rusty cleaned up their dinner dishes.

When she was finished, she swept the floor—more to give herself something to do than because it needed it. Unbelievable as it seemed, she'd come to take pride in how neatly she had arranged and maintained the cabin.

Eventually she ran out of chores and stood awkwardly in the center of the room while deciding what to do with herself. Cooper was hunched in his chair, broodily staring into the fireplace as he steadily drank. The most sensible thing to do would be to make herself scarce, but their cabin had only one room. A walk was out of the question. She wasn't a bit sleepy, but bed was her only alternative.

"I, uh, think I'll go to bed now, Cooper. Good night."

"Sit down."

Already on her way to her bed, she was brought up short. It wasn't so much what he'd said that halted her, but the manner in which he'd said it. She would prefer a strident command to that quiet, deadly request.

Turning, she looked at him inquisitively.

"Sit down," he repeated.

"I'm going—"

"Sit down."

His high-handedness sparked a rebellious response, but Rusty quelled it. She wasn't a doormat, but neither was she a dope. Only a dope would tangle with Cooper while he was in this frame of mind. Huffily, she crossed the room and dropped into the chair facing his. "You're drunk."

"You're right."

"Fine. Be ridiculous. Make a fool of yourself. I couldn't care less. But its embarrassing to watch. So if you don't mind, I'd rather go to bed."

"I do mind. Stay where you are."

"Why? What difference does it make? What do you want?"

He took a sip from his cup, staring at her over the dented rim of it. "While I'm getting plashtered, I want to sit here and shtare at you and imagine you . . ." He drank from the cup again, then said around a juicy belch, "Naked."

Rusty came out of her chair as though an automatic spring had ejected her. Apparently no level of drunkenness could dull Cooper's reflexes. His arm shot out. He grabbed a handful of her sleeve, hauled her back, and pushed her into the chair.

"I told you to shtay where you are."

"Let go of me." Rusty wrested her arm free. She was as apprehensive now as she was angry. This wasn't a silly drunk's prank, or an argumentative drunk's unreasonableness. She tried convincing herself that Cooper wouldn't hurt her, but then she really didn't know, did she? Maybe alcohol was the catalyst that released his controlled violence. "Leave me alone," she said with affected courage.

"I don't plan on touching you."

"Then what?"

"Call this a masochistic kind of . . . self-fulfillment." His eyelids drooped suggestively. "I'm sure you can substitute the correct name for it."

Rusty went hot all over with embarrassment. "I know the correct name for *you*. Several, in fact."

He laughed. "Save them. I've heard them all. Instead of thinking up dirty names to call me," he said, after sipping from his mug, "let's talk about you. Your hair, for instance."

She crossed her arms over her middle and looked toward the ceiling, a living illustration of supreme boredom.

"You know what I thought about the first time I saw your hair?" He was undaunted by her uncooperative spirit and refusal to answer. Leaning forward from the waist, he whispered, "I thought about how good it would feel sweeping over my belly."

Rusty jerked her eyes back to his. His were glazed, and not entirely from liquor. They didn't have the vacuous look of the seasoned drunk. The dark centers of them were brilliant, fiery. His voice, too, was now clear. He wasn't slurring his words. He made it impossible for her to misunderstand him—even to pretend to.

"You were standing in the sunshine out on the tarmac. You were talking to a man . . . your father. But then I didn't know he was your father. I watched you hug him, kiss his cheek. I was thinking, 'That lucky bastard knows what it's like to play with her hair in bed.' "

"Don't, Cooper." Her fists were clenched at her sides. She was sitting as tall and straight as a rocket about to be launched.

"When you got on the plane, I wanted to reach out and touch your hair. I wanted to grab handfuls of it, use it to move your head down even with my thighs."

"Stop this!"

Abruptly he ceased speaking and took another draught of whiskey. If anything, his eyes grew darker, more sinister. "You like hearing that, don't you?"

"No."

"You like knowing you've got that kind of power over men."

"You're wrong. Very wrong. I felt extremely self-conscious about being the only woman on that airplane."

He muttered an obscenity and took another drink. "Like today?"

"Today? When?"

He set his cup aside without spilling a single drop. His coordination, like his reflexes, was still intact. He was a mean, nasty drunk, but he wasn't a sloppy one. He leaned forward, beyond the edge of his chair, putting his face within inches of hers.

"When I came in and found you bundled up naked in that blanket."

"That wasn't calculated. It was an error in judgment. I had no way of knowing you would come back so soon. You never do. You're usually away for hours at a time. That's why I decided to take a sponge bath while you were gone."

"I knew the minute I came through the door that you had bathed," he said in a low, thrumming voice. "I could smell the soap on your skin." His eyes moved down over her, as though seeing bare skin rather than her heavy, cable-knit sweater. "You favored me with a peek at your breast, didn't you?"

"No!"

"Like hell."

"I didn't! When I realized the blanket had slipped, I—"

"Too late. I saw it. Your nipple. Pink. Hard."

Rusty drew in several uneven breaths. This bizarre discussion was having a strange effect on her. "Don't say any more. We promised each other not to be abusive."

"I'm not being abusive. Maybe to myself, but not to you."

"Yes, yes, you are. Please, Cooper, stop this. You don't know—"

"What I'm saying? Yes, I do. I know exactly what I'm saying." He looked directly into her eyes. "I could kiss your nipples for a week and never get tired of doing it."

The whiskey huskiness of his voice barely made the words audible, but Rusty heard them. They intoxicated her. She swayed unsteadily under their impact. She whimpered and shut her eyes in the hopes of blocking out the outrageous words and the mental pictures they inspired.

His tongue moving over her flesh, soft and wet, tender and ardent, rough and exciting.

Her eyes popped open and she glared at him defensively. "Don't you dare speak to me like that."

"Why not?"

"I don't like it."

He gave her a smug and skeptical smile. "You don't like me telling you how I've wanted to put my hands all over you? How I've fantasized about your thighs being opened for me? How I've lain in that damn bed night after night listening to your breathing and wanting to be so deep inside you that—"

"Stop it!" Rusty leaped from her chair and pushed past him, trying to make good an escape out the door of the cabin. She would survive the bitter cold far better than she would his heat.

Cooper was too quick for her. She never reached the door. Before she'd taken two steps, he had her locked in an inescapable embrace. He arched her back as he bent over her. His breath struck her fearful features hotly.

"If it was my destiny to be stranded in this godforsaken place, why did it have to be with a woman who looked like you? Huh?" He shook her slightly as though expecting a logical explanation. "Why'd you have to be so damn beautiful? Sexy? Have a mouth designed for loving a man?"

Rusty tried to wiggle free. "I don't want this. Let me go."

"Why couldn't I be trapped here with someone ugly and sweet? Somebody I could have in bed and not live to regret it. Somebody who would be grateful for my attention. Not a shallow little tart who gets off by driving men crazy. Not a socialite. Not *you*."

"I'm warning you, Cooper." Gritting her teeth, she struggled against him.

"Somebody far less attractive, but *useful*. A woman who could cook." He smiled nastily. "I'll bet you cook all right. In bed. That's where you cook. I'll bet that's where you serve up your best dishes."

He slid his hands over her buttocks and brought her up hard against himself, thrusting his hips forward and making contact with her lower body.

"Does it give you a thrill, knowing you do that to me?"

It gave her a thrill, but not the kind of which he spoke. This intimacy with his hardness stole her breath. She grabbed his shoulders for support. Her eyes clashed with his. For seconds, they held there.

Then Rusty broke their stare and shoved him away. She despised him for putting her through this. But she was also ashamed of her own, involuntary reaction to everything he'd said. It had been fleeting, but for a moment there, her choice could have gone either way.

"Keep away from me," she said in a voice that trembled with purpose. "I mean it. If you don't, I'll turn that knife you gave me on you. Do you hear me? Don't lay a hand on me again." She strode past him and threw herself face down on her bed, using the coarse sheet to cool her fevered cheeks.

Cooper was left standing in the center of the room. He raised both hands and plowed them through his long hair, painfully raking it back off his face. Then he slunk back to his chair in front of the fireplace and picked up the jug and his tin cup.

When Rusty dared to glance at him, he was still sitting there morosely sipping the whiskey.

She panicked the following morning when she saw that his bed hadn't been slept in. Had he wandered out during the night? Had something terrible happened to him? Throwing off the covers—she didn't remember pulling them up over herself last night—she raced across the floor and flung open the door.

She slumped against the jamb in relief when she saw Cooper. He was splitting logs. The sky was clear. The sun was shining. What had been icicles hanging from the eaves the day before were now incessant drips. The temperature was comparatively mild. Cooper wasn't even wearing his coat. His shirttail was hanging out loose, and when he turned around Rusty saw that his shirt was unbuttoned.

He spotted her, but said nothing as he tossed several of the split logs onto the mounting pile near the edge of the porch. His face had a greenish cast and there were dark crescents beneath his bloodshot eyes.

Rusty stepped back inside, but left the door open to let in fresh air. It was still cold, but the sunshine had a cleansing effect. It seemed to dispel the hostility lurking in the shadows of the cabin.

Hastily Rusty rinsed her face and brushed her hair. The fire in the stove had gone out completely. By now she was skilled at adding kindling and starting a new one. In minutes she had one burning hot enough to boil the coffee.

For a change, she opened a canned ham and fried slices of it in a skillet. The aroma of cooking pork made her mouth water; she hoped it would tantalize Cooper's appetite, too. Instead of oatmeal, she cooked rice. She would have traded her virtue for a stick of margarine. Fortunately she didn't have an opportunity to barter it, so she settled for drizzling the ham drippings over the rice, which miraculously came out just right.

Splurging, she opened a can of peaches, put them in a bowl, and set them on the table with the rest of the food. She could no longer hear the crunching sound of splitting logs, so she assumed Cooper would be in shortly.

She was right. He came in moments later. His gait was considerably more awkward than usual. While he was washing his hands at the sink, Rusty took two aspirin tablets from the first-aid kit and laid them on his plate.

He stared down at them when he reached the table, then took them with the glass of water beside his plate. "Thanks." Gingerly he settled himself into his chair.

"You're welcome." Rusty knew better than to laugh, but the careful way he was moving was indicative of how severe his hangover was. She poured a cup of strong, black coffee and passed it to him. His hand was shaking as he reached for it. The log-splitting exercise had been self-imposed punishment for his whiskey-drinking binge. She was glad he hadn't chopped off a toe. Or worse.

"How do you feel?"

Without moving his head, he looked over at her. "My eyelashes hurt."

She held back her smile. She also resisted the compulsion to reach across the table and lift the sweaty strands of hair off his forehead. "Can you eat?"

"I think so. I should be able to. I spent what seemed like hours, uh, out back. If the lining of my stomach is still there, it's all that's left."

While he sat with his shoulders hunched and his hands resting carefully on either side of his plate where he'd planted them, she dished up the food. She even cut his ham into bite-size pieces before scooting the plate in front of him. Taking a deep breath, he picked up his fork and took a tentative bite. When he was certain that it was going to stay down, he took another, then another, and was soon eating normally.

"This is good," he said after several minutes of silence.

"Thank you. Better than oatmeal, for a change."

"Yeah."

"I noticed the weather is much warmer."

Actually, what she had noticed was that the exercise had caused the hair on his chest to curl damply. He'd rebuttoned most of the buttons on his shirt before coming to the table, but it was open far enough for her to get a glimpse of that impressive chest.

"We might get lucky and have a few more days of this before the next storm blows through."

"That would be nice."

"Hmm. I could get a lot done around here."

They'd never had a pointless, polite conversation before. This exchange of meaningless chitchat was more awkward than any of their arguments had been, so both dropped it. In a silence so profound they could hear the water dripping off the eaves outside, they finished their meal and drank their second cups of coffee.

When Rusty stood up to clear the table, Cooper said, "I think the aspirin helped. My headache's almost gone."

"I'm glad."

He cleared his throat loudly and fiddled with the knife and fork he'd laid on his empty plate. "Look, about last night, I, uh, I don't have an excuse for it."

She smiled at him with understanding. "If I could have stood the taste of that whiskey, I might have gotten drunk myself. There have been numerous times since the crash when I've wanted that kind of escape. You don't have to apologize."

Moving back to the table, she reached for his plate. He caught her hand. The gesture, unlike anything else he'd done since she met him, was unsure, hesitant. "I'm trying to apologize to you for the things I said."

Staring down at the crown of his head, where his hair grew around a boyish swirl, Rusty asked softly, "Did you mean them, Cooper?"

She knew what she was doing. She was inviting him to make love to her. She wanted him to. There was no sense in fooling herself any longer. He appealed to her like no man ever had. And apparently the attraction was mutual.

They would never maintain their sanity if they didn't satisfy this physical craving. They might live through the winter without becoming lovers, but by spring they would both be raving maniacs. This passionate wanting, unreasonable as it was, could no longer be suppressed.

A relationship between them would be unworkable under ordinary circumstances. Their circumstances were far from ordinary. It simply wasn't practical to examine whether their life-styles or politics or philosophies were compatible. It didn't matter. What mattered—very much so—was a basic human need for intimacy with the opposite sex.

Cooper raised his head slowly. "What did you say?"

"I asked if you meant them—the things you said."

His eyes didn't even flicker. "Yes. I meant them."

He was a man of action, not of words. He reached up and curled his fingers around the back of her neck, pulling her head down for his kiss. He made a sound like that of a feasting wild animal as he used his lips to rub hers apart. His tongue went searching inside her mouth. Rusty welcomed it.

He stood up, stumbling and off balance. This time his chair did topple backward. It landed on the floor with a crash. Neither of them noticed. His arms slid around her waist, hers around his neck. He drew her body tightly against his. Where hers was bowed, his arched to complement it.

"Oh, God." He tore his mouth from hers and pressed it against her neck. The fingers of one hand ravaged her hair, threading through it and weaving it between his fingers. It became hopelessly ensnared in his grip, which was exactly what he wanted. He pulled her head back and stared down into her face. His was taut with desire.

She met his gaze without shyness. "Kiss me again, Cooper."

His mouth claimed hers again, hotly and hungrily. It drew breath from her. As he kissed her, his hand moved to the front of her slacks. He fumbled with the button and zipper until they were undone. When his hand slid into the elastic waistband of her panties, Rusty gasped. She had thought there would be a sensual buildup, a flirtatious progression, extended foreplay.

She didn't regret that there wouldn't be. His boldness, his impatience, was a powerful aphrodisiac. It set off explosions of desire deep within her. She tilted her hips forward and filled his palm with her softness.

He muttered swearwords that were in themselves arousing because they so explicitly expressed the height of his arousal. Like a Rod Stewart song, they were viscerally sexy;

one couldn't hear them without thinking of a male and a female mating.

He struggled with the fly of his jeans until his manhood was freed—a hot, hard fullness probing between her thighs. "I feel your hair against me," he rasped in her ear. "It's so soft."

The erotic message made Rusty weak. She leaned back against the edge of the table and lowered her hands to his hips, inside his jeans. "Please, Cooper, now."

One swift and sure stroke planted him solidly inside her. She gasped at the splendid pleasure/pain. He caught his breath and held it. They clung together like the survivors of a catastrophe—which, in fact, they were—as though their very existence depended on never letting go of each other. Oneness was essential to survival.

It was impossible to say who moved first. Perhaps it was simultaneous. After that initial instant of sheer delight in his total possession, Cooper began to delve deeper yet. He ground his hips against hers, extending himself, stretching her, his goal seemingly to be to reach the very nucleus of her soul.

Rusty, crying out in ecstasy, flung her head back. He randomly kissed her exposed throat and moved his mouth over her breasts, though she was still wearing her sweater.

But love play was unnecessary. Nothing could heighten this fire. Cooper's plunging body became hotter and harder with each savage thrust.

Then he had no choice in the matter.

"You're a very beautiful woman."

Rusty gazed up at her lover. One of her arms was folded beneath her head. The other hand was draped over his shoulder. Her pose was provocative. She wanted it to be. She didn't mind that her breasts were fully revealed and wantonly inviting. She wanted to display them for his entertainment. She enjoyed seeing his eyes turn lambent every time he looked at them and their pouting tips.

Maybe he'd been right all along. She'd shown a marked lack of modesty since she'd met him. Maybe she had been deliberately seductive because she had wanted him from the beginning. She had wanted this—this languishing aftermath of a coupling that had left her replete.

"You think I'm beautiful?" she asked coyly, running her fingers through his hair and smiling like the cat who had just lapped up the cream.

"You know I do."

"You don't have to sound so angry about it."

His fingers trailed down the groove between her ribs all the way to her navel. "I am, though. I didn't want to give in to your charms. I lost the battle with my own lust."

"I'm glad you did." She raised her head and kissed his mouth softly.

He dusted his fingertips over her navel. "For the time being, so am I."

Rusty didn't want them to be restricted to a time limit. "Why 'for the time being'?"

It hadn't taken them long to undress and make up the pallet in front of the fire. Stretched out naked on the pile of furs, hair a rumpled heap of reddish curls, lips rosy and wet from frequent kissing, eyes drowsy with lovemaking, Rusty looked like a conquering vandal's battle prize. Cooper had never waxed poetic, surely not right after having sex. The thought brought an involuntary smile to his lips.

He surveyed her alluring body. "Never mind."

"Tell me."

"It has something to do with you and me and who we are. But I really don't want to talk about that now." He bent his head low and kissed the ginger curls between her thighs. They were damp. They smelled and tasted of himself and he felt his body respond. Her low moan worked as surely as a velvet-fisted caress on his rising sex. He sighed his pleasure. "Did you know that you're very small?" he whispered into the fleecy delta. Her thighs relaxed and parted. His fingers slipped inside her.

"I am?"

"Yes."

"I'm not all that experienced."

He gazed down at her doubtfully, but her face was guileless. Abruptly he asked, "How many?"

"How indelicate!"

"How many?"

Rusty wrestled with her decision to tell him. Finally, eyes evasive, she said quietly, "Less than I could count on one hand."

"In a year?"

"Total."

Cooper stared down at her, searching for any trace of duplicity in her eyes. God, he wanted to believe her, but couldn't. His probing caress was telling him what his mind wasn't ready to accept, what he should have known the moment he entered her, but couldn't reconcile with his image of her.

"Less than five?"

"Yes."

"Less than three?" She looked away. "Just one?" She nodded. His heart did an odd little dance, and the emotion that surged through him felt like happiness. But he'd known so little of it, he couldn't be sure. "And you didn't live with him, did you, Rusty?"

"No." She tossed her head to one side and bit her lower lip at his thumb's indolent stroking. The callused pad of it had been gifted with a magical and intuitive touch that paid honor to a woman's body.

"Why not?"

"My father and brother wouldn't have approved."

"Does everything you do have to meet with your father's approval?"

"Yes...No...I...I...Cooper, please stop," she gasped breathlessly. "I can't think while you're doing that."

"So don't think."

"But I don't want to...to, you know...oh, please...no..."

After the last shimmering beam of light had finally burned out, she opened her eyes and met his teasing smile. "That wasn't so bad, was it?"

She discovered that she had just enough energy to answer his smile and reach up and touch his mustache with her fingertips. "I didn't want to do that so soon. I wanted to look at you some more."

"I guess that ends the discussion of you and your father."

Her brows drew into a frown. "It's very complex, Cooper. He was devastated when Jeff was killed. So was I. Jeff was...." She searched for the all-encompassing word. "He was wonderful. He could do everything."

Cooper brushed her lips with his mustache. "Not everything," he said mysteriously. "He couldn't—" He bent down and whispered what Jeff couldn't do with him, using a street word that brought color rising all the way to Rusty's hairline. But she blushed with pleasure, not with affront. "So, see? There's no reason for you to feel inferior to your brother."

Before she could expound on the subject, he sealed her lips closed with an arousing, eating kiss. "Now, what was that about looking at me?"

Her breath was insufficient. She drew in a deep, long one before saying, "I haven't looked my fill." Her eyes, shining as brightly as copper pennies, roved down his chest. She lifted her hand to touch him, glanced up at him as though asking permission, then laid her fingers against the springy hair.

"Go on, coward. I don't bite." The glance she gave him was eloquently sensual. He laughed. "Touché. I do. But not all the time." He leaned down and whispered, "Only when I'm buried inside the sweetest silk I've ever found between two thighs."

While she explored, he nibbled her ear and took love bites out of her neck. When her fingers flitted across his nipple, he sucked in a sharp breath. She jerked her hand back quickly. He recaptured it and pressed it back against his chest.

"That wasn't alarming or painful," he explained in a hoarse, thick voice. "It's like connecting two live wires. I wasn't prepared for the shock. Do it again. All you want."

She did. And more. She dallied with him until his breath became choppy. "Something else needs your attention, but we'd better not," he said, catching her hand on its downward slide. "Not if we want to take this one slow and easy."

"Let me touch you."

Against such a breathy request, he exercised no willpower. He squeezed his eyes shut and withstood her curious caresses until he couldn't bear anymore. Then he lifted her hand off him and satisfied them both with a fervent kiss.

"My turn." One of her arms was still bent behind her head. Her breasts rose off her chest, perfect domes crowned with delicate, pink crests. He covered each with a hand and squeezed. "Too hard?" he asked in response to Rusty's change in facial expression.

"Too wonderful." She sighed.

"That night I kissed you...here..." He touched the curving softness of her breast.

"Yes?"

"I meant to make the mark."

Her sleepy eyelids opened wide. "You did? Why?"

"Because I'm mean, that's why?"

"No, you're not. You just want everyone to think you are."

"It works, doesn't it?"

She smiled. "Sometimes. Sometimes I've thought you were very mean. Other times I knew you were feeling a lot of pain and that being deliberately mean was your only way of coping with it. I think it goes back to your days as a POW."

"Maybe."

"Cooper?"

"Hmm?"

"Make another mark if you want to."

His eyes darted up to hers. Then he moved above her and kissed her mouth thoroughly while his hands continued to massage her breasts. He brushed her wet and swollen lips with his mustache before dragging it down her neck, nipping her lightly with his teeth as he went. He kissed his way across her collarbone and down her chest until he reached the upper curve of her breast.

"I'm responsible for the bruises on your bottom. Then the passion mark. I guess in a primitive way I wanted to brand you mine. I don't have to put a mark on you now," he said, moving his lips lightly over her skin. "You belong to me. For a little while, anyway."

Rusty wanted to take issue with his choice of words and tell him that she would belong to him for as long as he liked, but his roving lips emptied her mind of the correct phrases. He kissed every inch of her breasts, avoiding the nipples. Then he licked them all over and at once, like a greedy child with a quickly melting ice-cream cone. When Rusty didn't think she could stand any more, she clutched handfuls of his hair and pulled his mouth directly above one of the achy, stiff peaks.

His tongue flicked over it, lightly, deftly, until her head was thrashing from side to side. He used his mustache to tickle and tease. When he closed his lips around her nipple and surrounded it with the scalding, tugging pressure of his mouth, she cried his name out loud.

"Oh, baby, you're nice." He moved his head from one side of her body to the other. His mouth was ravenous, but tender.

"Cooper?"

"Hmm?"

"Cooper?"

"Hmm?"

"*Cooper*?" She curled her fingers around his ears and pulled his head up even with hers. "Why'd you do it?"

"Do what?"

He avoided looking at her by staring at a spot beyond the top of her head. "You know what." She wet her lips anxiously. "Why did you...withdraw...before...?"

She felt apprehensive and disappointed, just as she had earlier when, at the last possible heartbeat, he'd cheated her out of the ultimate high, that of feeling him come inside her.

He became perfectly still. For a moment she was afraid she'd made him angry and that he was going to leave the pallet. After a long, tense moment, he cut his eyes back to hers. "I guess you're due an explanation." She said nothing. He released her name on a sigh. "We might be here for a long time. I don't think either of us wants or needs another mouth to feed."

"A baby?" Her voice was hushed with awe. She played with the idea of having a baby and didn't find it repugnant at all. In fact her lips formed a winsome smile. "I hadn't thought of that."

"Well, I had. We're both young, healthy adults. I know you're not using a contraceptive because I know everything that we brought into this cabin with us. Am I right?"

"Yes," she said timidly, like a child confessing a small transgression.

"I didn't pack anything to take with me to the hunting lodge."

"But it probably won't even happen."

"We can't be sure. I'm taking no chances. So—"

"But if it should," she interrupted excitedly, "we'd be found before the child was born."

"Probably, but—"

"Even if we weren't, I'd be the one responsible for feeding it."

This talk about a child had his stomach churning. His mouth was set in its familiar, firm, hard line. It softened now when he saw how earnest Rusty was. Almost naive. "That's just it," he said roughly, his mouth moving toward her breasts. "I can't stand the thought of sharing you with anyone."

"But—"

"I'm sorry. That's the way it's got to be."

She wanted to protest and pursue the argument. But he used his hands and lips and tongue with such prurient talent that they dissolved in a mutual, simultaneous orgasm before she realized that once again he had withdrawn from her just in time.

They kept each other so sated with sex that they didn't get hungry or cold or tired. They made love all that day and into the evening. Finally, exhausted, they wrapped themselves in fur and each other, and slept.

Only the unexpected rat-a-tat drumbeat of helicopter blades could have disturbed their dreams.

Ten

He was going to miss the chopper. He knew that. He al-
ways did. But he kept running anyway. He always did that,
too. Jungle foliage blocked his path. He clawed his way
through it toward the clearing. He was running so hard his
lungs were on fire. His breathing sounded loud to his own
ears.

But he could still hear the rotating blades of the chopper.
Close. So close. Noisy.

I've got to make it this time, *he cried to himself.* I've got
to make it or I'll be captured again.

But he knew he wouldn't make it, although he kept run-
ning. Running. Running . . .

As always, after having the nightmare, Cooper sat up,
chest heaving with exertion and drenched with sweat. God,
it had been real this time. The racket of those chopper
blades seemed—

Suddenly he realized that he could still hear the helicopter. Was he awake? Yes, he was. There lay Rusty, sleeping
peacefully beside him. This wasn't Nam; this was Canada.
And, by God, he heard a helicopter!

He scrambled to his feet and crossed the cabin's chilly
floor with running footsteps. Since the day they'd missed the
search plane, the flare gun had remained on a shelf next to

the door. He grabbed it on his way out. When he dashed across the porch and leaped to the ground, he was still naked, but the flare gun was clutched tightly in his right hand.

Shading his eyes with his left, he scanned the sky. The sun was brilliant and just even with the tops of the trees. His eyes teared because it was so bright. He couldn't see a damn thing. He only had six flares. He mustn't waste them. Each one had to count. But he could still hear the chopper. So he acted on impulse and fired two of the flares directly overhead.

"Cooper, is it—"

"A chopper."

Rusty ran out onto the porch and tossed him a pair of jeans. When she had awakened, first with the intuitive knowledge that her lover was no longer lying beside her, then with the sound of the helicopter, she had hastily pulled on her tattered slacks and bulky sweater. Now she, too, shaded her eyes and searched the sky in every direction.

"He must have seen the flares," Cooper cried excitedly. "He's coming back."

"I don't see him. How do you know?"

"I recognize the sound."

Apparently he did. Within seconds, the helicopter swept over the tops of the trees and hovered above the cabin. Cooper and Rusty began waving their arms and shouting, even though it was obvious that they'd been spotted by the two men sitting in the chopper. They could even see their wide smiles through the bubble.

"They see us! Oh, Cooper, Cooper!"

Rusty launched herself against him. He caught her in a fierce bear hug and, lifting her off her feet, swung her around. "We made it, baby, we made it!"

The clearing surrounding the cabin was large enough to accommodate the helicopter. It set down. Hand in hand, Rusty and Cooper ran toward it. She was heedless of the twinge of pain in her leg. The pilot in the right-hand chair unbuckled his seat belt and stepped out. Ducking under the rotating blades, he ran to meet them.

"Miz Carlson, ma'am?" His Southern accent was as thick as corn syrup. Rusty bobbed her head up and down, suddenly shy and speechless. Timidly she clung to Cooper's arm.

"Cooper Landry," Cooper said, sticking out his hand and pumping the pilot's in a hearty handshake. "We're damn sure glad to see you guys."

"We're kinda glad to see you, too. Miz Carlson's daddy hired us to look for her. The authorities weren't doing the job to his satisfaction."

"That sounds like Father," Rusty shouted over the clapping sound of the turning blades.

"Y'all the only ones who made it?" They nodded somberly. "Well, unless y'all want to stick around, let's git you home. Your daddy sure is gonna be glad to see ya."

At the mention of the young woman's father, the congenial pilot gave Cooper a worried glance, taking in his unfastened jeans. It was obvious that they'd been pulled on in haste and that the man wearing them was naked underneath. Rusty had the debauched, disheveled look of a woman who'd been making love all night. The pilot summed up the situation readily enough; it didn't have to be spelled out to him.

They returned to the cabin only long enough to dress properly. Cooper retrieved his expensive hunting rifle. Beyond that, they came away empty-handed. As she went through the door for the last time, Rusty gave the cabin a wistful backward glance. Originally she had despised the place. Now that she was leaving it, she felt a trace of sadness.

Cooper didn't seem to share her sentiment. He and the pilot were laughing and joking, having discovered that they were veterans of the same war and that their tours of duty had overlapped. Rusty had to run to catch up with them.

When she did, Cooper slipped an arm around her shoulders and smiled down at her. That made everything all right. Or at least better.

"I'm Mike," the pilot told them as he assisted them into their seats. "And that's my twin brother Pat." The other pilot saluted them.

"Pat and Mike?" Cooper shouted. "You gotta be kidding?"

That seemed hilariously funny and they were all laughing uncontrollably as the chopper lifted off the ground and skimmed the tops of the trees before gaining altitude.

"The crash site was spotted by a search plane several days ago," Mike shouted back at them and pointed down.

Rusty viewed the sight. She was surprised that they had covered so much distance on foot, especially with Cooper dragging her in the handmade travois. She would never have survived if it hadn't been for him. What if he had died in the crash? Shuddering at the thought, she laid her head on his shoulder. He placed his arm around her and pulled her close. Her hand curled around the inside of his thigh in a subconscious gesture of trust.

"The other five died on impact," Cooper told the pilots. "Rusty and I were sitting in the last row. I guess that's why we lived through it."

"When the report came back that the plane wasn't burned or anything, Mr. Carlson insisted on searching for survivors," Mike said. "He hired my brother and me out of Atlanta. We specialize in rescue missions." He propped his elbow on the back of his seat and turned his head to address them. "How'd you happen onto the cabin?"

Cooper and Rusty exchanged a troubled glance. "We'll save that story and tell it only once, if you don't mind," Cooper said.

Mike nodded. "I'm gonna radio that you've been rescued. Lots of people have been lookin' for ya. The weather's been a real bitch. Sorry, Miz Carlson."

"That's okay."

"We were grounded until yesterday when the weather cleared. Didn't see anything. Then got an early start again this morning."

"Where are you taking us?" Cooper asked.

"Yellowknife."

"Is my father there?"

Mike shook his head. "He's in L.A. My guess is that he'll have y'all hustled down there before the day is out."

That was good news to Rusty. She couldn't say why, but she had dreaded having to relate the details of her ordeal to her father. Knowing that she wouldn't have to face him right away came as a relief—perhaps because of what had happened last night. She hadn't had time to analyze it. She wanted to savor the experience she had had with Cooper.

Their rescue had been an intrusion. She'd been glad about it, of course. Still, she wanted to be alone with her thoughts. The only person she wanted to distract her was Cooper. With that thought, the uncharacteristic shyness stole over her again and she snuggled against him.

He seemed to read her mind. He tipped her face up and peered at her closely. Bending his head, he kissed her soundly on the lips, then pressed her head against his chest. He gathered her hair in a gentle fist. His actions were both protective and possessive.

They stayed in that position for the remainder of the flight. Neither pilot tried to engage them in conversation, but respected their need for privacy. Pertinent questions could wait.

"You've drawn quite a crowd." Mike glanced at them over his shoulder and nodded toward the ground as they approached the airport, which was small when compared to metropolitan airports, but large enough to accommodate jet aircraft.

Rusty and Cooper saw that the airport below was teeming with people. The milling crowd was showing no respect for restricted areas of the tarmac. Vans labeled as portable television-broadcast units were parked end to end. In this remote area of the Northwest Territories, such media hype was virtually unheard of.

Cooper muttered a curse. "Who the hell is responsible for this?"

"The plane crash made big news," Mike told him with an apologetic smile. "Y'all were the only survivors. I reckon everybody wants to hear what y'all've got to say about it."

The instant Pat set the chopper down, the crowd of reporters surged forward against the temporary barriers. Policemen had a difficult time forcing them back. Several official-looking men ran forward. The helicopter's twirling blades plastered their business suits against their bodies and slapped their neckties against their faces. The rotors finally wound down.

Mike jumped to the concrete and helped Rusty climb down. She cowered bashfully against the side of the helicopter until Cooper jumped down beside her. Then, after profusely thanking the twin pilots from Georgia, they moved forward. Their hands were clasped together tightly.

The men who greeted them were representatives of the Canadian Aviation Safety Board and the National Transportation Safety Board. The U.S. agency had been invited to investigate the crash since the passengers involved were all American.

The bureaucrats deferentially welcomed Cooper and Rusty back to civilization and escorted them past the squirming, shouting wall of reporters whose behavior was anything but civilized. They bombarded them with questions fired as rapidly as machine-gun bullets.

The dazed survivors were escorted through one of the building's employee entrances, down a corridor, and into a private suite of offices that had been provided for their use.

"Your father has been notified, Miss Carlson."

"Thank you very much."

"He was delighted to hear that you are well," the smiling official told her. "Mr. Landry, is there anyone we should notify for you?"

"No."

Rusty had turned to him, curious to hear his reply. He had never mentioned a family, so she had assumed that there was none. It seemed terribly sad to her that no one had been waiting for Cooper's return. She longed to reach out and lay a compassionate hand along his cheek. But the officials were crowded around them.

One stepped forward. "I understand you were the only two to survive the crash."

"Yes. The others died immediately."

"We've notified their families. Some are outside. They want to speak with you." Rusty's face turned as white as the knuckles of her fingers, which were still linked with Cooper's. "But that can wait," the man said hastily, sensing her distress. "Can you give us a clue as to the cause of the crash?"

"I'm not a pilot," Cooper said shortly. "The storm was a factor, I'm sure. The pilots did everything they could."

"Then you wouldn't blame the crash on them?" the man probed.

"May I have a glass of water, please?" Rusty asked softly.

"And something to eat," Cooper said in that same clipped tone. "We haven't had any food this morning. Not even coffee."

"Surely, right away." Someone was dispatched to order them a breakfast.

"And you'd better bring in the proper authorities. I've got the deaths of two men to report."

"What two men?"

"The ones I killed." Everyone froze. He had succeeded in winning their undivided attention. "I'm sure someone should be notified. But first, how about that coffee?" Cooper's voice rang with authority and impatience. It was almost amusing how it galvanized everyone into action. For the next hour, the officials flapped around them like headless chickens.

They were brought huge breakfasts of steak and eggs. More than anything on the tray Rusty enjoyed the fresh orange juice. She couldn't drink enough of it. As they ate, they answered the endless rounds of questions. Pat and Mike were brought in to verify the location of the cabin relative to the crash site. While the weather was still cooperating, crews were dispatched to view the wreckage and exhume the bodies that Cooper had buried.

In the midst of the chaos a telephone receiver was thrust into Rusty's hand and her father's voice boomed into her ear. "Rusty, thank God. Are you all right?"

Tears filled her eyes. For a moment she couldn't speak. "I'm fine. Fine. My leg feels much better."

"Your leg! What happened to your leg? Nobody told me anything about your leg."

She explained as best she could in brief, disjointed phrases. "But it's fine, really."

"I'm not taking your word for it. Don't worry about anything," he told her. "I'll handle everything from here. You'll be brought to L.A. tonight and I'll be at the airport to meet you. It's a miracle that you survived."

She glanced at Cooper, and said softly, "Yes, a miracle."

Around noon they were taken across the street to a motel and assigned rooms in which to shower and change into clothes provided by the Canadian government.

At the door to her room, Rusty reluctantly let go of Cooper's arm. She couldn't bear to let him out of her sight. She felt alien, apart. None of this seemed real. Everything and everybody swam toward her like distorted faces out of a dream. She had difficulty matching words to concepts. Everything was strange—except Cooper. Cooper alone was her reality.

He seemed no more pleased with the arrangements than she, but it would hardly be suitable for them to share a motel room. He squeezed her hand and said, "I'll be right next door."

He watched her enter her room and safely close and lock the door before he went to his own. Once inside, he dropped into the only chair and covered his face with his hands.

"Now what?" he asked the four walls.

If only he had held off for one more night. If only she hadn't asked that question of him yesterday morning after breakfast. If only she hadn't been so desirable in the first place. If only they hadn't been on the same airplane. If only it hadn't crashed. If only some of the others had survived and they hadn't been alone.

He could come up with thousands of "if onlys," and the bottom line would still be that they'd made love all day yesterday and last night until the wee hours.

He didn't regret it—not a single breathless second of it.

But he didn't know how in the hell he was going to handle it from here. Rightfully, he should pretend that it hadn't happened and ignore the shining recognition of mutual passion in her eyes. But that was just it: he couldn't ignore her melting looks.

Nor could he callously disregard her dependency on him. The rules they'd laid down in the cabin were still in effect. She hadn't acclimated yet. She was apprehensive. She had just survived a trauma. He couldn't subject her to another one so soon. She wasn't tough like him; she had to be treated with delicacy and tact. After the rough time he'd given her, he thought she deserved that much consideration.

Of course he was reconciled to having to turn his back on her. He wished she would turn hers on him first. That would relieve him of the responsibility of hurting her.

But dammit, she wouldn't. And he couldn't. Not yet. Not until it was absolutely necessary for them to part. Until then, even though he knew it was foolhardy, he'd go on being her Lancelot, her protector and lover.

God, he loved the role.

It was just too damn bad it was temporary.

The hot shower felt wonderful and worked to revive her physically and mentally. She scrubbed her hair with shampoo twice and rinsed it until it squeaked. When she stepped out of the tub, she felt almost normal.

But she wasn't. Normally she wouldn't have noticed how soft the motel towels were. She would have taken soft towels for granted. She was changed in other ways, too. When she propped her foot on the edge of the tub to dry, she noticed the unsightly, jagged scar running down her shin. She bore other scars. Deeper ones. They were indelibly engraved on her soul. Rusty Carlson would never be the same.

The clothes she'd been given were inexpensive and way oversize, but they made her feel human and feminine again. The shoes fit, but they felt odd and unusually light on her feet. It was the first time in weeks that she'd worn anything but hiking boots. Almost a week at the lodge and almost two since the crash.

Two weeks? Is that all it had been?

When she emerged from the motel room, Cooper was waiting outside her door. He had showered and shaved. His hair was still damp and well combed. The new clothes looked out of place on his rangy body.

They approached each other warily, shyly, almost apologetically. Then their eyes met, the familiarity sparked. And something else, too.

"You're different," Rusty whispered.

He shook his head. "No, I'm not. I might look different, but I haven't changed."

He took her hand and drew her aside, giving the people who would have rushed to cluster around them a "back off" glance. They moved out of hearing distance. Cooper said,

"In all this confusion, I haven't had a chance to tell you something."

Clean and smelling like soap and shaving cream, mouth giving off the fresh scent of peppermint, he was very handsome. Her eyes moved hungrily over him, unable to take in this new Cooper. "What?"

He leaned closer. "I love the way your tongue feels flicking over my navel."

Rusty sucked in a startled breath. Her eyes darted toward the group that was huddled a discreet distance away. They were all watching them curiously. "You're outrageous."

"And I don't give a damn." He inched even closer. "Let's give them something to speculate about." He curled his hand around her throat and placed his thumb beneath her chin to tilt it up.

Then he kissed her unsparingly. He took what he wanted and gave more than she would have had the audacity to ask for. Nor was he in any hurry. His tongue plumbed her mouth slowly and deliciously in a purely sexual rhythm.

When he finally pulled away, he growled, "I want to kiss you like that all over, but," he shot a look in the direction of their astounded observers, "that'll have to wait."

They were driven back to the airport, but Rusty never remembered leaving the motel. Cooper's kiss had entranced her.

The hours of the afternoon dragged on forever. They were catered another meal. Rusty ordered an enormous chef's salad. She was starved for cold, crisp, fresh vegetables, but found that she could only eat half of it.

Her lack of appetite was partially due to the breakfast she'd eaten only hours before, but mostly to her anxiety over the interrogation she and Cooper were put through regarding the deaths of Quinn and Reuben Gawrylow.

A court reporter was brought in to take down Cooper's testimony. He told how they had met the two recluses, were given shelter by them, promised rescue, and then were attacked. "Our lives were in danger," he said. "I had no choice. It was self-defense."

Rusty gauged the reactions of the policemen and saw that they weren't convinced. They murmured among themselves and kept casting suspicious glances toward Cooper. They began asking him about his stint in Vietnam and brought up the fact that he was a former POW. They asked him to recount the events leading to his escape from the prison camp. He refused, saying that it had no bearing on this issue.

"But you were forced to...to..."

"Kill?" Cooper asked with ruthless candor. "Yes. I killed a lot of them on my way out of there. And I'd do it again."

Telling looks were exchanged. Someone coughed uncomfortably.

"He's leaving out a vital point," Rusty said abruptly. Every eye in the room turned to her.

"Rusty, no," he said. His eyes speared into hers in a silent plea for caution and discretion. "You don't have to."

She looked back at him lovingly. "Yes, I do. You're trying to spare me. I appreciate it. But I can't let them think you killed those two men without strong motivation." She faced her listeners. "They, the Gawrylows, were going to kill Cooper and...and keep me."

Shock registered on the faces encircling the table where she was seated with Cooper. "How do you know that, Ms. Carlson?"

"She just knows it, okay? You might suspect me of lying, but you have no reason to think she is."

Rusty laid a restraining hand on Cooper's arm. "The older one, Quinn, attacked me." In plain language, she told them what Gawrylow had done to her that morning in the cabin. "My leg was still seriously injured. I was virtually helpless. Cooper returned just in time to prevent a rape. Gawrylow reached for a gun. If Cooper hadn't acted when and how he did, he would have been killed instead of Gawrylow. And I would still be at the old man's mercy.''

She exchanged a long stare of understanding with Cooper. She had never deliberately inflamed the hermits. He had known that all along. He silently asked her to forgive him his insults and she silently asked him to forgive her for ever being afraid of him.

Cooper's hand splayed wide over the top of her head and moved it to his chest. His arms wrapped around her. Ignoring everybody else in the room, they held each other tight, rocking slightly back and forth.

Half an hour later, Cooper was relieved of all legal responsibility for the deaths of the Gawrylows. Facing them now was their meeting with the victims' families. The weeping, somber group was led into the office. For nearly an hour Rusty and Cooper spoke with them and provided what information they could. The bereaved derived some comfort from the fact that their loved ones had died immediately and without having suffered. They tearfully thanked the survivors for sharing their knowledge about the crash. It was a moving experience for everyone involved.

The meeting with the media was something altogether different. When Rusty and Cooper were escorted into the large room that had been set up for the press conference, they were greeted by a restless crowd. A pall of tobacco smoke obscured the ceiling.

Seated behind a table with microphones, they answered the barrage of questions as thoroughly, but as concisely, as possible. Some of the questions were silly, some were intelligent, and some were painfully personal. When one gauche reporter asked what it was like to share a cabin with a total stranger, Cooper turned to one of the officials and said, "That's it. Get Rusty out of here."

The bureaucrat didn't move fast enough to suit him. Taking it upon himself to remove Rusty from the carnival atmosphere, he slipped his arm beneath hers and assisted her out of her chair. As they made their way toward the exit, a man came rushing up and shoved a business card into Cooper's face. It identified him as a reporter for a news-magazine. He offered them an enormous sum of money for exclusive rights to their story.

"But if that's not enough," he stammered hastily when Cooper glared at him with icy malevolence, "we'll up the ante. I don't suppose you took any pictures, did you?"

Emitting a feral growl, Cooper pushed the reporter aside and told him what he could do with his magazine, using descriptive words that couldn't be misunderstood.

By the time they were boarded onto the L.A.-bound jet, Rusty was so exhausted she could barely walk. Her right leg was aching. Cooper had to practically carry her aboard. He buckled her into her first-class seat next to the window and took the aisle seat beside her. He asked the flight attendant to bring a snifter of brandy immediately.

"Aren't you having any?" Rusty asked after taking a few fiery and restorative sips.

He shook his head. "I've sworn off the booze for a while." The corner of his mouth lifted into a slight smile.

"You're very handsome, Mr. Landry," she remarked softly, gazing up at him as though seeing him for the first time.

He removed the snifter from her listless fingers. "That's the brandy talking."

"No, you are." She raised her hand and touched his hair. It slid through her fingers silkily.

"I'm glad you think so."

"Dinner, Ms. Carlson, Mr. Landry?"

They were surprised to realize that the airplane was already airborne. They'd been so preoccupied with each other that they hadn't even noticed the takeoff. Which was just as well. The helicopter ride hadn't been so bad for her because she hadn't had time to anticipate it. But as the day stretched out, the thought of flying to Los Angeles had filled Rusty with apprehension. It would be a while, if ever, before she was a completely comfortable flyer.

"Dinner, Rusty?" Cooper asked. She shook her head. To the flight attendant he said, "No, thanks. They fed us several times today."

"Buzz me if you need anything," she said graciously before moving down the aisle. They were the only passengers in the first-class cabin. When the flight attendant returned to the galley, they were left alone for the first time since being rescued.

"You know, it's funny," Rusty said musingly, "we were together so much that I thought I'd welcome the time when we could be apart. I thought I missed being with other people—" she fingered the pocket of his shirt "—but I hated the crowds today. All that pushing and shoving. And every time I lost sight of you, I panicked."

"Natural," he whispered as he tucked a strand of hair behind her ear. "You've been dependent on me for so long, you're in the habit. That'll go away."

She angled her head back, "Will it, Cooper?"

"Won't it?"

"I'm not sure I want it to."

He said her name softly before his lips settled against hers. He kissed her ardently, as though this might be his last chance. There was a desperation behind his kiss. It persisted when Rusty looped her arms around his neck and buried her face in the hollow of his shoulder.

"You saved my life. Have I thanked you? Have I told you that I would have died without you?"

Cooper was frantically kissing her neck, her ears, her hair. "You don't need to thank me. I wanted to protect you, to take care of you."

"You did. Well. Very well." They kissed again until they were forced to break apart breathlessly. "Touch me."

He watched her lips whisper the words. They were still glistening from their kiss. "Touch you? Here? Now?"

She nodded rapidly. "Please, Cooper. I'm frightened. I need to know you're here—really and truly here."

He opened the coat that the Canadian government had supplied and slipped his hand inside. He covered her breast. It felt womanly and warm and full beneath her sweater.

He laid his cheek against hers and whispered, "Your nipple is already hard."

"Hmm."

His fingers played with the tight little bead through the knit. "You don't seem surprised."

"I'm not."

"Are they always like this? Where were you when I was fourteen?"

She laughed softly. "No, they're not always like this. I was thinking about last night."

"Last night lasted a lifetime. Be specific."

"Remember when . . ." She whispered a sultry reminder.

"Lord, yes," he groaned, "but don't talk about that now."

"Why?"

"If you do, you'll have to sit on my lap."

She touched him. "To cover this?"

"No, Rusty," he said through gritted teeth. And when he told her what they would be doing if she sat on his lap, she chastely removed her hand.

"I don't think that would be proper at all. For that matter, neither is what you're doing. Maybe you'd better stop." He withdrew his hand from her sweater. By now both her breasts were showing up hard and pointed beneath it. They gazed at each other, their eyes reflecting a sense of loss. "I wish we hadn't been so stubborn. I wish we'd made love before last night."

He sighed deeply. "I've thought about that, too."

A sob rose in her throat. "Hold me, Cooper." He clasped her tightly and burrowed his face in her hair. "Don't let me go."

"I won't. Not now."

"Not ever. Promise."

Sleep claimed her before she got his promise. It also spared her from seeing the bleak expression on his face.

It seemed that the entire population of the city was waiting for their arrival at LAX. They had landed only briefly in Seattle and hadn't had to deplane. None of the boarding passengers had joined them in first class. That takeoff had been uneventful.

Now, anticipating a mob scene, the senior flight attendant advised them to let all the other passengers disembark first. Rusty welcomed the delay. She was terribly nervous. Her palms were wet with perspiration. Jitters like this were foreign to her. At ease on every social occasion, she couldn't imagine why she was sick with anxiety now. She didn't want to release her grip on Cooper's arm, although she kept flashing insincere, confident smiles up at him. If only she could slip back into her regular life without a lot of fuss.

But it wasn't going to be that easy. The moment she stepped through the opening of the jet way and entered the terminal, her worst expectations were realized. She was momentarily blinded by television lights. Microphones were poked into her face. Someone inadvertently bumped her sore shin with a camera bag. The noise was deafening. But out of that cacophony, a familiar voice beckoned her. She turned toward it.

"Father?"

Within seconds she was smothered in his embrace. Her arm was jostled away from Cooper's. Even as she returned her father's hug, she groped for Cooper's hand, but she couldn't find it. The separation left her panicked.

"Let me review the damage," Bill Carlson said, pushing his daughter away and holding her at arm's length. The reporters widened the circle around them, but cameras snapped pictures of this moving reunion. "Not too bad, under the circumstances." He whipped the coat from around her shoulders. "As grateful as I am to the charitable Canadian government for taking such good care of you today, I think you'll feel much better in this."

One of his lackeys materialized and produced a huge box, from which Carlson shook out a full-length red fox coat exactly like the one she'd been wearing when the plane crashed. "I heard about your coat, darling," he said as he proudly draped the fur around her shoulders, "so I wanted to replace it."

Oohs and aahs rose out of the crowd. Reporters pressed closer to take pictures. The coat was gorgeous but far too heavy for the balmy southern California evening. It felt like chain mail weighting her down. But Rusty was oblivious to it, to everything, as her eyes frantically probed the circle of light surrounding her in search of Cooper. "Father, I want you to meet—"

"Don't worry about your leg. It will be seen to by expert doctors. I've arranged a room for you at the hospital. We're going there immediately."

"But Cooper—"

"Oh, yes, Cooper Landry, isn't it? The man who also survived the crash. I'm grateful to him, of course. He saved your life. I'll never forget that." Carlson spoke in a booming voice that was guaranteed to be overhead by the newspaper reporters and picked up by microphones.

Diplomatically his assistant wielded the long coat-box to clear a path for them through the throng of media people. "Ladies and gentlemen, you'll be notified if anything else comes out about the story," Carlson told them as he ushered Rusty toward a golf cart that was waiting to transport them through the terminal.

Rusty looked everywhere, but she didn't see Cooper. Finally she spotted his broad-shouldered form walking away from the scene. A couple of reporters were in hot pursuit. "Cooper!" The cart lurched forward and she grabbed the seat beneath her for balance. "Cooper!" she called again. He couldn't hear her above the din.

She wanted to leap off the cart and chase after him, but it was already in motion and her father was speaking to her. She tried to assimilate his words and make sense of them, but it seemed that he was speaking gibberish.

She fought down her rising panic as the cart rolled down the concourse, beeping pedestrians out of the way. Finally Cooper was swallowed up by the crowd and she lost sight of him altogether.

Once they were inside the limousine and cruising toward the private hospital where Carlson had arranged for a room, he clasped Rusty's clammy hand. "I was very afraid for you, Rusty. I thought I'd lost you, too."

She rested her head on her father's shoulder and squeezed his arm. "I know. I was as worried about how you'd take the news of the crash as I was about my own safety."

"About our tiff that day you left—"

"Please, Father, don't let's even think about that now." She lifted her head and smiled up at him. "I might not have survived the gutting of that ram, but I survived a plane crash."

He chuckled. "I don't know if you remember this—you were very young—but Jeff sneaked out of his cabin at Boy Scout camp one summer. He spent the entire night in the woods. He got lost and wasn't found until well into the next day. But that little scrapper wasn't the least bit scared. When we found him, he had made camp and was calmly fishing for his dinner."

Rusty returned her head to his shoulder, her smile gradually fading. "Cooper did all that for me."

She felt the sudden tension in her father's body. He usually bristled like that when something didn't meet with his approval. "What kind of man is this Cooper Landry, Rusty?"

"What kind?"

"A Vietnam veteran, I understand."

"Yes. He was a POW, too, but managed to escape."

"Did he . . . handle you well?"

Ah, yes, she was thinking. But she capped the fountain of passionate memories that bubbled inside her like uncorked champagne. "Yes, Father. Very well. I wouldn't have survived without him."

She didn't want to tell him about her personal involvement with Cooper so soon after her return. Her father would have to be apprised of her feelings gradually. They might be met with resistance, because Bill Carlson was an opinionated man.

He was also intuitive. One didn't easily pull the wool over his eyes. Keeping her tone as casual as possible, Rusty said, "Will you try to locate him for me tonight?" It wasn't an unusual request. Her father had contacts all over the city. "Let him know where I am. We got separated at the airport."

"Why is it even necessary for you to see this man again?"

He might just as well have asked her why it was necessary for her to go on breathing. "I want to thank him properly for saving my life," she said as a diversion.

"I'll see what I can do," Carlson told her just as the chauffeur wheeled under the porte cochere of the private clinic.

Even though her father had paved the way, it was two hours later before Rusty was left alone in her plush room. Decorated with original works of art and contemporary furniture, it resembled a chic apartment more than it did a hospital room. She lay in a firm, comfortable, mechanized bed with soft pillows beneath her head. She was wearing a new designer nightgown, one of several her father had packed in the suitcase that had been waiting for her when she checked in. All her favorite cosmetics and toiletries had been placed in the bathroom. She had the staff at her beck and call. All she had to do was pick up the phone on her nightstand.

She was miserable.

For one thing, her leg was sore as a result of the surgeon's examination. As a safety precaution X rays had been taken, but they revealed no broken bones. "Cooper said nothing was broken," she quietly informed the doctor. He had frowned over the jagged scar. When he lamented the crude stitching that had been done, Rusty jumped to Cooper's defense. "He was trying to save my leg," she snapped.

Suddenly she was fiercely proud of that scar and not all that excited about seeing it erased, which, she was told, would require at least three reconstructive operations—maybe more. To her, the scar was like a badge of courage.

Besides, Cooper had spent a great deal of time with it the night before, kissing the raised, puckered skin and telling her that it didn't turn him off in the slightest and, in fact, made him "horny as hell" every time he looked at it. She had contemplated telling *that* to the pompous plastic surgeon.

She hadn't. Indeed, she hadn't said much of anything. She simply didn't have the energy. All she could think about was how blessed it was going to be when she was left alone to go to sleep.

But now that she had the opportunity, she couldn't. Doubts and fears and unhappiness were keeping her awake. Where was Cooper? Why hadn't he followed her? It had been a circus at the airport, but surely he could have stayed with her if he'd really wanted to.

When the nurse came in offering her a sedative, she gladly swallowed the pill. Otherwise she knew she'd never fall asleep without Cooper's hard, warm presence embracing her.

Eleven

❦❧

"I mean, my God! We couldn't believe it! Our Rusty in a plane crash!"

"It must have been dreadful."

Rusty looked up from the pillows of her hospital bed at the two well-dressed women and wished they would vanish in a puff of smoke. As soon as her breakfast tray had been carried out by an efficient and ebullient nurse, her two friends had breezed into her room.

Reeking of exotic perfume and avid curiosity, they said they wanted to be the first to commiserate. Rusty suspected that what they really wanted was to be the first to hear the delicious details of her "Canadian caper," as one had called it.

"No, I couldn't say it was much fun," Rusty said tiredly.

She had awakened long before breakfast was served. She was accustomed to waking up with the sun now. Thanks to the tranquilizing pill she'd been given the night before, she had slept soundly. Her lack of animation stemmed from dejection more than fatigue. Her spirits were at an extremely low ebb, and her friends' efforts to raise them were having the opposite effect.

"As soon as you get out of here, we're treating you to a day of self-indulgence at the salon. Hair, skin, massage. Just look at your poor nails." One lifted her listless hand, clicking her tongue against the roof of her mouth. "They're ravaged."

Rusty smiled wanly, remembering how upset she'd been when Cooper had pared off her fingernails with his hunting knife. "I didn't get around to having a manicure." It was meant to be facetious, but her friends were nodding sympathetically. "I was too busy trying to stay alive."

One shook her intentionally tousled blond head and shuddered delicately, causing the Hermès scarf around her neck to slip. The dozen or so silver bangle bracelets on her wrist jingled like the harness on a Christmas reindeer. "You were so brave, Rusty. I think I would rather have died than go through all that you did."

Rusty was about to refute that remark, when she remembered that not too long ago she could have said something that shallow. "I always thought I would, too. You'd be amazed how strong the human animal's survival instincts are. In a situation like the one I was in, they take over."

But her friends weren't interested in philosophy. They wanted to hear the nitty-gritty. The get-down-and-get-dirty good stuff. One was sitting on the foot of Rusty's bed; the other was leaning forward from the chair beside it. They looked like scavenger birds perched and ready to pick her bones clean the second she succumbed.

The story of the crash and the events following it had appeared on the front page of that morning's newspaper. The writer had, with only a few minor errors, meticulously chronicled Rusty's and Cooper's ordeal. The piece had been serious in tone and journalistically sound. But the public had a penchant for reading between the lines; it wanted to hear what had been omitted. Her friends included, the public wanted the facts fleshed out.

"Was it just *awful*? When the sun went down wasn't it terrifyingly dark?"

"We had several lanterns in the cabin."

"No, I mean outside."

"Before you got to the cabin. When you had to sleep outdoors in the woods."

Rusty sighed wearily. "Yes, it was dark. But we had a fire."

"What did you eat?"

"Rabbits, mostly."

"Rabbits! I'd *die*."

"I didn't," Rusty snapped. "And neither would you."

Now, why had she gone and done that? Why hadn't she just left it alone? They were looking wounded and confused, having no idea why she had jumped down their throats. Why hadn't she said something cute, something glib, such as telling them that rabbit meat is served in some of the finest restaurants?

Following on the heels of that thought, of course, came one of Cooper. A pang of longing for him seized her. "I'm awfully tired," she said, feeling the need to cry and not wanting to have to explain why.

But subtlety didn't work with this duo. They didn't pick up on the hint to leave. "And your poor leg." The one with the bracelets clapped her hand to her cheek in horror. "Is the doctor sure he can fix it?"

Rusty closed her eyes as she answered, "Reasonably sure."

"How many operations will it take to get rid of that hideous scar?" Rusty felt the air stir against her face as the other friend waved frantically to the untactful speaker. "Oh, I didn't mean it that way. It's not that hideous. I mean—"

"I know what you mean," Rusty said, opening her eyes. "It is hideous, but it's better than a stump, and for a while I was afraid that's what I'd end up with. If Cooper—"

She broke off, having inadvertently spoken his name. Now that it was out, the carrion birds flocked to it, grasping it in their avidly curious talons.

"Cooper?" one asked innocently. "The man who survived the crash with you?"

"Yes."

The two women exchanged a glance, as though mentally tossing a coin to see who was going to pose the first of numerous questions about him.

"I saw him on the TV news last night. My God, Rusty, he's gorgeous!"

"'Gorgeous'?"

"Well not gorgeous in the *perfect* sense. Not *model* gorgeous. I mean rugged, manly, sweaty, hairy, sexy kind of gorgeous."

"He saved my life," Rusty said softly.

"I know, my dear. But if one's life must be saved, better it be by someone who looks like your Cooper Landry. That mustache!" She grinned wickedly and licked her chops. "Is what they say of mustaches true? Remember the joke?"

Rusty did remember the joke. Her cheeks went pink while her lips went pale. What they said about mustaches *was* true.

"Are his shoulders really this broad?" The friend held her hands a yard apart.

"He's rather brawny, yes," Rusty admitted helplessly. "But he—"

"Are his hips really this narrow?" The hands closed to less than a foot apart. The ladies giggled.

Rusty wanted to scream. "He knew things to do that I would never have thought about. He built a travois, using my fur coat, and dragged me away from the crash site—for miles. I didn't even realize how far until I saw the distance from the helicopter."

"There's something deliciously dangerous about him." One friend gave a delicate shiver. She hadn't heard a single word Rusty had said. "Something threatening in his eyes. I've always found that primitive streak wildly sexy."

The one sitting in the chair closed her eyes in a near swoon. "Stop. You're making me hot."

"This morning's paper said he killed two men in a fight over you."

Rusty nearly got out of her bed. "That's not what the paper said at all!"

"I put two and two together."

"It was self-defense!"

"Honey, calm down." She patted Rusty's hand. "If you say it was self-defense, then it was self-defense." She winked down at Rusty. "Listen, my hubby knows Bill Friedkin. He thinks your story would make a terrific movie. He and Friedkin are having lunch next week and—"

"A movie!" Rusty was aghast over the thought. "Oh, no. Please tell him not to say anything. I don't want anything to come of this. I just want to forget about it and get on with my life."

"We didn't mean to upset you, Rusty." The one who had been sitting in the chair rose to stand beside the bed. She laid a comforting hand on Rusty's shoulder. "It's just that we're your two best friends. If there *was* something dreadful that you wanted to discuss, some—you know—*personal* aspect of the disaster that you couldn't tell your father, we wanted to make ourselves available."

"Like what?" Rusty shrugged off her friend's hand and glared up at them. They exchanged another telling glance.

"Well, you *were* alone with that man for almost two weeks."

"And?" Rusty asked tetchily.

"And," she said, drawing a deep breath, "the paper said it was a one-room cabin."

"So?"

"Come on, Rusty." The friend's patience gave out. "The situation lends itself to all kinds of speculation. You're a very attractive young woman, and he's positively yummy and certainly virile. You're both single. You were hurt. He nursed you. You were almost totally dependent on him. You thought you might be stranded up there for the duration of the winter."

The other took up the slack and said excitedly, "Living together like that, in such close proximity, in the wilderness—well, it's positively the most romantic thing I ever heard of. You know what we're getting at."

"Yes, I know what you're getting at." Rusty's voice was cold, but her brown eyes were smoldering. "You want to know if I slept with Cooper."

Just then the door swung open and the topic of their discussion came striding in. Rusty's heart nearly jumped out of her chest. Her friends spun around, reacting to the radiant smile that broke across her face. He barely took notice of them. His gray eyes found and locked upon Rusty. The sizzling look they exchanged should have answered any questions regarding their level of intimacy.

Rusty finally composed herself enough to speak. "Uh, Cooper, these are two of my closest friends." She introduced them by name. He gave each of the women a disinterested, terse nod to acknowledge the introductions.

"Oh, Mr. Landry, I'm *so* honored to meet you," one of them gushed, round-eyed and breathless. "The *Times* said that you are an escaped POW. That just blows my mind. I mean, all that you've been through already. Then to survive a plane crash."

"Rusty claims that you saved her life."

"My husband and I would like to give the two of you an intimate little dinner party when Rusty gets up and around. Please say you'll let us."

"When did you decide that?" the other asked with pique. "*I* wanted to give them a dinner party."

"I spoke first."

The silly chatter was irritating and embarrassing. Their squabbling made them sound like the two stepsisters in *Cinderella*. "I'm sure Cooper can't stay long," Rusty interrupted, noticing that he was growing increasingly impatient. As was she. Now that he was here, she wanted to get rid of her so-called friends so she could be alone with him.

"We've stayed long enough," one of them said as she gathered up her handbag and coat. She bent over Rusty and kissed the air just above her cheek, whispering, "You sly thing, you. You won't get away with this. I want to know *everything*."

The other one leaned down and said, "I'm sure he was well worth the plane crash. He's divine. So raw. So... Well, I'm sure I don't have to tell *you*."

They stopped on their way to the door to say goodbye to Cooper. One even tapped his chest with a flirtatious hand as she reminded him about the dinner party she was planning in his honor. They glided out, smiling smugly at Rusty over their shoulders before the door closed on them.

Cooper watched them go, then approached the bed. "I'm not going to any damned dinner party."

"I didn't expect you to. Once the novelty has worn off, I'll advise her to drop that idea."

Looking at him proved to be hazardous. She was dismayed to feel tears stinging her eyes. Self-consciously she brushed them off her cheeks.

"Something wrong?"

"No, I'm..." She hesitated to tell him, but decided to take the plunge. The time for secrets between them was long past. Bravely she lifted her eyes back to his. "I'm just very glad to see you."

He didn't touch her, although he might just as well have. His gaze was as possessive as a caress. It passed down her form lying beneath the thin blanket, then moved back up again. It lingered on her breasts, which were seductively outlined by the clinging silk nightgown.

She nervously raised her hand and fiddled with the lace neckline. "The, uh, the gown was waiting here for me when I checked in."

''It's nice.''

''Anything is better than long johns.''

''You look all right in long johns.''

Her smile wavered. He was here. She could see him, smell his soapy clean smell, hear his voice. He was wearing new clothes—slacks and a casual shirt and jacket. But they weren't responsible for his distant attitude. She didn't want to acknowledge it, but it was undeniably there—as obvious to her as an unbreachable wall.

''Thank you for coming to see me,'' she said for lack of anything better. ''I asked my father to locate you and tell you where I was.''

''Your father didn't tell me anything. I found you on my own.''

She took heart. He'd been looking for her. Maybe all night. Maybe while she'd lain sleeping a drug-induced sleep, he'd been combing the city streets in a frantic search.

But then he shot down her soaring hopes by adding, ''It was in the morning paper that you were here. I understand that a plastic surgeon is going to correct the stitches I made.''

''I defended your stitching.''

He shrugged indifferently. ''It worked, that's all I care about.''

''That's all I care about, too.''

''Sure.''

''It is!'' She sat up straighter, angry over his righteous condescension. ''It wasn't my idea to come straight here from the airport. It was my father's. I would rather have gone home, checked my mail, watered my plants, slept in my own bed.''

''You're a big girl. Why didn't you?''

''I just told you. Father had made these arrangements. I couldn't demand that he change them.''

''How come?''

"Don't be obtuse. And why shouldn't I want this scar removed?" she cried angrily.

He glanced away, gnawing on the corner of his mustache. "You should. Of course you should."

Slumping with misery, Rusty settled back on her pillows and blotted her eyes with the corner of the sheet. "What's wrong with us? Why are we behaving like this?"

His head came back around. He wore a sad expression, as though her naiveté was to be pitied. "You shouldn't have to go through the rest of your life with that scar on your leg. I didn't mean to suggest that you should."

"I'm not talking about the scar, Cooper. I'm talking about everything. Why did you disappear at the airport last night?"

"I was there, in plain sight."

"But you weren't with me. I called out. Didn't you hear me?"

He didn't answer directly. "You didn't seem to be lacking attention."

"I wanted *your* attention. I had it until we stepped off the airplane."

"We could hardly do in that crowd what we were doing on the airplane." His eyes raked down her insultingly. "Besides, you were otherwise occupied." His mouth was set in a cynical smirk again. It looked unfamiliar now because Rusty hadn't seen that expression since they'd made love.

She was bewildered. Where and when had things between them gone wrong? "What did you expect to happen when we arrived in L.A.? We were and are news, Cooper. It wasn't my fault that the reporters were there. And my father. He was worried sick about me. He helped fund our rescue. Did you think he'd treat my return casually?"

"No." He raked his fingers through his hair. "But did it have to be such a goddamn sideshow? Why the big production? That coat, for instance."

"That was a very thoughtful thing for him to do."

It embarrassed her even now to recall her father's flamboyant gesture, but she sprang to defend him. The coat had been an expression of his love and joy at having her safely returned to him. That it had been a tasteless display of affluence wasn't the point. It was aggravating that Cooper couldn't see that and simply overlook her father's idiosyncrasies.

Cooper was moving around the room restlessly, as though he found it confining. His motions were abrupt and self-conscious, like those of a man ill at ease because his clothes didn't fit him well. "Look, I've got to go."

"Go? Now? Why? Where are you going?"

"Home."

"To Rogers Gap?"

"Yeah. Back to where I belong. I've got a ranch to look after. No telling what shape I'll find it in when I get there." Almost as an afterthought he glanced down at her right leg. "What about your leg? Is it going to be all right?"

"Eventually," she replied dully. *He's leaving. He's going. Away from me. Possibly forever.* "It's going to take a series of operations. The first of them is being done tomorrow."

"I hope I didn't do you more harm than good."

Her throat was tight with emotion. "You didn't."

"Well, I guess this is goodbye." He edged toward the door, trying not to make it look like an escape.

"Maybe sometime I can drive up to Rogers Gap and say hello. You never can tell when I might get up that way."

"Yeah, sure. That'd be great." His forced smile told her otherwise.

"How . . . how often do you come to L.A.?"

"Not very often," he was honest enough to say. "Well, so long, Rusty." Turning on the heels of his new shoes, he reached for the door handle.

"Cooper, wait!" He turned back. She was sitting up in bed, poised to chase after him if necessary. "Is this how it's going to end?"

He nodded curtly.

"It can't. Not after what we've been through together."

"It has to."

She shook her head so adamantly that her hair flew in every direction. "You don't fool me anymore. You're being insensitive to protect yourself. You're fighting it. I know you are. You want to hold me just as much as I want to hold you."

His jaw knotted as he ground his teeth together. At his sides, his hands formed fists. He warred with himself for several seconds before losing the battle.

He lunged across the room and pulled her roughly into his arms. Lowering himself onto the side of the bed, he hugged her against him tightly. With their arms wrapped around each other, they rocked together. His face was buried in the cinnamon-colored hair. Hers was nestled against his throat.

"Rusty, Rusty."

Thrilling to the anguish in his voice, she told him, "I couldn't go to sleep last night without a sedative. I kept listening for your breathing. I missed being held in your arms."

"I missed feeling your bottom against my lap."

He bent his head at the same moment she lifted hers and their mouths sought each other. Their kiss was desperate with desire. He plowed all ten fingers through her hair and held her head still while he made love to her open mouth with his tongue.

"I wanted you so bad last night, I thought I'd die," he groaned when they moved apart.

"You didn't want to be separated from me?"

"Not that way."

"Then why didn't you answer me when I called out to you at the airport? You heard me, didn't you?"

He looked chagrined, but nodded his head yes. "I couldn't be a performer in that circus, Rusty. I couldn't get away from there fast enough. When I came home from Nam, I was treated like a hero." He rubbed a strand of her hair between his fingers while he reflected on the painful past. "I didn't feel like a hero. I'd been living in hell. In the bowels of hell. Some of the things I'd had to do... Well, they weren't very heroic. They didn't deserve a spotlight and accolades. *I* didn't deserve them. I just wanted to be left alone so I could forget it."

He tilted her head back and pierced her with a silvery-gray stare. "I don't deserve or want a spotlight now, either. I did what was necessary to save our lives. Any man would have."

She touched his mustache lovingly. "Not any man, Cooper."

He shrugged away the compliment. "I've had more experience at surviving than most, that's all."

"You just won't take the credit you deserve, will you?"

"Is that what you want, Rusty? Credit for surviving?"

She thought of her father. She would have enjoyed hearing a few words of praise for her bravery. Instead he had talked about Jeff's Boy Scout escapade and told her how well her brother had reacted to a potentially fatal situation. Comparing her to Jeff hadn't been malicious on her father's part. He hadn't meant to point out how she fell short of Jeff's example. But that's what it had amounted to. What would it take, she wondered, to win her father's approval?

But for some reason, winning his approval didn't seem as important as it once had been. In fact, it didn't seem important at all. She was far more interested in what Cooper thought of her.

"I don't want credit, Cooper. I want..." She stopped short of saying "you." Instead, she laid her cheek against his chest. "Why didn't you come after me? Don't you want me anymore?"

He laid his hand over her breast and stroked it with his fingertips. "Yes, I want you." The need that made his voice sound like tearing cloth wasn't strictly physical.

Rusty perceived the depth of his need because she felt it too. It came out of an emptiness that gnawed at her when he wasn't there. It caused her own imploring inflection. "Then why?"

"I didn't follow you last night because I wanted to speed up the inevitable."

"The inevitable?"

"Rusty," he whispered, "this sexual dependency we feel for each other is textbook normal. It's common among people who have survived a crisis together. Even hostages and kidnap victims sometimes begin to feel an unnatural affection for their captors."

"I know all that. The Stockholm syndrome. But this is different."

"Is it?" His brows lowered skeptically. "A child loves whoever feeds him. Even a wild animal becomes friendly with someone who leaves food out for it. I took care of you. It was only human nature that you attach more significance—"

Suddenly and angrily, she pushed him away. Her hair was a vibrant halo of indignation, her eyes bright with challenge. "Don't you dare reduce what happened between us with psychological patter. It's crap. What I feel for you is real."

"I never said it wasn't real." Her feistiness excited him. He liked her best when she was defiant. He yanked her against him. "We've always had this going for us." He cupped her breast again and impertinently swept his thumb across the tip.

She wilted, murmuring a weak "Don't," which he disregarded. He continued to fondle her. Her eyes slid shut.

"We get close. I get hard. You get creamy. Every damned time. It happened the first time we laid eyes on each other in the airplane. Am I right?"

"Yes," she admitted.

"I wanted you then, before we ever left the ground."

"But you didn't even smile, or speak to me, or encourage me to speak to you."

"That's right."

"Why?" She couldn't take any more of his caresses and stay sensible. She moved his hand aside. "Tell me why."

"Because I guessed then what I know for fact now: we live worlds apart. And I'm not referring to geography."

"I know what you're talking about. You think I'm silly and superficial, like those friends of mine you just met. I'm not!"

She laid her hands on his forearms and appealed to him earnestly. "They irritated me, too. Do you know why? Because I saw myself—the way I used to be. I was judging them just as you did me when we first met.

"But please be tolerant toward them. Toward me. This is Beverly Hills. Nothing is real. There are areas of this city I couldn't relate to. The Gawrylows' cabin was beyond my realm of comprehension. But I'm changed. I really am. I'm not like them anymore."

"You never were, Rusty. I thought so. I know better now." He framed her face between his hands. "But that's the life you know. It's the crowd you run with. I couldn't. Wouldn't. Wouldn't even want to try. And you wouldn't belong in my life."

Hurt by the painful truth of what he was saying, she reacted with anger and threw off his hands. "Your life! What life? Shut away from the rest of the world? Alone and lonely? Using bitterness like an armor? You call that a life? You're right, Cooper. I couldn't live like that. The chip on my shoulder would be too heavy to bear."

His lower lip narrowed to a thin, harsh line beneath his mustache. She knew she'd hit home, but there was no victory in it.

"So there you have it," he said. "That's what I've been trying to tell you. In bed we're great, but we'd never make a life together."

"Because you're too damned stubborn to try! Have you even considered a compromise?"

"No. I don't want any part of this scene." He spread his hands wide to encompass the luxurious room and all that lay beyond the wide window.

Rusty aimed an accusing finger at him. "You're a snob."

"A snob?"

"Yes, a snob. You snub society because you feel superior to the masses. Superior and righteous because of the war and your imprisonment. Scornful because you see all that's wrong with the world. Locked up there on your solitary mountain, you play God by looking down on all of us who have the guts to tolerate each other despite our human failings."

"It's not like that," he ground out.

"Isn't it? Aren't you just a trifle self-righteous and judgmental? If there's so much wrong with our world, if you ridicule it that much, why don't you do something to change it? What are you accomplishing by withdrawing from it? Society didn't shun you. You shunned it."

"I didn't leave her until she—"

"*Her?*"

Cooper's face cleared of all emotion and became as wooden and smooth as a mask. The light in his eyes flickered out. They became hard and implacable.

Shocked, Rusty laid a hand against her pounding heart. *A woman was at the source of Cooper's cynicism.* Who? When? A hundred questions raced through her mind. She wanted to ask all of them, but for the time being she was occupied only with enduring his icy, hostile stare. He was furious with himself and with her. She had goaded him into resurrecting something he had wanted to keep dead and buried.

Her overactive heart pumped jealousy through her system as rich and red as her blood. Some woman had wielded enough influence over Cooper to alter the course of his life. He might have been a happy-go-lucky chap before this unnamed she-wolf got her claws into him. For his bitterness to be this lasting, she must have been some woman. He was still feeling her influence. Had he loved her that much? Rusty asked herself dismally.

A man like Cooper Landry wouldn't go long without having a woman. But Rusty had imagined his affairs to be fleeting, physical gratification and little else. It had never occurred to her that he'd been seriously involved with someone. But he had been, and her departure from his life had been wrenching and painful.

"Who was she?"

"Forget it."

"Did you meet her before you went to Vietnam?"

"Drop it, Rusty."

"Did she marry someone else while you were a prisoner?"

"I said to forget it."

"Did you love her?"

"Look, she was good in the sack, but not as hot as you, okay? Is that what you're itching to know—how the two of you compare? Well, let's see. She wasn't a redhead, so she lacked your fiery spirit. She had a great body, but it didn't come close to yours."

"Stop it!"

"Her breasts were fuller, but no more responsive. Nipples? Larger and darker. Thighs? Hers were just as smooth, but not nearly as strong as yours." He stared at the spot where hers came together. "Yours can squeeze the life out of a man."

She covered her mouth to trap a sob of anguish and outrage. Her breath was coming as hard and fast as his. They glared at each other with an animosity as fierce as the passion they'd shared while making love.

It was into that seething atmosphere that Bill Carlson made his inopportune entrance. "Rusty?"

She jumped at her father's voice. "Father!" His name came out as a gusty exhalation. "Come...good morning. This..." She discovered that her mouth was dry and the hand she raised to gesture toward Cooper was trembling. "This is Cooper Landry."

"Ah, Mr. Landry." Carlson extended his hand. Cooper shook it. He did so firmly, but with a noticeable lack of enthusiasm and a great deal of dislike. "I've had several people trying to track you down." Cooper offered no explanations as to his whereabouts overnight, so Carlson blustered on. "I wanted to thank you for saving my daughter's life."

"No thanks is necessary."

"Of course it is. She means the world to me. The way she tells it, you meant the difference between her life and death. In fact she's the one who urged me to locate you last night."

Cooper glanced down at Rusty, then back at Carlson, who was reaching into the breast pocket of his suit coat. He withdrew a white envelope. "Rusty wanted to say thank-you in a special way."

He handed the envelope to Cooper. Cooper opened it and glanced inside. He stared at the contents for a long moment before lifting his eyes to Rusty. They were frigid with contempt. One corner of his mustache curled into a nasty smile. Then, in one vicious motion, he ripped the envelope and the cashier's check inside in half. He tossed the two halves into the valley of her thighs.

"Thanks all the same, Miss Carlson, but on our last night together I was paid in full for my services."

Twelve

~~~ ❧❧❧ ~~~

Turning back to his daughter after watching Cooper storm from the room, Carlson said, "What an unpleasant individual."

"Father, how could you have offered him money?" Rusty cried in dismay.

"I thought you wanted and expected me to."

"Whatever gave you that impression? Cooper... Mr. Landry... He is a proud man. Do you think he saved my life for profit?"

"I wouldn't be surprised. He's an unlikeable character from what I've heard of him."

"You asked around?"

"Certainly. As soon as he was identified as the man with you when you were rescued. Being marooned with him couldn't have been easy for you."

"We had our differences," Rusty replied with a rueful smile. "But he could have deserted me and saved himself at any time."

"He wasn't about to. Not when there might be a reward for saving you."

"He didn't know that."

"He's clever. He deduced that I'd spare no expense to rescue you if you were still alive. Maybe he was offended by the amount." He picked up the ripped check and studied it. "I thought it was a generous reward, but maybe he's greedier than I suspected."

Rusty closed her eyes and let her head fall back onto the pillows in defeat. "Father, he doesn't want your money. He's all too glad to be rid of me."

"The feeling is mutual." Carlson sat down on the edge of her bed. "However, it's unfortunate that we can't capitalize on your mishap."

Her eyes came open again. "'Capitalize'? What in the world are you talking about?"

"Don't jump to conclusions until you've heard me out."

She'd already jumped to several conclusions, none of which were to her liking. "You're not referring to a movie are you?" When her friend had mentioned the idea, she'd been appalled.

Carlson patted her hand. "Nothing so crass, my dear. We've got more style than that."

"Then, what?"

"One of your problems has always been your lack of vision, Rusty." Affectionately, he cuffed her on the chin. "Your brother would have immediately seen the enterprising possibilities this situation has opened up to us."

As usual, the comparison to her brother left her feeling inferior. "Like what?"

Patiently Carlson explained. "You've made a name for yourself in real estate. And not by riding my coattails, either. I might have placed a few opportunities in your path, but you took advantage of them."

"Thank you, but what is this leading to, Father?"

"In your own right, you're something of a celebrity in this town." She shook her head scoffingly. "I mean it. Your name is well-known in important circles. And in recent days your name and picture have appeared in newspapers and on television. You've been made into a sort of folk heroine.

That kind of free publicity is as good as money in the bank. I propose that we use this disaster to our advantage."

On the verge of panic, Rusty wet her lips. "You mean promote the fact that I survived an airplane crash to generate business?"

"What could it hurt?"

"You must be joking!" He wasn't. There was nothing in either his expression or demeanor to indicate that he was only fooling. She bowed her head, shaking it. "No, Father. Absolutely not. The idea doesn't appeal to me at all."

"Don't say no right away," he said patronizingly. "I'll get our advertising agency to work up a few ideas. I promise not to move on any of them until you've been consulted and I have your approval."

He was suddenly a stranger to her. The voice, the face, the polished manner—all were familiar. But she didn't really know the heart and soul of the man behind the veneer. She didn't know him at all.

"I'll never approve. That plane crash killed five people. *Five men*, Father. I met their families—their grieving widows and children and parents. I talked to them. I offered them my heartfelt condolences. To turn their misfortune to my own advantage—" she shuddered with repugnance "—no, Father. That's something I can't do."

Bill Carlson pulled on his lower lip, as he always did when he was deep in thought. "Very well. For the time being, we'll table that idea. But another has occurred to me."

He pressed both her hands between his. Rusty got the distinct impression that she was being restrained as a precautionary measure, as if what he was about to suggest would precipitate a fit.

"As I've told you, I had Mr. Landry thoroughly checked out yesterday. He owns a large ranch in a beautiful area of the Sierras."

"So he's said."

"No one has developed the land around it."

"That's the beauty of it. The region has remained virtually untouched. I fail to see what that has to do with us."

"Rusty, what's the matter with you?" he asked teasingly. "Have you become a conservationist after two weeks in the woods? You're not going to circulate petitions accusing builders of raping the land every time a new tract of homes goes up, are you?"

"Of course not, Father." His teasing bordered on criticism. There was a trace of reproach behind his smile. Rusty didn't want to disappoint him, but she hastened to eliminate any ideas he was nursing regarding Cooper and enterprise. "I hope you aren't considering any commercial development in Mr. Landry's part of the state. I can promise you, he wouldn't welcome it. In fact he'd fight you."

"Are you sure? How does the idea of a partnership strike you?"

She stared at him incredulously. "A partnership between Cooper and me?"

Carlson nodded. "He's a war veteran. That's very promotable. You survived a plane crash together and endured unbelievable hardships in the Canadian wilds before you were rescued. That, too, has high drama and marketability. The buying public will eat it up."

Everyone, even her own father, seemed to regard the plane crash and the life-threatening experiences following it as a grand adventure, a melodrama starring Cooper and herself in the principal roles—*The African Queen* set in a different time and locale.

Carlson was too caught up in his plans to notice Rusty's negative reaction to them. "I could make a few calls and by dark today put together a group of investors who would love to build condos in that area. There's a ski lift at this Rogers Gap, but it's ill-managed. We'd modernize and improve that and build around it.

"We'd bring Landry into it, of course. That would smooth the way with the other locals. He's not a mixer, but my investigators reported back that he wields a lot of influence. His name means something up there. Once the condos are under construction, you could start selling them. We'd all stand to make millions."

Her objections to his proposal were too many to enumerate, so she didn't even try. She had to shoot down the idea before it even took off. "Father, in case you didn't get the message a minute ago, Mr. Landry isn't interested in making money." She picked up the two halves of the check and shook them in front of his face as a reminder. "Making money off a real-estate venture will be anathema to him. He loves that country up there. He wants it left alone, kept the way it is, unspoiled by land developers. He loves the way nature developed it."

"He might play lip service to that Walden Pond philosophy," her father remarked skeptically. "But every man has his price, Rusty."

"Not Cooper Landry."

Carlson stroked his daughter's cheek. "Your naiveté is endearing."

The twinkle in his eyes was familiar and alarming. It indicated that he was on the scent of a Big Deal. In a community of capitalist sharks, her father was among those with the most deadly jaws. She grasped his hand and squeezed it hard. "Promise me, *promise*, that you won't do this. You don't know him."

"And you do?" The glint in his eyes dimmed and the lids narrowed. Gradually she released his hands. He backed away from her suspiciously, as though he'd just learned that what was confining her to the hospital bed might be contagious.

"I haven't posed any questions that might have been embarrassing for you to answer, Rusty. I wanted to spare us both that. However, I'm not blind. Landry is almost a caricature of the macho male. He's the kind of belligerent loner that women swoon over and fancy themselves able to tame."

He cupped her chin and tilted it up so he could read her eyes. "Surely you're too intelligent to fall for a pair of broad shoulders and a broody disposition. I hope that you didn't form any sort of emotional attachment to this man. That would be most unfortunate."

Unwittingly her father had echoed Cooper's theory—that their feelings were due largely to their dependency on each other. "Under the circumstances, wouldn't forming an attachment to him be natural?"

"Yes. But the circumstances have changed. You're no longer isolated with Landry in the wilderness; you're home. You have a life here that mustn't be jeopardized by a juvenile infatuation. Whatever happened up there," he said, hitching his perfectly groomed head in the direction of the window, "is over and should be forgotten."

Cooper had said as much, too. But it wasn't over. Not by a long shot. And it couldn't be forgotten. What she felt for him wasn't going to weaken and eventually die from lack of nurturing. She hadn't formed a psychological dependency on him that would disappear as she gradually resumed her previous life.

She'd fallen in love. Cooper was no longer her provider and protector, but something so much more. He was the man she loved. Whether they were together or apart, that would never change.

"Don't worry, Father. I know exactly what I feel for Mr. Landry." That was the truth. Let her father draw his own conclusions.

"Good girl," Carlson said, patting her shoulder. "I knew I could count on you to come out of this stronger and smarter than ever. Just like your brother, you've got your head on straight."

She had been home for a week after spending almost a week in the hospital recovering from the first operation on her shin. The scar didn't look much better than it had before the surgery, but the doctor had assured her that after the series of operations, it would be virtually undetectable.

Aside from a little tenderness in her leg, she felt perfectly fine. The bandages had been removed, but the surgeon had advised her to keep clothing off the leg and to continue to use crutches for support.

She had regained the few pounds she'd lost after the plane crash. She spent a half hour or so each day lying in the sun on the redwood deck of her pool to restore her light tan. Her friends had been true to their promise, and since she couldn't easily get to a salon, they'd brought the salon to her. A hairdresser had trimmed and conditioned and restored her hair to its usual glossy sheen. A manicurist had resculptured her nails. She'd also massaged a pound of cream into Rusty's dry, rough hands.

As she watched the manicurist smoothing away the scaly redness, Rusty thought about the laundry she had washed by hand, then hung up to dry on a crude outdoor clothesline. It had always been a contest to see if the clothes would dry before they froze. It hadn't been all that bad. Not really. Or did memory always make things seem better than they actually had been?

That could be applied to everything. Had Cooper's kisses really been that earth-moving? Had his arms and whispered words been that comforting in the darkest hours of the night? If not, why did she wake up frequently, yearning for his nearness, his warmth?

She had never been so lonely.

Not that she was ever alone—at least not for prolonged periods of time. Friends dropped in to bring trifling presents that would hopefully amuse her because she seemed so morose. Physically she was coming along nicely, but her spirits hadn't bounced back yet.

Friends and associates were worried about her. Since the airplane crash, she was not her usual, jovial self at all. They kept her stuffed with everything from Godiva chocolates to carry-out tacos to covered dishes from Beverly Hills's finest restaurants, prepared especially for her by the head chefs who knew personally what her favorite foods were.

She had lots of time on her hands, but she was never idle. Her father's prediction had come true: she was suddenly a celebrity real-estate agent. Everybody in town who wanted to sell or buy sought her advice on the fluctuating market trends. Each day she took calls from prospective clients, including an impressive number of movie and television people. Her ear grew sore from the hours spent on the telephone. Ordinarily she would have leaped over the moon for a client list of this caliber. Instead she was plagued with an uncharacteristic ennui that she couldn't explain or overcome.

Her father hadn't said any more about developing the area around Rogers Gap. She hoped that idea was officially a dead issue. He came by her house each day, ostensibly to check on her progress. But Rusty suspected, perhaps unfairly, that her father was more interested in quickly harvesting this crop of new business than in her recovery.

The lines around his mouth became tense with impatience, and his jocular encouragement for her to get back to work was beginning to sound forced. Even though she was following doctor's orders, she knew that she was stretching her recovery time for as long as she could. She was determined, however, not to return to her office until she felt good and ready.

On this particular afternoon, she groaned in dread when the doorbell pealed through her house. Her father had called earlier to say that because of a business commitment he wouldn't be able to come by that day. Rusty had been relieved. She loved her father but had welcomed the break from his daily visit, which never failed to exhaust her.

Obviously his meeting had been canceled and she wasn't going to get a reprieve after all.

Hooking her arms over her crutches, she hobbled down the hallway toward her front door. She'd lived in this house for three years. It was a small, white stucco building with a red tile roof, very southern California in design, tucked into an undercliff and shrouded with vividly blooming bougain- villea. Rusty had fallen in love with it the minute she saw it.

Propping herself up on one crutch, she unlatched and opened the door.

Cooper said nothing. Neither did she. They just stared at each other for a long time before she silently moved aside. He stepped through the arched doorway. Rusty closed the door and turned to face him.

"Hi."

"Hi."

"What are you doing here?"

"I came to see about your leg." He looked down at her shin. She stuck it out for his inspection. "It doesn't look much better."

"It will." His skeptical gaze moved up to meet hers. "The doctor has promised it will," she said defensively.

He still seemed doubtful, but let the subject drop. He took in his surroundings, pivoting slowly. "I like your house."

"Thank you."

"It's a lot like mine."

"Really?"

"Mine looks sturdier, maybe. Not decorated as fancy. But they're similar. Large rooms. Lots of windows."

She felt she had recovered enough to move. Upon seeing him, her one good knee, which she relied on for support, had threatened to buckle beneath her. Now, she felt confi- dent enough to move forward and indicated for him to fol- low her. "Come on in. Would you like something to drink?"

"Something soft."

"Lemonade?"

"Fine."

"It'll only take a minute to make."

"Don't bother."

"No bother. I was thirsty for some anyway."

She maneuvered herself through the dining room and into the kitchen at the back of the house. He followed. "Sit down." She nodded toward the butcher-block table that formed an island in the center of the kitchen and moved toward the refrigerator.

"Can I help?" he asked.

"No thanks. I've had practice."

She turned her head, ready with a smile, and caught him staring at the backs of her legs. Thinking that she was going to be alone all day, she'd dressed in a ragged pair of cutoffs and hadn't bothered with shoes. The tails of a chambray shirt were knotted at her waist. She'd pulled her hair up into a high, scraggly ponytail. The effect was a Beverly Hills version of Daisy Mae.

Caught staring at her smooth, bare legs, Cooper shifted guiltily in his chair. "Does it hurt?"

"What?"

"Your leg."

"Oh. No. Well, some. Off and on. I'm not supposed to walk or drive or anything like that yet."

"Have you gone back to work?"

Her ponytail swished against her neck as she shook her head. "I'm conducting some business here by telephone. The messenger services love me. I've kept them busy. But I haven't quite felt up to dressing and going to the office."

She took a can of lemonade concentrate out of the refrigerator where she'd had it thawing. "Have you been busy since you got home?"

She poured the thick pink concentrate into a pitcher and added a bottle of chilled club soda. When some of it splashed on the back of her hand, she raised it to her mouth and sucked it off. That's when she turned with the question still in her eyes.

Like a hawk, Cooper was watching every move. He was staring at her mouth. Slowly, she lowered her hand and turned back to her task. Her hands were trembling as she took glasses down out of the cabinet and filled them with ice cubes.

"Yeah, I've been busy."

"How was everything when you got back?"

"Okay. A neighbor had been feeding my livestock. Guess he would have gone on doing that indefinitely if I'd never turned up."

"That's a good neighbor." She had wanted to inject some levity into the conversation, but her voice sounded bright and brittle. It didn't fit the atmosphere, which was as heavy and oppressive as a New Orleans summer. The air was sultry; she couldn't draw enough of it into her lungs.

"Don't you have any help running your ranch?" she asked.

"Off and on. Temporary hands. Most of them are ski bums who only work to support their habit. When they run out of money they work a few days so they can buy lift tickets and food. The system works for both them and me."

"Because you don't like a lot of people around."

"Right."

An abysmal depression came over her. She staved it off by asking, "Do you ski?"

"Some. Do you?"

"Yes. Or I did." She glanced down at her leg. "I may have to sit this season out."

"Maybe not. Since the bone wasn't broken."

"Maybe."

And that, it seemed, was all they had to say. By tacit agreement, they ended the inane small talk and did what they really wanted to do—look at each other.

His hair had been cut, but was still unfashionably long. She liked the way it brushed the collar of his casual shirt. His jaw and chin were smoothly shaven, but if one single hair in his mustache had been altered, she couldn't tell it. The lower lip beneath it was as stern and unyielding as ever. If anything, the grooves bracketing his mouth looked deeper, making his face appear more unrelievedly masculine. She couldn't help but wonder what particular worry had carved those lines deeper.

His clothes weren't haute couture, but he would turn heads on Rodeo Drive and be a refreshing change from the dapper dressers. Blue jeans still did more for a male physique than any other garment ever sewn together. They did more for Cooper's body than for most. Of course, there was more to work with—so much more that the bulging denim between his thighs made Rusty's stomach flutter.

His cotton shirt was stretched over a chest she still dreamed about. The sleeves had been rolled back to reveal his strong forearms. He had carried a brown leather bomber jacket in with him. It was now draped over the back of his chair, forgotten. Indeed, he seemed to have forgotten everything except the woman standing only a few feet, yet seemingly light-years, away from him.

His eyes tracked down her body, stripping her as they went. As though he were actually peeling away layer after layer of clothing, her skin began to burn with fever. By the time his eyes paused on the uneven, stringy hems of her cutoffs, where the soft threads tickled her bare thighs, Rusty was warm and moist.

His gaze moved back up to her face and the desire he saw registered there reflected his own. His eyes were like magnets drawing her into their field. On her crutches, she closed the distance between them, never breaking their stare. He didn't either. As she drew nearer, he had to tilt his head back to maintain eye contact. It seemed to take a lifetime but was actually only a few seconds before she stood directly in front of him, leaning on her crutches for support.

She said, "I can't believe you're really here."

Groaning, he lowered his head and pressed it hard against her breasts. "Rusty. Damn you. I couldn't stay away."

Overwhelming emotions caused her eyes to close. Her head tipped forward in total surrender to her love for this complex man. She whispered his name.

He folded his arms around her waist and nuzzled his face in the soft, fragrant valley between her breasts. His hands opened wide over her back, drawing her body closer even though she couldn't move her feet.

"I've missed you," she admitted hoarsely. She didn't expect him to make a similar confession, and he didn't. But the ardency of his embrace was unspoken evidence of how much he'd missed her. "I'd hear your voice and turn, expecting you to be there. Or I'd start to say something to you before I realized you weren't there."

"God, you smell good." Openmouthed, he gnawed on the soft inner curves of her breasts, catching cloth and all between his strong, white teeth.

"You smell like the mountains," she told him, kissing his hair.

"I've got to have—" he was frantically untying the knot at her waist "—just one—" it came undone and he ripped the buttons apart "—bite." His mouth fastened on the fleshy part of her breast, which was overflowing the cup of her brassiere.

At the first hot contact of his mouth with her skin, she arched her back and moaned. Her knuckles turned white where they gripped the handles of her crutches. She longed to drop them and plunge her fingers into his hair. She felt it dusting her skin when he turned his head and kissed her other breast. He took gentle love bites through the sheer cups of her brassiere and delicately sipped at the tips.

She released a keening sound much like a sob. It was both frustrating and thrilling not to have the use of her hands. The sense of helplessness was titillating. "Cooper," she gasped imploringly.

He reached around her and unhooked her bra strap, working it down as far as it would go before the straps got caught in her sleeves. But that was sufficient. He had completely uncovered her. His eyes drank their fill before his lips surrounded one taut, pink crest and drew it into his mouth. He sucked it lovingly, then sponged the very tip of it with his tongue before drying it with his mustache. His whole face moved over her breasts, rubbing them with cheek and chin and mouth and nose and brow. Rusty, leaning precariously on her crutches, chanted his name with religious fervor.

"Tell me what you want. Anything," he said huskily. "Tell me."

"I want you."

"Woman, you've got me. What do you want?"

"To touch. To be touched."

"Where?"

"Cooper..."

"*Where?*"

"You know where," she cried.

He brusquely unsnapped her cutoffs and slid down the zipper. Her brief panties did little more than cover the triangle of curls. He wanted to smile, but his face was too set with passion, so he couldn't. He merely growled his approval as he pulled down the panties along with her cutoffs. He kissed the gingery down.

Rusty's strength deserted her. She let go of the crutches. They clattered to the floor. She fell forward slightly, breaking her fall by placing her hands on Cooper's shoulders. As she did so, he slid off the seat of the chair and sank to his knees in front of her.

She caught her lower lip between her teeth to keep from screaming with pleasure as he parted her dewy flesh with his thumbs and buried his tongue in the softness.

He didn't stop there. He didn't stop at all. Not after the first wave of ecstasy swept over her. Not even after the second had claimed her. He didn't stop until her body was glistening with a fine sheen of perspiration, until tendrils of russet hair were clinging damply to her temples and cheeks and neck, until she was quivering with aftershocks.

Only then did he rise to his feet and take her in his arms. "Which way?" His face was softer than she'd ever seen it as it bent over hers. The guarded chill was no longer in his eyes. In its place were sparks of some strong emotion she dared to hope was love.

She raised her hand and pointed in the general direction of the bedroom. He found it without difficulty. Since she'd spent a great deal of time in that room recently, it had a homey, lived-in aspect that apparently appealed to him. He smiled as he carried her through the doorway. Gently he stood her on her left leg and threw back the covers on the bed. "Lie down."

She did, watching as he went into the bathroom. She heard water running. Moments later, he came back carrying a damp cloth. He didn't say a word, but his eyes spoke volumes as he drew her into a sitting position and eased off her blouse. Removing her brassiere only required sliding the straps off her arms. She sat before him totally naked, and marvelously unashamed.

He ran the cool, damp cloth over her arms and shoulders and around her neck. After he had eased her back onto the pillows, he raised her arms over her head and washed the shallow cups of her armpits. She purred in surprised satisfaction; he ducked his head and kissed her moaning mouth.

He moved the cloth over her chest, then her breasts. Her nipples drew up again and he smiled. He touched a rosy whisker-burn on her tender flesh.

"I always seem to leave a mark on you," he said with a trace of regret. "I'm sorry."

"I'm not."

His eyes glowed hotly as they moved down her stomach to her navel. He licked the sweat out of it before bathing the rest of her abdomen with the cloth. Then he washed her legs, being careful of her new scar. "Turn over."

Rusty gazed up at him inquisitively, but she turned over on her stomach and rested her cheek on her stacked hands. Leisurely, he washed her entire back with the cloth. At the small of her back, he paused, then ran the cloth over the cheeks of her bottom.

"Hmm," she sighed.

"That's for me to say."

"Go right ahead."

"Hmm." He spent far more time than was necessary to wash away any perspiration. He sponged the backs of her legs all the way down to the soles of her feet, which he discovered were ticklish. On his way back up, he lingered to taste the backs of her knees.

"Just relax a minute," he told her as he left the bed to undress.

"Easy for you to say. You haven't been subjected to heavy petting."

"Brace yourself, baby. You've got more coming."

Rusty wasn't quite braced for him to lie naked and warm along the length of her back. She drew in a jagged breath and shivered with the startling impact of his hair-roughened skin against the smoothness of her back. His opened thighs sandwiched hers. Her bottom fit snugly against his sex. It was solid with desire and as smooth as velvet-sheathed steel as it rubbed against her.

He covered the backs of her hands with his palms, interlacing their fingers, and used his nose to move aside her ponytail so his lips could get to her ear.

"I can't do anything for wanting you," he whispered gruffly. "Can't work. Sleep. Eat. There's no comfort in my getaway house anymore. You ruined it for me. The mountains aren't beautiful anymore. Your face has blinded me to them."

He rocked against her and made an upward thrust, settling himself more firmly against her. "I thought I'd work you out of my system, but so far I've failed. I even went to Vegas and bought a woman for the evening. When we got to the hotel room, I just sat there staring at her and drinking, trying to work up desire. She practiced some of her fanciest tricks, but I felt nothing. I couldn't do it. Didn't want to. Finally I sent her home before she became as disgusted with me as I was with myself."

He buried his face in the back of her neck. "You redheaded witch, what'd you do to me up there? I was fine, understand? Fine, until you came along with your wet-satin mouth and silky skin. Now my life isn't worth a damn. All I can think about, see, hear, touch, smell, taste, is you. *You.*"

He rolled her over and pinned her beneath him. His mouth slanted against hers. He parted her lips with his hard, invasive, possessive tongue. "I've got to have you. Got to. Now."

He ground his body against hers as though to meld them into one. Nudging her knees apart and giving one long, smooth, plunging motion of his hips, he delved into the giving folds of her womanhood.

Groaning with pleasure, he lowered his head to her chest. He called upon every prince of Heaven and hell to release him from his torment. His breath fell hot and labored on her breasts and when the nipples responded, he loved them with his mouth.

His skin was flushed. It burned her hands as she moved them over the rippling, supple muscles of his back and hips. She cupped his hard buttocks and drew him deeper yet. He moaned her name and brought their mouths together again. His kiss was carnally symbolic.

Rusty didn't feel vanquished by his virile power, though she could well have. On the contrary, she felt free and unfettered, strong enough to fly, to soar to the limits of the universe. Just as her body was opened to him, so was her heart and soul. Love poured out of them abundantly. He must feel it. He must know.

She was sure he did, because he was saying her name in cadence to his thrusts. His voice was raw with emotion. But a heartbeat before he lost his ability to reason, she felt him about to withdraw.

"No! Don't you dare."

"Yes, Rusty, yes."

"I love you, Cooper." She crossed her ankles at the small of his back. "I want you. All of you."

"No, no," he groaned in misery as well as ecstasy.

"I love you."

Clenching his teeth and baring them, he threw his head back and surrendered to orgasm with a long, low, primal groan that worked its way up from the bottom of his soul. He filled this woman who loved him with his hot, rich seed.

Thirteen

Sweat dripped from his face. He was drenched in it. His body hair was curled with it. He collapsed atop her. She held him tightly. Her maternal instinct asserted itself; she wanted to cuddle him like a child.

It was an endless forever before he regained enough strength to move, but neither was in a hurry for him to leave her. Finally, he rolled away from her and lay on his back, replete. Rusty gazed at his beloved face. His eyes were closed. The lines on either side of his stern mouth had relaxed considerably since he'd come through her front door.

She laid her head on his chest and smoothed her hand over his stomach, combing through the crinkled, damp hair. "It wasn't just me you withdrew from, was it?" Somehow she knew that this was the first time in a long time that Cooper had completed the love act.

"No."

"It wasn't because I might get pregnant, was it?"

"No, it wasn't."

"Why did you make love that way, Cooper?" He opened his eyes. She stared down into them. They were guarded. He, who she had assumed was fearless, was afraid of her, a naked woman, lying helplessly beside him, utterly fascinated by him and under his spell. What threat could she possibly represent?

"Why did you impose that kind of discipline on yourself?" she asked gently. "Tell me."

He stared at the ceiling. "There was a woman."

Ah, *the* woman, Rusty thought.

"Her name was Melody. I met her soon after I got back from Nam. I was messed up. Bitter. Angry. She—" he made a helpless gesture "—she put things back into perspective, gave focus to my life. I was attending college on the GI bill. We were going to get married as soon as I finished. I thought that everything was going well for us. It was."

He closed his eyes again and Rusty knew he was approaching the difficult part of the story. "Then she got pregnant. Without my knowledge, she had an abortion." His hands curled into fists and his jaw grew rigid with fury. Rusty actually jumped when he turned to her abruptly.

"She killed my baby. After all the death I'd seen, she..." His breathing became so harsh that Rusty was afraid he'd go into cardiac arrest. She laid a comforting hand on his chest and softly spoke his name.

"I'm so sorry, Cooper, darling. I'm so sorry."

He breathed deeply, until he had filled his lungs with sufficient air. "Yeah."

"You've been angry at her ever since."

"At first. But then I came to hate her too much to be angry at her. I'd shared so many confidences with her. She knew what was going on inside my head, how I felt about things. She'd urged me to talk about the prison camp and everything that happened there."

"Did you feel that she abused that confidence?"

"Abused and betrayed it." With the pad of his thumb, he caught a tear rolling down Rusty's cheek and swept it away. "She'd held me in her arms while I cried like a baby, telling her about buddies I'd seen...killed," he finished in a hoarse whisper.

"I'd told her about the hell I went through to escape and then what I did to survive until I was rescued. Even after that, after I'd described how I'd lain in a heap of rotting, stinking corpses to keep from being recaptured—"

"Cooper, don't." Rusty reached for him and drew him close.

"She went out and had our baby destroyed. After I'd seen babies torn apart, probably had killed some myself, she—"

"Shh, shh. Don't."

Rusty cradled his head against her breasts and crooned to him as she smoothed his hair. Tears blurred her vision. She felt his suffering, and wished she could take it all on herself. She kissed the crown of his head. "I'm sorry, my darling. So very sorry."

"I left Melody. I moved to the mountains, bought my livestock, built my house."

And a wall around your heart, Rusty thought sadly. No wonder he'd spurned society. He'd been betrayed twice— once by his country, which didn't want to be reminded of its mistake, and then by the woman he had loved and trusted.

"You didn't take a chance on any woman getting pregnant by you again."

He worked his head free and looked into her eyes. "That's right. Not until now." He placed his hands on either side of her face. "Until you. And I couldn't stop myself from filling you." He kissed her hard. "I wanted it to last forever."

Smiling, she turned her head and bit the meaty part of his hand just below his thumb. "I thought it was going to."

He smiled, too, looking boyishly pleased with himself. "Really?"

Rusty laughed. "Really."

He slid his hand between her thighs and worked his fingers through the nest of russet curls before intimately palming her sex. "I left a special mark on you this time. You're carrying part of me inside you." He raised his head off the pillow and brushed his mouth across her kiss-swollen lips.

"That's what I wanted. I wouldn't have let you leave me this time."

"Oh, no?" There was an arrogant, teasing glint in his eyes. "What would you have done?"

"I would have given you one hell of a fight. That's how much I wanted you. All of you."

He pulled her lower lip between his teeth and worried it deliciously with his tongue. "One of the things I like most about you . . ." His mouth went for her neck.

"Yes?"

"Is that you always look like you've just been royally . . ." He finished his sentence with a gutter word that only he could make sound sexy.

"Cooper!" Pretending to be offended, Rusty sat back on her heels and placed her hands on her hips.

He laughed. The wonderful, rare sound of his laughter was so encouraging that she assumed an even prissier expression. He only laughed harder. His laughter was real, not tainted by cynicism. She wanted to draw it around her like a blanket. She wanted to bask in it as one would the first hot day of summer. She'd made Cooper Landry laugh. That was no small feat, particularly in the past few years. Probably few could lay claim to having made this man laugh.

His mouth was still split into a wide grin beneath his mustache. He mimicked her in an old maid's whine. "Cooper!" Piqued by his imitation of her, she smacked his bare thigh. "Hey, it's not my fault that you've got bedroom hair and smoky brown eyes." He reached out and ran his thumb along her lower lip. "I can't help it if your mouth always looks recently kissed and begging for more; if your breasts are always aquiver."

"'Aquiver'?" she asked breathlessly as he cupped one.

"Hmm. Is it my fault that your nipples are always primed and ready?"

"In fact it is."

That, he liked. Smiling, he plucked at the dusky pearl, rolling it gently between his fingers.

"But primed and ready for what, Cooper?"

He leaned forward and, using his lips and tongue, demonstrated.

Rusty felt the familiar sensations unwinding in her midsection like a spool of silk ribbon. Sighing, she clasped his head and pushed it away from her. He looked at her in bewilderment, but didn't resist as she pressed him back against the pillows. "What are we doing?" he asked.

"I'm going to make love to you for a change."

"I thought you just did."

She shook her tousled head. At some point her ponytail had come down. "You made love to me."

"What's the difference?"

Smiling a feline smile, her eyes full of promise, she stretched out alongside him and began nibbling his neck. "Wait and see."

In the peaceful aftermath, they lay together, their arms and legs entangled. "I thought only hookers knew how to do that right." His voice was still scratchy from crying out her name, and he barely had the energy to strum her spine with his fingertips.

"Did I do it right?"

He tilted his head back and gazed down at the woman who lay sprawled across his chest. "Don't you know?"

Her eyes were glazed with love as she looked up at him and shook her head with shy uncertainty.

"That's the first time you ever . . . ?" She nodded yes. He hissed a soft curse and drew her up for a gentle, loving kiss. "Yeah. You did it just fine," he said with a trace of humor when he finally released her lips. "Just fine."

After a long silence, Rusty asked him, "What kind of family life did you have?"

"Family life?" As he collected his thoughts, he absently rubbed his leg against her left one, ever careful not to bump the sore one. "It's been so long ago I barely remember. Practically all I remember of my dad was that he went to work every day. He was a salesman. His job finally caused a massive heart attack that killed him instantly. I was still in elementary school."

"Mother never got over being mad at him for dying prematurely and leaving her a widow. She never got over being mad at me for...existing, I guess. Anyway, all I meant to her was a liability. She had to work to support us."

"She never remarried?"

"No."

His mother had probably blamed her blameless son for that, too. Rusty could paint in the numbered spaces and get the complete picture. Cooper had grown up unloved. It was little wonder that now, when a hand was extended to him in kindness, he bit it instead of accepting it. He didn't believe in human kindness and love. He'd never experienced them. His personal relationships had been fouled with pain, disillusionment, and betrayal.

"I joined the Marines as soon as I graduated from high school. Mother died during my first year in Nam. Breast cancer. She was the kind of woman who was too stubborn to have that lump checked before it was too late."

Rusty stroked his chin with her thumbnail, occasionally dipping it into the vertical cleft. She was filled with remorse for the lonely, unloved child he'd been. Such unhappiness. By comparison she'd had it so easy.

"My mother died, too."

"And then you lost your brother."

"Yes. Jeff."

"Tell me about him."

"He was terrific," she said with an affectionate smile. "Everybody liked him. He was friendly—the kind of person who never met a stranger. People were automatically drawn to him. He had outstanding leadership qualities. He could make people laugh. He could do everything.''

"You've been reminded of that often enough.''

Quickly her head popped up. "What's that supposed to mean?''

Cooper seemed to weigh the advisability of pursuing this conversation, but apparently decided in favor of it. "Doesn't your father continually hold your brother up as an example for you to follow?''

"Jeff had a promising future in real estate. My father wants that for me, too.''

"But is it *your* future he wants for you, or your brother's future?''

She disengaged herself and swung her legs over the side of the bed. "I don't know what you mean.''

Cooper caught a handful of her hair to keep her from leaving the bed. He came up on his knees behind her where she sat on the edge of it. "Like hell you don't, Rusty. Everything you've said about your father and brother leads me to believe that you're expected to fill Jeff's shoes.''

"My father only wants me to do well.''

"What *he* considers well. You're a beautiful, intelligent woman. A loving daughter. You have a career, and you're successful. Isn't that enough for him?''

"No! I mean, yes, of course it's enough. It's just that he wants me to live up to my potential.''

"Or Jeff's.'' She tried to move away, but he held her back by her shoulders. "Like that hunting trip to Great Bear Lake.''

"I told you that that was my idea, not Father's.''

"But why did you feel that it was necessary to go? Why was it your responsibility to uphold the tradition he had shared with Jeff? You only went because you thought it might please your father.''

"What's wrong with that?''

"Nothing. If it was strictly a gesture of self-sacrifice, of love. But by going, I think you set out to prove something to him; I think that you wanted your father to see that you're as marvelous as Jeff was."

"Well, I failed."

"That's my point!" he shouted. "You don't like hunting and fishing. So what? Why should that make you a failure?"

She managed to wrest herself free. Once she was on her feet, she spun around to face him. "You don't understand, Cooper."

"Obviously I don't. I don't see why being exactly what you are isn't enough for your father. Why do you continually have to prove yourself to him? He lost his son: unfortunate; tragic. But he's still got a daughter. And he's trying to shape her into something she isn't. You're both obsessed with Jeff. Whatever else he did, I'm fairly sure he didn't walk on water."

Rusty aimed an accusing finger at him. "You're a fine one to preach about other people's obsessions. You nurse your hurt obsessively. You actually take pleasure in your despair."

"That's nuts."

"Precisely. It's easier for you to sit up there on your mountain than it is to mix with other human beings. Then you might have to open yourself up a little, let people get a peek at the man you are inside. And that terrifies you, doesn't it? Because you might be found out. Somebody might discover that you're not the hard, cold, unfeeling bastard you pretend to be. Someone might decide that you're capable of giving and receiving love."

"Baby, I gave up on the idea of love a long time ago."

"Then what was that all about?" She gestured toward the bed.

"Sex." He made the word sound as dirty as possible.

Rusty recoiled from the ugliness of his tone, but tossed her head back proudly. "Not to me. I love you, Cooper."

"So you said."

"I meant it!"

"You were in the throes of passion when you said it. That doesn't count."

"You don't believe that I love you?"

"No. There's no such thing."

"Oh, there is." She played her trump card. "You still love your unborn child."

"Shut up."

"You grieve for it still because you loved it. You still love all those men you saw die in that prisoner-of-war camp."

"Rusty..." He came off the bed and loomed over her threateningly.

"You watched your mother spend her life nursing her anger and bitterness. She thrived on her misfortune. Do you want to waste your life like that?"

"Better that than to live like you, constantly striving to be someone you're not."

Hostility crackled between them. It was so strong that at first they didn't even notice the doorbell. It wasn't until Bill Carlson called out his daughter's name that they realized they weren't alone.

"Rusty!"

"Yes, Father." She dropped back onto the edge of the bed and started yanking on her clothes.

"Is everything okay? Whose beat-up old car is that out front?"

"I'll be right out, Father."

Cooper was pulling on his clothes with considerably more composure than she. She couldn't help but wonder if this was the first time he had found himself in an awkward situation like this, maybe with the untimely appearance of a husband.

Once they were dressed, he helped her to her feet and handed her her crutches. Together they went through the bedroom door and down the hall. Red-faced, knowing that her hair was in wild tumble and that she smelled muskily of sex, Rusty entered the living room.

Her father was impatiently pacing the hardwood floor. When he turned around and saw Cooper, his face went taut with disapproval. He treated Cooper to a frigid stare before casting his judgmental eyes on his daughter.

"I hated to let a day go by without coming to see you."

"Thank you, Father, but it really isn't necessary for you to stop by every day."

"So I see."

"You...you remember Mr. Landry."

The two men nodded to each other coolly, taking each other's measure like opposing champion warriors who would decide the outcome of a battle. Cooper kept his mouth stubbornly shut. Rusty couldn't speak; she was too embarrassed. Carlson was the first to break the stressful silence.

"Actually, this is an opportune meeting," he said. "I have something to discuss with both of you. Shall we sit down?"

"Surely," Rusty said, flustered. "I'm sorry. Uh, Cooper?" She gestured toward a chair. He hesitated, then dropped into the overstuffed armchair. His insolence grated on her raw nerves. She gave him a baleful look, but he was staring at her father. He'd watched the Gawrylow men with that same kind of suspicious caution. The memory disturbed Rusty. What correlation between them and her father was he making in his mind? She moved toward a chair near Carlson.

"What do you want to discuss with us, Father?"

"That land deal I mentioned to you a few weeks ago."

Rusty's lungs caved in. She could feel each membrane giving way, collapsing one on top of the other. Her cheeks paled, and her palms became immediately slick with nervous perspiration. A choir of funeral bells started tolling in her ears. "I thought we had that all settled."

Carlson chuckled amiably. "Not quite. But now we do. Now the investors have had a chance to put some concrete ideas on paper. They'd like to present these ideas for Mr. Landry's consideration."

"Somebody want to tell me what the hell is going on?" Cooper rudely interrupted.

"No."

"Of course." Carlson overrode his daughter's negative reply and seized the floor. In his typically genial manner, he outlined his ideas for developing the area around Rogers Gap into an exclusive ski resort.

Summing up, he said, "Before we're done, working with only the most innovative architects and builders, it will rival Aspen, Vail, Keystone, anything in the Rockies or around Lake Tahoe. In several years I'll bet we could swing the Winter Olympics our way." Leaning back in his chair and smiling expansively, he said, "Well, Mr. Landry, what do you think?"

Cooper, who hadn't so much as blinked an eye during Carlson's recital, slowly rolled off his slouching spine and came to his feet. He circled the island of furniture several times as though considering the proposal from every angle. Since he owned some of the land that would be used— Carlson had done his homework—and had been offered the salaried, figurehead position as local coordinator of the project, he stood to make a great deal of money.

Carlson glanced at his daughter and winked, assured of capitulation.

"What do I think?" Cooper repeated.

"That's what I asked," Carlson said jovially.

Cooper looked him straight in the eye. "I think *you* are full of garbage, and I think your *idea* sucks." He dumped those words in the middle of the floor like a ton of bricks, then added, "And for your information, so does your daughter."

He gave Rusty a look that should have turned her to stone. He didn't even deign to slam the door shut behind himself after he stamped out. They heard his car roar to life, then the crunch of gravel as he steered out of her driveway.

Carlson harrumphed and said, "Well, I see that I was right about him all along."

Knowing that she would never recover from the wound Cooper had inflicted on her, Rusty said dully, "You couldn't be more wrong, Father."

"He's crude."

"Honest."

"A man without ambition or social graces."

"Without pretenses."

"And apparently without morals. He took advantage of your solitude and confinement."

She laughed softly. "I don't remember exactly who dragged whom into the bedroom, but he certainly didn't force me into bed with him."

"So you *are* lovers?"

"Not anymore," she said tearfully.

Cooper thought she had betrayed him, too, just like that other woman, Melody. He thought she had been her father's instrument, using bedroom tactics to turn a profit. He would never forgive her, because he didn't believe that she loved him.

"You've been his lover all this time? Behind my back?"

She started to point out that at the ripe old age of twenty-seven she shouldn't have to account to her father for her private life. But what was the use? What did it matter? The starch had gone out of her. She felt sapped of strength, of energy, of the will to live.

"When we were in Canada, yes. We became lovers. When he left my hospital room that day, he went home and hasn't been back since. Not until this afternoon."

"Then apparently he has more sense than I gave him credit for. He realizes that the two of you are completely incompatible. Like most women, you're looking at the situation through a pink fog of romance. You're letting your emotions rule you instead of your head. I thought you were above that female frailty."

"Well, I'm not, Father. A female is what I happen to be. And I have all the frailties, as well as all the strengths, that go with being a woman."

He came to his feet and crossed the room. He gave her a conciliatory hug. She was standing on her crutches so he didn't notice how stiffly she held herself in resistance to his embrace. "I can see that Mr. Landry has upset you again. He truly is a scoundrel to have said what he did about you. You're better off without him, Rusty, believe me.

"However," he continued briskly, "we won't let his lack of charm keep us from doing business with him. I intend to move forward with our plans in spite of his objections to them."

"Father, I beg you—"

He laid a finger against her lips. "Hush, now. Let's not talk anymore tonight. Tomorrow you'll feel better. You're still emotionally overwrought. Having surgery so soon after the plane crash probably wasn't such a good idea. It's perfectly understandable that you're not quite yourself. One of these days you'll come to your senses and return to being the old Rusty. I have every confidence that you won't disappoint me."

He kissed her forehead. "Good night, my dear. Look over this proposal," he said, withdrawing a file folder from his lizard briefcase and laying it on the coffee table. "I'll drop by tomorrow morning, eager to hear your opinion."

After he left, Rusty locked up her house and returned to the bedroom. She bathed, languishing in a hot bubble bath. She'd taken one every day since the doctor had said it was okay to get her leg wet. But once she was dried, lotioned, and powdered, she still hadn't rid her body of the traces of Cooper's lovemaking.

She was pleasantly sore between her thighs. The blemish he'd left on her breast still showed up rosily, as indelible as a tattoo. Her lips were tender and puffy. Every time she wet them with her tongue, she could taste him.

Looking at herself in the mirror, she admitted that he was right. She *did* look as if she'd just been engaged in rowdy lovemaking.

Her bed seemed as large and empty as a football field during the off-season. The linens still smelled like Cooper. In her mind she relived every moment they'd spent together that afternoon—the giving and taking of pleasure; the exchange of erotic dialogue. Even now, his whispered, naughty words echoed through her mind, causing her to flush hotly all over.

She yearned for him and could find no comfort in the thought that her life would be a series of empty days and joyless nights like this one.

She'd have her work, of course.

And her father.

Her wide circle of friends.

Her social activities.

It wouldn't be enough.

There was a great big hole where the man she loved should be.

She sat up in bed and clutched the sheet against her, as though the realization she'd just had would get away from her if she didn't hold on to it until she could act upon it.

Her choices were clear. She could either roll over and play dead. Or she could fight for him. Her main adversary would be Cooper himself. He was mule-headed and mistrustful. But eventually she would wear him down and convince him that she loved him and that he loved her.

Yes, he did! He could deny it until he gasped his dying breath, but she would never believe that he didn't love her—

because right after her father had made that hateful disclosure, just before Cooper's face had hardened with contempt, she'd seen incredible pain there. She wouldn't have the power to hurt him that badly unless he loved her.

She lay back down, glowing in her resolution and knowing exactly what she had to do the following morning.

Her father was taken off-guard. A strategist as shrewd as General Patton, he had slipped up. He hadn't expected a surprise attack.

When she made her unannounced appearance in his office the next morning, he glanced up from his highly polished, white lacquered desk and exclaimed, "Why, Rusty! What . . . what a lovely surprise."

"Good morning, Father."

"What are you doing out? Not that the reason matters. I'm delighted to see you up and around."

"I had to see you and didn't want to wait to be worked into your busy schedule."

He chose to ignore the note of censure in her voice and walked around his desk with his hands outstretched to take hers. "You're feeling much better—I can tell. Did Mrs. Watkins offer you coffee?"

"She did, but I declined."

He regarded her casual clothes. "Apparently you're not going to your office."

"No, I'm not."

He cocked his head to one side, obviously waiting for an explanation. When none was forthcoming he asked, "Where are your crutches?"

"In my car."

"You drove here? I didn't think—"

"Yes, I drove myself. I wanted to walk in here under my own steam and stand on my own two feet."

He backed away from her and propped his hips against the edge of his desk. Casually he crossed his ankles and folded his arms over his middle. Rusty recognized the stance. It was the tactical one he assumed when he was backed into a corner but didn't want his rivals to know that he was. "I take it you read the proposal." With a smooth motion of his head, he indicated the folder she was carrying under her arm.

"I did."

"And?"

She ripped the folder in two. Tossing the remnants on the glassy surface of his desk, she said, "Lay off Cooper Landry. Drop the Rogers Gap project. Today."

He laughed at her sophomoric gesture and shrugged helplessly, spreading his arms wide in appeal. "It's a little late for that, Rusty dear. The ball has already started rolling."

"Stop it from rolling."

"I can't."

"Then you're in a real jam with these investors you collected, Father—" she leaned forward "—because I'm going to privately and publicly resist you on this. I'll have every conservationist group in the country beating down your door in protest. I don't think you want that."

"Rusty, for Heaven's sake, come to your senses," he hissed.

"I did. Sometime between midnight and 2:00 a.m., I realized that there's something much more important to me than any real-estate deal. Even more important to me than winning your approval."

"Landry?"

"Yes." Her voice rang with conviction. She was not to be swayed.

But Carlson tried. "You'd give up everything you've worked for to have him?"

"Loving Cooper doesn't take anything away from what I've done in the past or will do in the future. Love this strong can only embellish, not tear down."

"Do you realize how ridiculous you sound?"

She didn't take offense. Instead she laughed. "I guess I do. Lovers often babble nonsensically, don't they?"

"This is no laughing matter, Rusty. If you do this, it's an irreversible decision. Once you give up your position here, that's it."

"I don't think so, Father," she said, calling his bluff. "Think how bad it would be for business if you fired your most effective employee." She produced a key from the pocket of her nylon windbreaker. "To my office." She slid the key across his desk. "I'll be taking an indefinite leave of absence."

"You're making a fool of yourself."

"I made a fool of myself at Great Bear Lake. I did that for love, too." She turned on her heels and headed for the door.

"Where are you going?" Bill Carlson barked. He wasn't accustomed to someone walking out on him.

"To Rogers Gap."

"And do what?"

Rusty faced her father. She loved him. Very much. But she could no longer sacrifice her own happiness for his. With staunch conviction she said, "I'm going to do something that Jeff could never do: I'm going to have a baby."

Fourteen

Rusty stood on the cliff and breathed deeply of the cool, crisp air. She never tired of the scenery. It was constant, and yet ever changing. Today the sky was like a blue china bowl turned upside down over the earth. Snow still capped the mountain peaks against the horizon. The trees ranged in color from the blue-green of the evergreens to the delicate green of trees on the verge of spring budding.

"Aren't you cold?"

Her husband came up behind her and wrapped his arms around her. She snuggled against him. "Not now. How's the foal?"

"He's having breakfast—to his and his mother's mutual contentment."

She smiled and tilted her head to one side. He inched down the turtleneck of her sweater and kissed her beneath her ear. "How's the other new mother on the place?"

"I'm not a new mother yet." She glowed with pleasure as he ran his large hands over her swollen abdomen.

"Looks that way to me."

"You think this new figure of mine is amusing, don't you?" She frowned at him over her shoulder, but it was hard to maintain that expression when he was gazing at her with such evident love.

"I love it."

"I love you."

They kissed. "I love you, too," he whispered when he lifted his mouth off hers. Words he had found impossible to say before, now came easily to his lips. She had taught him how to love again.

"You had no choice."

"Yeah, I remember that night you showed up on my threshold looking as bedraggled as a homeless kitten in a rainstorm."

"Considering what I'd just come through I thought I looked pretty good."

"I didn't know whether to kiss you or paddle you."

"You did both."

"Yeah, but the paddling didn't come until much later."

They laughed together, but he was serious when he said, "No fooling, I couldn't believe you drove all that way alone through that kind of weather. Didn't you listen to your car radio? Didn't you hear the storm reports? You escorted in the first heavy snowstorm of the season. Every time I think about it, I shudder." He pulled her closer, crossing his hands over her breasts and nuzzling his face in her hair.

"I had to see you right then, before I lost my nerve. I would have gone through hell to get here."

"You very nearly did."

"At the time, it didn't seem so bad. Besides, I had survived a plane crash. What was a little snow?"

"Hardly a 'little snow.' And driving with your injured leg too."

She shrugged dismissively. To their delight the gesture caused her breasts to rise and fall against his hands. Murmuring his appreciation, he covered them completely and massaged them gently, aware of the discomfort they'd been giving her lately as a result of her pregnancy.

"Tender?" he asked.

"A little."

"Want me to stop?"

"Not on your life."

Satisfied with her answer, he propped his chin on the top of her head and continued to massage her.

"I'm glad the operations on my leg have to be postponed until after the baby gets here," she said. "That is, if you don't mind looking at my unsightly scar."

"I always close my eyes when we're making love."

"I know. So do I."

"Then how do you know mine are closed?" he teased. They laughed again, because neither of them closed his eyes while they were making love; they were too busy looking at each other, looking at themselves together, and gauging each other's level of passion.

As they watched a hawk lazily circling in downward spirals, Cooper asked, "Remember what you said to me the instant I opened the door that night?"

"I said, 'You're going to let me love you, Cooper Landry, if it kills you.'"

He chuckled at the memory and his heart grew warm, as it had that night, when he thought about the courage it had taken for her to come to him and make that bizarre announcement. "What would you have done if I had slammed the door in your face?"

"But you didn't."

"Assuming I had."

She pondered that for a moment. "I'd have barged in anyway, stripped off all my clothes, pledged everlasting love and devotion, and threatened you with violence if you didn't love me back."

"That's what you did."

"Oh, yeah," she said around a giggle. "Well, I'd have just kept on doing that until you stopped refusing."

He planted his lips against her ear. "You went down on bended knee and asked me to marry you and give you a baby."

"How well your memory serves you."

"And that's not all you did while you were on your knees."

She turned in his arms and said sweetly, "I didn't hear you complaining. Or were all those garbled phrases coming out of your mouth complaints?"

He laughed, throwing back his head and releasing a genuine burst of humor—something he did frequently now. There were times when he lapsed into the moody, withdrawn man he'd been. His mind carried him back to haunting phases of his life where she couldn't go. Her reward lay in the fact that she could bring him out again. Patiently, lovingly, she was eradicating his disturbing memories and replacing them with happy ones.

Now she kissed his strong, tanned throat and said, "We'd better go in and get ready for our trip to L.A."

They made one round-trip a month to the city, during which they spent two or three days at Rusty's house. While there, they ate in fine restaurants, went to concerts and movies, shopped, and even attended an occasional social gathering. Rusty stayed in touch with her old friends, but was delighted with the new friendships Cooper and she had cultivated as a couple. When he wanted to, he could ooze charm and engage in conversation on a wide range of subjects.

Also while they were there, she handled business matters that demanded her attention. Since her marriage, she'd been promoted to vice-president in her father's real-estate company.

Cooper worked as a volunteer counselor in a veterans' therapy group. He'd initiated several self-help programs that were being emulated in other parts of the country.

Now, with their arms around each other's waist, they walked back toward the house that was nestled in a grove of pines. It overlooked a spectacular valley. Horses and cattle grazed in the mountain pastures below the timberline.

"You know," he said as they entered their glass-walled bedroom, "talking about that night you arrived has gotten me all hot and bothered." He peeled off his shirt.

"You're always hot and bothered." Rusty peeled her sweater over her head. She never wore a bra when they were at home alone.

Eyeing her enlarged breasts, he unsnapped his jeans and swaggered toward her. "And it's always your fault."

"Do you still desire me, even though I'm misshapen?" She gestured at her rounded tummy.

For an answer, he took her hand and pulled it into his open fly. She squeezed his full manhood. He groaned softly. "I desire you." Bending his knees, he kissed one of her creamy breasts. "As long as you're you, I'll love you, Rusty."

"I'm glad," she sighed. "Because, just like after the plane crash, you're stuck with me."

Compelling Debut Author

TAYLOR SMITH

Catapults you into a world where deception is
the rule

Guilt by Silence

In the flash of an eye, Mariah Bolt's world came
crashing down. Confronted by the destruction of her
family and too many unanswered questions, she's
determined to prove that her husband's accident was a
carefully planned attempt at murder. As she probes
deeper into what really happened, she realizes that she
can trust no one—not the government, not her husband,
not even Paul Chaney, the one person willing to help
her. Because now Mariah is the target.

Available this June at your favorite retail outlet.

MIRA The brightest star in women's fiction

Bestselling Author

Introduces you to the woman called

Everybody loves Red—whoever she is. A haunted
teenager who defied the odds to find fame as a top model.
A pretty face who became a talented fashion photographer.
A woman who has won the love of two men. Yet, no
matter how often she transforms herself, the pain of Red's
past just won't go away—until she faces it head on....

Available this July, at your favorite retail outlet.

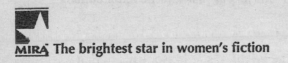

Bestselling Author

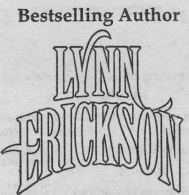

Dares you to enter a wonderland of passion and sin in

Meet the Connellys:

Matt—the charismatic, scandal-ridden senator determined to hide the truth.

Lee—the wife who drowns her sorrows in the bottle.

Terry—the prodigal son, who always gets what he wants, at all costs.

Beth—the jet-setting daughter who can no longer run from the past or her family.

And the one man who can bring it all tumbling down—
Case McCandless, town sheriff sworn to ferret out the truth, and destined to find love with the enemy.

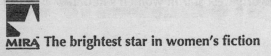